PRAISE FOR *GO ASK* ~~FANNIE~~
and ELISABETH H~~YDE~~

"A book full of huge-hearted mistake makers that you'll want to call your own—*Go Ask Fannie* is a rousing reminder that the only way to truly forgive another person is to first forgive yourself."

—Courtney Maum, author of *Touch* and
I Am Having So Much Fun Without You

"Wonderful characters, a gorgeous sense of time and place, and elegant storytelling make *Go Ask Fannie* an utter delight. The members of this loving, raging, totally compelling family may not like one another all the time, but I adored them all from the first page. Elisabeth Hyde has written a funny, joyous novel, heartbreaking and heartwarming all at once and in the very best ways."

—Laurie Frankel, author of *This is How It Always Is*

"What does it mean to be a family? What are the secrets we hide? In this poignant, often funny, yet serious novel, Elisabeth Hyde mines the mysteries and paradoxes of our most intimate connections. How we hurt, disappoint, and lie to one another, and how despite it all we are inextricably joined. In the end Elisabeth Hyde has served us up a recipe for love, one that the reader will feast on for a long time."

—Mary Morris, author of *The Jazz Place*

"Writing in a style both affecting and realistic, Hyde gives readers a family that could mirror their own, including the characters, the conversations, and the treasured family keepsake. With all the feels of a *This Is Us* episode, Hyde's latest novel will delight readers."

—*Booklist*

"Hyde's insightful and engaging novel is highly recommended, especially for readers who enjoy family sagas by Sue Miller and Anne Tyler."

—*BookPage*

"In this heartfelt story, family conflict and love intertwine."
   —*The Tennessean*

"Hyde always produces character-driven books that ooze authenticity."
   —*5280* magazine

"[Hyde] is here an accomplished, assured and painstaking archae-ologist of a multilayered family history, of its secrets, vulnerabilities and regrets. A richly rewarding read."
   —*Sunday Times* (UK)

"The writing is superb and compelling. . . . Excellent plotting and a story which just seems to happen without effort."
   —*The Bookbag* (UK)

"[Hyde's] prose is vigorous and natural, her perception subtle, her voice and those of her characters all-American."
   —*The New York Times Book Review*, Editors' Choice

"Like Anne Tyler, Hyde captures the quirky, heartbreaking core of a character and puts it on the page with shining prose . . . in a novel full of originality and sparkle."
   —*Publishers Weekly*

Go Ask Fannie

ELISABETH HYDE

G. P. Putnam's Sons
New York

PUTNAM

G. P. PUTNAM'S SONS
Publishers Since 1838
An imprint of Penguin Random House LLC
penguinrandomhouse.com

Copyright © 2018 by Elisabeth Hyde
Penguin supports copyright. Copyright fuels creativity, encourages diverse voices,
promotes free speech, and creates a vibrant culture. Thank you for buying an authorized
edition of this book and for complying with copyright laws by not reproducing, scanning,
or distributing any part of it in any form without permission. You are supporting
writers and allowing Penguin to continue to publish books for every reader.

The Library of Congress has catalogued the G. P. Putnam's Sons
hardcover edition as follows:

Names: Hyde, Elisabeth, author.
Title: Go ask Fannie/by Elisabeth Hyde.
Description: New York : G. P. Putnam's Sons, 2018.
Identifiers: LCCN 2017034257 | ISBN 9780735218567 (hardcover) |
ISBN 9780735218628 (epub)
Classification: LCC PS3558.Y38 G66 2018 | DDC 813/.54—dc23
LC record available at https://lccn.loc.gov/2017034257
p.   cm.

First G. P. Putnam's Sons hardcover edition / April 2018
First G. P. Putnam's Sons trade paperback edition / April 2019
G. P. Putnam's Sons trade paperback ISBN: 9780735218611

Printed in the United States of America
1 3 5 7 9 10 8 6 4 2

BOOK DESIGN BY MEIGHAN CAVANAUGH

For JLH

Go Ask Fannie

Prologue

IF I GIVE HER ENOUGH ROPE, SHE'LL HANG HERSELF, HE thought.

George Blaire didn't consider himself a mean person, but put him in a car with his older sister, Ruth, and instantly he felt like he was thirteen again and plotting schemes to trip her up. This was because Ruth was perpetually blind to her bossy, snobbish nature, and George enjoyed nothing more than catching her unawares. *Is there a reason you don't eat iceberg lettuce, Ruth? You think I should use how much salt, Ruth?*

True, he could go overboard. As a nurse in the intensive care unit at a midsized hospital, he dealt with a fair amount of stress, and one day, after he'd not only witnessed a thirty-five-year-old woman die of sepsis but been assaulted by her husband for not having done enough to save her life—after that very long day, he happened to have a snappy phone conversation with Ruth in which he teased her about getting a facial every week. And Ruth, traumatized by acne as a teenager, first went silent and then said, "Really, George?" in a shaky, tearful voice, which made George ask himself what particular neural defect would cause a younger brother to value the callous taunt over some heartfelt empathy.

Such was their dynamic, however. And so as they drove north from the Manchester airport on Friday night, with dusk softening the sky and thickening the stands of pine along the highway, he merely had to ask what she wanted to do over the weekend, and Ruth began outlining her plans, using the words "first," "second," and "third," which prompted him to wonder aloud whether those were bullet points, capital letters, or Roman numerals. Oh, that got her goat.

And just past Concord, with its steepled skyline and golden dome, all he had to do was tease her about the amount of money she spent grooming her thirteen-year-old golden retriever, and she was suddenly declaring that the grooming bills were nothing compared to the doggie acupuncture. "It was Morgan's idea," she protested, once George had stopped choking on his coffee.

But the best moment came as they were heading up the long driveway to the old red farmhouse where their father lived, just north of Franconia Notch, and he reminded her that arriving with a preset agenda for the weekend was not going to make their father very happy.

"Well, *George*," she remarked, reapplying lipstick using the little mirror on the visor, "my primary purpose in life is not to make people happy."

The bald admission hovered like a snarl of gnats, and George didn't have to say anything at all to make his point: even Ruth herself lapsed into silence, unnerved by her own bitchiness.

Bingo.

WHAT BOTHERED RUTH was that here was her brother, an ICU nurse with presumably a fair amount of compassion, yes? affirmatively trying to point out all the ways her life was different from his. Big fat Washington, DC, versus little old New Hampshire. High income versus meh. Hillary versus Bernie. Did he really have to make her feel so stupid when she talked about taking an Uber back to the airport on Monday? ("Not really Uber country, Ruth," he'd chuckled.) Did he have to make her feel so guilty about the chef she and Morgan had recently hired to handle dinners during the hectic weeknights when the boys had soccer, music lessons, and homework, and needed something other than a clam box of sushi at eight p.m.? *Stop treating me like your neurotic older sister,* she wanted to say to him. *Start treating me like a human.*

But if she said that, he would call her out on being bossy again, and she would be made to feel bad, bad, and really, really bad.

It didn't help that her day had gone poorly from the start. First Caleb got a bloody nose at the breakfast table and had to be convinced that no, it was not cancer, and yes, the stain would come out of his new Abercrombie sweatshirt. Then on the way out to the car, Kyle dropped his shoebox diorama of Machu Picchu, and all the little Incans toppled off the carefully molded Andean mountaintop. She got into her office to find an unanticipated stack of civil investigative demands from the Justice Department, and very unmindfully ate two glazed donuts for lunch, so that by the time she left for the airport, she was having to mainline a protein drink, which took care of her dizziness but had the effect of making her somewhat aggressive, so that when a barrel-chested man cut in front of her while going through security, she calmly asked if he'd been born an asshole or just recently become one. Then she cut in front of him, which due to his protests drew the attention of security, who pulled her aside and subjected her to a wand-down while the asshole breezed on through. Finally, as if this weren't bad enough, upon boarding she discovered that not only was he on her flight, he was sitting right in front of her, which allowed him to tip his seat back into her personal space, preventing her from opening her laptop, which prompted her to jostle, push, and tug at his seat any chance she could, forcing him to speak to the flight attendant, and when Ruth heard herself protest "But *he* started it," she knew she had reached one of the lower moments of her adult life.

And now with George on her case for feeding the boys too much sushi? She had a lot to accomplish this weekend, and it wasn't going to help if George was going to direct his energy toward making her feel bad, bad, and really, really bad, all weekend long.

LIZZIE, THE YOUNGEST, felt like she was going to explode.

Bless her father, but he'd taken to calling her over every little thing these days. *I can't find the salad spinner. The remote isn't working. I forgot my password.* Because she lived just twenty minutes away—as opposed to George, an hour away down in Concord, and

Ruth, three hours by plane in Washington, DC—it all fell upon her. Didn't he realize she had a life? That she had papers to read, recommendation letters to write, and hiring-committee work to tend to? She truly loved her weekly visits, and she truly loved cooking him a big pot of soup with plenty of leftovers, but she couldn't help but think sometimes that his constant requests reflected an assumption that her work as a fully tenured professor of literature at a nearby college wasn't quite as important as that of her siblings.

Although to be fair, maybe she was just hypersensitive these days. Physically, she was still a bit off, she reminded herself. That accounted for a lot. But with everyone convening at her father's house for the weekend—Ruth with a suitcase full of to-dos, George wanting to show off the photos of his latest marathon—she feared simply being overwhelmed by the busyness of it all. Ruth would call family meetings, George would push people to go for a run with him, and her father would probably decide to take advantage of all three of them being around to help move the behemoth buffet out of the dining room and into the shed so he could sand it down and restain it before posting it on Craigslist.

The flip side of her proximity was that it would give her an out during the weekend. Twenty minutes and she could be back at her very modest, asbestos-sided home, with space and time to herself. She'd agreed to feed the neighbor's cats for the next two days, and she had a rash of papers to grade, plus a mound of applicants' resumés to wade through for a position that had opened up at her college. Not that she wanted to avoid her family, but she sensed that it would be a weekend of mild friction, with everybody wedded to their own agendas.

An idea came to her then: maybe the best way to avoid all that potential strife would be to go through family photos. Or letters. Something not too overwhelming—like their mother's recipes, actually. Which reminded her to get the cookbook back from her ex-boyfriend Gavin, who'd been holding on to it for the last four months. Because without something calming for them to focus on, she just felt like she was going to lose it.

AND EIGHTY-ONE-YEAR-OLD MURRAY BLAIRE—a retired attorney, a state legislator, a two-day congressman-elect, and now an amateur farmer—anticipated the arrival of his three children that Friday night in mid-September and hoped for the best. He had some serious matters to discuss this weekend, and he wanted things to run smoothly. But harmony, that Artful Dodger in so many families, had its way of eluding his family as well, and after cleaning up the stacks of unread magazines, the piles of newspapers; after vacuuming the dust kitties from under the guest beds and scrubbing out the pan he'd burned last night and putting away the shellac and the turpentine and, finally, changing into unstained clothes, he steeled himself by knocking back a double gin and tonic before they arrived. Then he brushed his teeth, gargled, combed his hair, and sat down at the kitchen table to wait as gravity drew his children back into his orbit for the next three days.

PART ONE

2016

1.

Squabblety-Budgets

"COME IN, COME IN," MURRAY EXCLAIMED, OPENING THE kitchen door wide. He glanced at his watch. "You made excellent time! How was the traffic? Ruth, is that all you brought?"

Ruth propped her large floppy tote against her carry-on bag and kissed her father hello. "I always travel light, Dad, you know that." She looked around. "Where's Lizzie?"

"She called and said she'll be down tomorrow morning," Murray replied. "Something about wanting to get some papers graded tonight. George"—and he clasped his son's arm—"thanks for doing airport duty."

"Nice sweater, Dad," said Ruth. "Is it new?"

Murray glanced down, as though he'd forgotten what he was wearing. "This? No, just dug it out of the back of the closet. Mothballs and all."

"Well, you look good in red, Dad," said Ruth.

Murray beamed. It pleased him when Ruth took note of his grooming efforts, not because he was out to impress her, but because he knew Ruth had a tendency to keep tabs on how well he was taking care of himself. This would give him a nice bold check in the "Keeps Up Appearances" column.

"I have dinner all ready," he told them. On the stove was a pot of chili, along with a pan of cornbread made from a mix Ruth had brought him from Santa Fe, probably years ago. He'd prepared a salad as well—though that, too, had been easy, coming prewashed in a bag so all he did was dump it in a bowl. "We can eat any time."

"Let me check in with Morgan first," said Ruth, taking out her phone.

"You already checked in with him," George said. "Three times in the car already."

"I want him to know we arrived," Ruth said, and her index finger skittered across the screen. Murray looked on, somewhat appalled: What color was her nail polish, exactly? Blue-green? In a law firm? It looked vampirish to Murray.

Ruth, having sent her text, placed her phone on the table. "Okay, *now* I'll take a glass of wine."

"Wow, fancy stuff," George observed, as Murray got a bottle of white wine from the refrigerator.

"Is this the right one?" Murray asked Ruth, showing her the bottle.

"Wait—you *told* him to get you that wine?" George said. "Seriously?"

"Zip it, George," said Ruth.

George took the bottle from Murray's hand before he could uncork it. He eyed the label. "How much did this cost?"

"I said drop it, George," Ruth warned.

"Nothing wrong with splurging every once in a while," Murray said lamely—wishing George would, in fact, drop the issue. The wine had actually cost over twenty dollars at the state liquor store, far more than what Murray might have spent on a bottle for himself, but Ruth had been specific and he didn't want her to be disappointed. He'd only bought one bottle, anyway. It wasn't like he was going to keep her supplied all weekend long. "Do you want some, George?"

"No, I'll just take a *Bud*," quipped George, emphasizing the common-man's brand, which Murray thought was an unnecessary dig, since George knew that Murray always kept a few craft beers in the refrigerator for his son.

But if it was a dig, Ruth did not snap back, and they sat down to Murray's dinner and for the rest of the evening they made light, frivolous, for the most part happy conversation: George telling them about his knee injury; Ruth filling them in on the soccer camps the boys had attended this summer, and the awards they'd received, and their week at the Delaware shore where Kyle forgot sunscreen one day and ended up with a blistering sunburn that Ruth still got choked up about, because now if he got skin cancer it would be her fault. Murray, for his part, just sat and listened. He wished Lizzie were here, too, but he had to admit, he was grateful for all this harmony. Ruth and George seemed to be making an effort.

If only the whole weekend could be just like this, he thought. *Any ideas, Lillian? Would you scold, if things started heating up? Let them duke it out themselves? Or would you escape to your room upstairs and write about it?*

AS IT WOULD TURN OUT, the next morning would find Murray wondering what toxic wind had blown in during the night, because when he came downstairs around eight, he found Ruth and George arguing at the breakfast table about who should inherit their grandfather's army parka. Over toast they argued about the percentage by which Donald Trump was going to lose. ("Epic," George predicted. Murray himself wasn't so sure.) Over eggs, they fought about how to deal with Lizzie, who was posting unflattering childhood pictures of them all on Facebook.

By nine o'clock they'd moved on to finances; as Murray was making a second pot of coffee, Ruth was trying to convince George he should be putting more money into his retirement account, and George was getting prickly, Murray could tell, not just because he probably wasn't putting enough aside, but because Ruth could be so bossy.

Squabblety-budgets, Lillian used to call them when they fought like this. *Yackety-yacks*. Their voices sounded like the Sunday morning news shows. *Stop it!* he wanted to shout. But then an idea occurred to him, so simple he wondered why he hadn't thought of it before: he reached up and removed his hearing aid and slipped it into his pocket. And that was it; that was better. Without the device, his children's voices receded and Murray felt happy. Let them argue for the time being. Slowly the coffee began to burble up in the old percolator and Murray felt happier still. He looked out the window.

It was a cloudless day, the blue peaks of the Franconia Range deeply shadowed from the low morning sun. Down the hill, just visible over the roof of his barn, lay a brilliant swash of yellow. Murray had put in two acres of sunflowers three years ago, almost as much an experiment in color as an agricultural endeavor. The flowers grew chest-high, as big as dinner plates, drooping heavily at this time of year from the weight of their seeded centers. Standing in his field, under a cerulean sky and surrounded by a sea of gold, Murray Blaire felt like Van Gogh.

The coffee smelled good, rich, nutty. It occurred to him that he might have given the army parka to the thrift shop.

"I said Dad!" Ruth exclaimed.

"Don't shout!" Murray snapped. (Oh, he hated getting snappy!)

Ruth then said something that Murray couldn't quite make out. He wondered if he could slip his hearing aid back in without her noticing, now that she had zeroed in on him for something. Ruth had a way of noticing all the *would*s, *could*s, and *should*s he did or didn't do, many of which had to do with the safety of living alone; she thought he should use his hearing aid all the time, for instance, though what that had to do with safety, Murray couldn't say.

Yet wasn't this tendency the reason he'd urged her to come up for a long weekend, to be honest? Because she also noticed those *would*s and *should*s about everyone else, too, and she would notice them about Lizzie. More specifically, what Lizzie could and should be doing to get out of what Murray perceived to be a bad relationship.

For the past year and a half, Lizzie had been seeing an older man named Gavin Langley, technically married but separated from his wife. Originally from New York, he'd bought a place near Lizzie in the hamlet of Sugar Hill, a nineteenth-century clapboard farmhouse that he'd gutted and remodeled with local stone and timber. Murray had visited the place once, when Gavin invited the locals to come and admire his renovations; this was before Murray knew that any kind of relationship existed with Lizzie, and he'd stood and nibbled cheddar cheese, wondering how soon he could extricate himself from the man's ostentatious attempts to garner admiration under the guise of neighborly generosity. Eventually Murray learned of his daughter's involvement with the man, but things had reached a point this past month where Murray suspected all was not well, for Lizzie's moods had grown increasingly dark lately. Something was going on. And Murray, as her father, felt quite helpless to investigate.

"Dad, focus, please!" implored Ruth.

Fine. Ignoring his daughter's watchful eye, Murray fitted his hearing aid back in, poured himself some coffee, and went to sit at the old drop-leaf table with Ruth and George. Ruth was wearing baggy gray sweats, and she'd clipped her hair up in back so that it fell over on itself, like a rooster tail. George wore a black T-shirt that read "¿lɐɯɹoN ǝq ʎɥM."

"Now what's this all about?" said Murray.

"Will you please tell George why he should be saving more for retirement?" Ruth said.

"Nope," said Murray. "George is forty-five. He knows about compound interest."

"Forty-four," George pointed out.

"Where's Lizzie with the coffee cake, anyway?" said Murray. "She should be here by now." A shadow clouded his mind, as it always did when one of his kids didn't arrive on time. Anything could happen. Look at Lillian. Look at Daniel. Contrary to popular belief, lightning could always strike twice.

"Do you actually think you can live on Social Security?" Ruth asked George.

"I have a pension, Ruth," said George. "I am employed, you know."

Murray checked his watch. "Darn that girl. Somebody call her."

Both his children simultaneously reached for their phones. Murray got the feeling it was a race. Everything with his children was a competition, it seemed. "In the meantime, though, since I have you here, I want to talk about the situation."

"Which situation?" asked Ruth.

"Dad doesn't like Gavin," George told her.

"Oh, *that* one. I don't like Gavin either," said Ruth. "He's what, twenty-seven years older than she is, to begin with."

Murray rubbed his chin. He'd forgotten to shave that morning, he just realized. No doubt Ruth had noticed.

"My fear is that he's leading your sister on," he said. "Cultivating expectations. He's not serious about her, that much I can sense, and I'm afraid she's going to end up hurt." Murray was old-fashioned when it came to sex; he viewed women as more vulnerable than men, more likely to think that love was involved and apt to fall apart when things ended. He didn't know the exact terms of the relationship in question here, but he did know Gavin was still married, at least on paper. And he thought Ruth, as an older sister, could help empower Lizzie to extricate herself.

"I want you to talk to her, Ruth."

"Not me?" asked George, hurt.

"I already talked to her once this summer," said Ruth. "She didn't want to listen."

"Well, she definitely doesn't want to listen to her old man," Murray said. "You're her sister. You're a woman."

"She's actually closer to me," George pointed out.

"Fine, you talk to her," said Ruth.

"Stop it, the two of you," said Murray, convinced his children could find discord in a glass of milk. "This is my house. I hate it when you fight. Your mother would hate it, too. So stop it."

"Speaking of which," began Ruth.

"Uh-oh," said George, and Murray grunted. *Speaking of which,* they both knew, meant that Ruth was going to change the subject.

"I noticed a little mold in the bathroom, Dad. Behind the sink pedestal. Have you had the house tested for black mold?"

"I don't have black mold," said Murray. "I have blue mold."

"You still have to take care of it. Get Sandra to wipe down the walls with some vinegar. Also there's a huge wasp nest under the eaves."

"I'll take it down."

"No. You'll hire a professional. You're allergic to bees, Dad."

"I am?"

"Dad!"

"Then I'll spray it after dark."

"Why won't you just hire someone?" Ruth said.

"Is this why you came up here?" George asked her. "To tell him what to do about all the things that are wrong with his house?"

"Of course not. But at some point we're going to need to talk about a whole different living situation for Dad, and this is just the start."

"I keep a very clean house," said Murray. "I throw out my newspapers. I take out my garbage. Do I have mice in the walls? Yes. Squirrels in the attic? Maybe a few. So what? A little blue mold isn't going to kill me." He nodded at Ruth's cell phone. "Have you heard back from her?"

Ruth shook her head.

Murray sighed. Despite the coffee, he suddenly felt drowsy.

"I'm going to go lie down," he said. "Wake me when she gets here."

He left the room and shuffled toward the stairs, trying to remember his last bee sting. "You see?" he heard Ruth say. "How tired he gets? And it's only quarter past nine."

IN THE RELATIVE QUIET of his room, Murray lay down on his bed, which he hadn't yet made this morning: something else Ruth would notice. A few leaves on the maple tree outside his window had turned red, which reminded him that fall was upon him, which reminded him that winter was not far along, which made him sad. Winters had gotten so long at this point in his life.

Well, they were long because he couldn't ski anymore because of back problems, he reminded himself. He no longer snowshoed because of balance issues. All he could do was sit inside and read when the north wind blew. If he went for a walk, he risked slipping. If he drove, he might skid. Sometimes he felt like a hermit, living alone and talking to himself just to exercise his vocal cords.

What Murray really wanted this year was to go to Mexico for the winter. To find a small fishing village untainted by tourists, a place where he could rent a little stucco house and learn the language and eat the local food and shop at the local market. He'd heard that the town of Zihuatanejo on the Pacific was such a place, but when he Googled it, he saw restaurants and beaches and pleasure boats, and concluded that it would be too touristy for him. It would take some research to find the right place, but that was half the fun. He would leave in January, and return after mud season, in late April, so he could be there for the purple trilliums and the lady slippers, the turning over of the soil in his sunflower field, the things that made life worth living here in northern New England.

Murray kicked at his sheets so he wasn't lying on wrinkles and lumps. He settled himself and folded his hands over his diaphragm and felt his breath begin to steady. He really was worried about Lizzie. He couldn't say for sure that Gavin was responsible for this, but Lizzie had been acting differently lately. Jumpy and skittish, prone to talk about leaving her job and going off to live in India or Nepal for a year. She'd never spoken of those countries before and Murray took this to mean that they were places Gavin had tossed around. *Oh, Lizzie, he's just playing with you, can't you see that? Dump the guy, before he dumps you.*

Right now it was Lizzie who was occupying his thoughts, but that didn't mean Murray didn't worry about his other children as well. Ruth was a lawyer for a large firm, and he worried that she worked too hard. Sixty, seventy hours a week, she'd once told him. Her husband, Morgan, was also an attorney, but for some reason he managed to get home every day by six thirty, something Murray frequently pointed out to Ruth. "If Morgan can manage it, why can't you?"

She never had a good answer for him.

As for George—George had chosen nursing, a profession that provided clearly defined hours, a day job that gave him time to run the marathons he was continually training for. George, who'd always had a voracious appetite, had ballooned up in his twenties, and originally took up running to lose weight. Now, at a lean and sinewy 160, he was running up to six marathons a year. Nothing wrong with that. But George worked in intensive care, and Murray worried that he was around death too much. Several times a week his son had to pull the sheet up over yet another body, which had to be wearing, and George was a sensitive boy. Plenty to worry about there, too.

Still, Lizzie was the one he worried about the most. She'd always been an impetuous child, prone to outbursts and melodrama. He recalled her decision at age six to scalp her Barbie, how mad she'd been when she realized the hair wouldn't grow back. At the age of ten she told a teacher to go suck a dick. In college she ran off to Mexico for a winter, and now here she was talking about quitting a tenured position and going off to live in the Himalayas!

At times like this Murray wished Lillian were around, to read some calm sense into Lizzie's brain. His eyes fell upon the photograph of his wife on his bureau. Framed in brass, it showed a thirty-five-year-old Lillian in a wicker chair, wearing a pale yellow sleeveless dress, looking sultry with a cigarette between her long, elegant fingers. How much Lizzie resembled her these days, Murray thought. Lizzie's hair was brown and wavy instead of ash blond and straight like Lillian's, but she had the same blue eyes, the same thin lips that curled up at the edges, even when mad. He wished Lillian were here to help Lizzie see the folly of her ways. Lillian had always gotten the kids to listen, it seemed to him. But Lillian had been gone now for thirty-two years, so it was up to Ruth.

Murray was planning just how he could ensure that his two daughters could have some private time and space during the weekend, when he heard a car pull up outside. Finally, Lizzie was here. Hastily he climbed out of bed and drew up the covers. (It was a matter of pride for him; unmade beds spoke of illness, of an old man who'd given up. Next thing you knew, the house would smell like piss, and Ruth would be the first to notice that, too.)

Down in the kitchen he looked out the window and saw a bedraggled-looking Lizzie climbing out of her car with a bakery box in one hand and a six-pack in the other. She was wearing a pair of flowing, balloon-like pants that Murray did not find flattering.

"A little early for beer, isn't it?" he asked, opening the kitchen door for her.

"Depends on how you look at things," Lizzie said, pushing her way in.

"How come you're late?" George asked. "We're starving."

Lizzie set the bakery box on the table and opened a beer.

"Jeez," said Ruth. "At ten thirty?"

"I had a very rough morning," Lizzie said. "Don't 'jeez' me."

"What, was some student upset over a grade?" asked George.

"No," said Lizzie. "I had a big fight with Gavin."

"I'm sorry to hear that," said Murray, thinking: *Oh joy.*

"How big?" asked Ruth.

"Oh, pretty big."

"As in what, you broke up?"

"As in, I sent him to the ER," said Lizzie.

2.

In You Go

THE QUESTIONS THEN FOLLOWED SO QUICKLY—WHAT happened, how is he hurt, where is he hurt, and (from George) did he try and hurt you first?—that Lizzie wished she could just walk out the door, get in her car, and drive away. Drive to where, she didn't know, but she wasn't going to be able to stand getting the first degree by a lineup of interrogators.

On the other hand, what did she expect? That they were going to just sit there and go, *Mmm hmm, that's too bad, what shall we have for lunch?* A fight, Gavin in the hospital—there was a lot they wanted to know, and she couldn't blame them.

Note to self: breathe.

She quickly downed half a beer; then, knowing that Ruth would notice, she forced herself to slow down.

"Start at the beginning," Murray said.

"So a week ago Gavin and I actually agreed to stop seeing each other," she said. "I didn't mention it because . . . well, I just didn't."

George reached out to touch her shoulder. "That's got to be hard."

She shrugged his hand away. She didn't need George being *George* right now. "Not really," she said. "I just wish he hadn't dropped Mom's cookbook in a sink full of dirty water. Because if——"

"Wait—which cookbook?" Ruth asked.

This was the kicker. "Fannie Farmer."

Ruth coughed out a little squeak.

"Guy's a dead man," George declared flatly.

The reason for this immediate and decisive reaction to something so seemingly commonplace was that the cookbook in question—an old edition of Fannie Farmer's *The Boston Cooking School Cookbook*— had been Lillian's mainstay when the children were growing up; its dog-eared pages were filled with penciled notations in her handwriting, which had changed over the years, from the neat boxy script of a young careful bride to the wobbly curls and loops of a harried mother of four. Many of the notes involved shortcuts—*Use can of mushroom soup,* for instance. *Substitute Bisquick.* But it was not just cooking notes she wrote; she also jotted in the margins ideas for stories that came to her while preparing dinner. *Lucy/egg salad/ Mother/D.E.*—things that made no sense to the children but which they knew were significant enough for her not to forget before she had a chance to get to her typewriter up in the attic guest room. In addition to story ideas, she wrote out to-do lists and made embarrassing notes for difficult conversations. (*M does not cause ACNE!*) Fannie Farmer grew to be such an authority in her kitchen that the long-dead author became the go-to for anything Lillian couldn't answer.

George: "What's for dinner?"

Lillian: "I don't know, go ask Fannie."

Daniel: "Why can't we have pizza on Sunday night like normal people?"

Lillian: "I don't know, go ask Fannie."

Ruth: "What is *wrong* with this family?"

Lillian: "Ask Fannie."

They didn't have any of Lillian's stories—those had long since disappeared—and she'd never been much of a letter writer or journal keeper; but they had this tome full of notes, and thus it became a keepsake, a cherished legacy, far more than any diamond engagement ring or string of pearls. (For Ruth especially; she was the most sentimental one, when it came to their mother.) Over time they'd devised a plan for communal ownership: each would take custody for a year and then pass it on.

This had been Lizzie's year.

One unspoken assumption was that the cookbook should not be lent out; Lizzie had breached this pact, and Ruth picked up on it immediately. "What was Gavin doing with Mom's cookbook?"

"He happened to see it at my house one day, and he asked if he could borrow it because his own mother had had the same cookbook. I didn't think it would be a big deal. Then Dad got the flu, remember, and I forgot about the cookbook until last week. That's when I asked for it back."

"You *forgot* about it?" Ruth asked.

"Oh, shut up, Ruth, I was a little preoccupied, if you remember; Dad was pretty sick and nobody else stepped up, okay?"

Murray's spring flu had developed into pneumonia, and he'd been in the hospital for a week, hooked up to oxygen and IV antibiotics. Every evening Lizzie stopped by; George, to Lizzie's annoyance, was in Arizona for a race, and Ruth was in trial. And so like many times, it fell to Lizzie to care for her father—a state of affairs she actually cherished, simply for all the time it gave her with him; but she didn't need to be scolded when other matters—like getting a cookbook back—fell by the wayside.

"So Gavin said he didn't have it—which was bullshit, I knew it, and he knew that I knew it, so I kept asking him for it, and it became this big deal. He accused me of harassing him and told me if I didn't stop, he would go to the police."

"I don't like where this is going," said Murray.

Lizzie ignored him. Her father had a tendency to slip into Eeyore mode, and if she wasn't resilient, it could bring her down faster than a gloomy day in November.

"Anyway, I really wanted the cookbook back by this weekend," she said, "so we could go through it together. I thought it would be fun. So I went up to his house this morning. I was very nice. I had to press him and finally he says he'd look in one more place, and he goes into his office and what do you know, he finds it. Well! I could see right off that it's totally water damaged. Like the pages are all thick and ruffled and the cover's all warped. *That's* why he kept denying he had it. Anyway, he handed it back to me like no big deal, giving me this story about how he'd been making pancakes and accidentally knocked it into the sink."

"Are we going to cut into that coffee cake or just look at it?" George asked.

"So I'm holding the cookbook," Lizzie continued, "and I just got so pissed. It was, like, chemicals running through my veins. He said he'd buy us a new copy, but that's such bullshit because he knows it's full of Mom's notes."

"Go on," said Ruth warily. "You got pissed. What did you do?"

Lizzie took a sip of beer. "Shot him."

"Oh, ha ha," said Ruth, but her sarcasm belied a tiny fear that this might not be a joke after all. Lizzie was tempted to keep the fun going, but she knew that now was not the time for extended teasing.

"Just kidding, Ruth," she said. "No, actually"—and here she found herself wishing she'd never done it—"I poured hot water on his laptop."

Ruth hung her head with great drama, which put Lizzie on the defensive again.

"I know, but hey, it was right there on the island, next to this teakettle. Practically begging to be ruined, if you ask me. So I picked up the teakettle and started pouring. Oh come on!" Lizzie exclaimed in her defense. "You should see the cookbook! Mom's notes are all blurry now! He might as well have let it soak overnight!"

"No sense letting good food go to waste," George murmured, picking up a knife.

"I don't get it," said Ruth. "So why is Gavin in the ER?"

"Oh," said Lizzie. "That. Because when I started pouring, Gavin tried to grab it away from me, and the hot water spilled all over his hand and wrist. So now he's screaming in pain, and screaming at me to leave, and screaming at Jessica—that's his daughter—to Google what to do for scalding burns. And apparently if they involve your hands, you're supposed to go to the hospital. I thought that was over-kill, but maybe he has a low co-pay for ER visits, I don't know. In any case I left."

"Actually, scalding burns can be pretty serious," George said. "Some lady sued McDonald's for third-degree burns from their coffee."

Third degree? From hot liquid?

"What?" she demanded, for Ruth was shaking her head.

"I just wish you could have shown a little more impulse control," Ruth said.

Lizzie thought Ruth could take her condescending remark and shove it.

"And I hope he backed everything up," Ruth continued.

"Whose side are you on?" Lizzie demanded.

"Your side," said Ruth, "but I don't want to fuel the fire either. He's a jerk, I'm glad you agreed to end your relationship, but I wish you hadn't escalated things. If he lost his files he's not going to for-give you. At the very least you're going to have to buy him a new laptop."

Murray cleared his throat. "I think we all need to put emotion aside," he said. "Chances are he's got backups; as for your mother's cookbook, it's unfortunate but accidents happen. In any case, let's hope it's not a serious burn and everybody will move on. Regarding the breakup, I'm sorry about that, Lizzie, but I do think it's for the best. I don't think he was the right man for you."

Inwardly Lizzie rolled her eyes. Her father's words implied a more serious relationship than she and Gavin had ever had. And she didn't need her father's approval in any event.

"Somebody else have a piece," said George, "before I eat it all."

"Why aren't you fat?" Ruth asked.

"Why aren't you nice?" George asked.

Lizzie reached for another beer. Murray stopped her. "Don't you think one beer before noon is enough?"

"Zero beers before noon is enough," said Ruth.

"Oh, Ruth," sighed Lizzie, for this whole sequence of events was now bringing on a massive headache. She wished her older sister would have a beer—or better yet, a couple shots of bourbon. "Do you always have to be such a little angel?"

"I'll split one with you, if you want," offered George.

LIZZIE KNEW, of course, that Ruth was right; no beer before lunch was really a good idea, and she turned down George's offer and put on her sunglasses to help with the headache and went out to the yard feeling light-headed and almost as angry as she'd been standing in Gavin's kitchen, facing off with him. The cookbook was actually just the last straw in what had been a very difficult month. She felt a little dishonest for not sharing the whole story with her family, but the whole story was still just too raw.

She wished she'd counted to ten, though. It might have at least given her time to realize just how hot the water was.

She picked up a rake and although very few leaves had fallen, she worked at the lawn with a swift, choppy vengeance. She thought back to when she had met Gavin, after a literary reading a year and a half ago as part of a fund-raiser for a nearby library. It was a short list of local writers, though Gavin was certainly the most well known; in fact Lizzie was thinking of using a story he'd published in *The New Yorker* in her Modern Short Fiction class. Afterward, Lizzie approached the distinguished writer and said, "Mr. Langley, I'm a big fan of your work," and he hesitated, amused, then took her hand and thanked her, and amid a gaggle of admirers, he offered to get her a glass of wine and then herded her away from the group and challenged her, privately and with great solemnity, to tell him just why she was such a fan.

Lizzie was caught off guard.

"I guess it's because your characters are so universal," she finally managed to say, feeling extremely sophomoric, but it seemed sufficient for Gavin, because he broke into laughter, which deepened the craggy lines on his face, and he downed his wine and told her to wait right there while he got another glass. Which she did. Wait, that is. And halfway through that second glass, after they had exchanged further pleasantries, he suddenly leveled his gaze upon her, fell silent, then gruffly said, "Let's get out of here, shall we?" and set his glass down on a vestibular table and touched the small of her back with just enough pressure that she found herself heading out of the library, across the mud-rutted parking lot toward his car, a sleek black Mercedes SUV, whose soft leather seats tilted back and later, on a dark stretch of road, felt buttery smooth against her bare thighs as he buried his head in her lap.

She knew he was married, that he had a reputation. Yet she didn't care. She'd been alone for the last year, ever since Bruce, her boyfriend of nine years, had come home one summer night and announced to her that he was in love with another woman. It had shocked her, how unlovable she instantly felt—how old, how wrinkled and dried up and dead. So that when Gavin the very next morning had emailed her to come over to his place for coffee that afternoon, she rearranged her office hours so that she was not only free but hot and damp and starved for his touch, something that must have been apparent to Gavin upon her arrival at the big red sky-lit barn in which he wrote, because he wasted no time in rolling the great door shut and tearing off the clothes she had specially chosen to motivate him to do just that.

They began meeting once a week, usually on Thursday afternoons. Wine. Sex. She didn't want a serious, long-term relationship; she was still trying to figure out what went wrong with Bruce. No: she mostly wanted to feel like a sexual being again. It didn't hurt that Gavin was older, attractive in a rough, homely way. Plus he had star power, which she found sexy. She didn't like to admit it, but there it was. He dropped names. So-and-so was a friend. So-and-so wanted him to review a book. So-and-so was coming up for Thanksgiving. He had a wife, that was true, which gave Lizzie pause, but she lived in New York and Gavin assured her their marriage was a sham, in name only, stapled together by a couple of linked accounts at Merrill Lynch.

There was no danger of love here, that was clear on both sides. Nevertheless they found a lot to talk about on those Thursday afternoons, especially during the New Hampshire primary; both were Bernie supporters, but Lizzie thought he could win and Gavin did not. They talked about literature. They talked about articles in *The New Yorker.* There was the little problem of a boisterous ego on

Gavin's part, the fact that he could sometimes feel a little over-bearing on certain issues, but Lizzie was able to ignore it most of the time.

Until this past month.

In any case, given the brazenly sexual nature of their relationship and the lack of commitment, he was not someone she was dying to bring home to meet the family. However, her father got wind of things when Lizzie mentioned one gloomy Sunday afternoon that she couldn't come down and watch the Patriots with him because she had other plans. She thought the words "other plans" would slide by Murray, but Murray (who made no secret of the fact that he wished she would find someone to replace Bruce) deduced from those words a promising new relationship, and over the course of the next few weeks he kept hinting that Lizzie should bring this new gentleman over to the house for dinner at some point—an idea that mortified Lizzie. She kept putting things off until one afternoon she and Gavin risked a rare public appearance together at the liquor store, and who should walk in but Murray.

"*That's* who you've been seeing?" he demanded later that evening, and Lizzie remembered at that point her father's having been at Gavin's housewarming party, and instantly she regretted her decision to be seen in public with him.

"It's not serious, is it?"

Lizzie felt trapped. If she answered no, her father would either presume that she and Gavin were simply enjoying nineteenth-century afternoon strolls together, or else, on a more up-to-date assumption, he would be forced to recognize the unpleasant thought that his daughter went around having casual sex. But if she lied and answered that yes, they *were* serious, he would jump to the conclusion that this man might become his son-in-law someday. Which would never, ever happen, but the very notion itself would cause Murray a lot of stress.

Either way, her father wasn't going to like the answer.

"We just kind of hang out together sometimes," she told him lamely.

That, apparently, was enough for Murray to set aside his distaste and press her again to bring Gavin over to the house for dinner—something neither Gavin nor Lizzie wanted to do, but Lizzie finally convinced Gavin that they only needed to do it once, that it would get Murray off her back, and she and Gavin would then be free to continue their mutually-agreed-upon, uncommitted, sex-drenched encounters.

The dinner was a flop, to say the least. Gavin for some reason got it into his head that he had to ingratiate himself to Murray, to which end he offered to restack Murray's woodpile. That didn't go over well. Murray liked his woodpile the way it was, and he certainly didn't need some guy sixteen years his junior rearranging things. Then Gavin made the mistake of asking Murray about his decades-old congressional campaign, which Gavin knew about because he'd Googled Murray, and Murray cut him off before the question was barely out of his mouth. (Fortunately Gavin didn't bring up Lillian, or—God forbid—Daniel. Murray would have closed up like a tomb.) For his part, to make conversation Murray asked Gavin about his latest book, something Gavin hated to be asked about, since it wasn't going very well at the moment, and Gavin gave him some kind of snobby reply about how he never talked about his works in progress, and Lizzie tried to change the subject by talking about how Gavin was thinking of planting a field of sunflowers, and in this, the two men finally found common ground, which lasted all of five minutes.

Afterward Lizzie didn't hear the end of it.

"I don't know what you see in him," Murray grumbled, and what was Lizzie supposed to say, that she liked screwing Mr. Viagra for let-me-count-the-reasons?

"He's got an oversized ego and he's way too old for you," Murray went on. "Doesn't he have a daughter in her twenties? Find someone your own age," he told her, in a moment of uncharacteristic do-it-because-I-said-so bluntness.

Well, obviously she didn't follow that advice, did she?

A cloud moved swiftly over the sun, darkening the lawn, the white clapboard house, and its connecting shed, where Lizzie could see her father's hired man, Boyd, tinkering with a tractor. He waved, and she waved back. Boyd took care of Murray's dairy herd. Murray had bought the herd when he retired up to the north country ten years ago, but he quickly found he liked the *idea* of dairy farming better than he liked actually getting up at five every morning. So he'd hired Boyd.

In the shed, Lizzie found an old basket and loaded up her meager pile of leaves. They smelled of must and decay, and as she stood there, a memory washed over her—she was five again, and George and Daniel were burying her in a pile of leaves in the backyard. She recalled lying still, the weightlessness of the leaves, the smell of rot, the unbearable tickle against her neck . . . Daniel telling George— loudly, for Lizzie's sake—to watch out for the *big hairy baboochies* that lived in dead leaves . . .

She shook her head. Such a very long time ago. She glanced now through the patio doors into the kitchen, where she could see her father, Ruth, and George still at the table. Lizzie realized she was going to have to watch out for Ruth the whole weekend. Whenever Ruth came up from DC, she put on her Eldest Child Hat and tried to get everybody to agree with her. For instance, of late she'd been making noise about how Murray ought to be looking at retirement communities—for real, too, not as part of the joke they used to make out of it. "You turn seventy, Dad: in you go!" they used to cluck when he was in his sixties, able to make light of a distant possibility. They would tease him relentlessly—and each other as well. Forgot a name? In you go! Lost your keys? In you go!

But now with him being eighty-one, it was nothing to joke about. Lizzie herself didn't think her father was anywhere near needing to give up his freedom for the safety of an old folks' home. Murray, after all, still had his wits about him; he still drove, he still shopped and cooked and cleaned up after himself. For the most part he took care of his property, keeping the fields mowed and the house in decent repair. Along with Boyd, he still managed his small herd of cows, having installed a new milking system the year before. He still made it to doctors' appointments on time.

But whenever Ruth came home, she focused not on what Murray *could* do, but on what he *wasn't* doing. *Dad's garbage smelled, did you notice? Dad didn't shave this morning, did you notice? Dad hasn't gotten his snow tires on yet, he hasn't filed his taxes, he hasn't picked up his mail in a week. And he forgets things all the time!* All right, it was true; there'd been some disturbing signs. A few months ago he got lost driving back from Concord, which should never have happened since it was a straight shot up I-93, but Murray had gotten off at the wrong exit and ended up in the wild, dark woods of Thornton Gore. Another time he left some carrots on high and went off to fold some laundry and realized his mistake only when the smoke alarm went off; the pot was so charred he had to throw it away. Ruth liked to focus on these things. And despite the fact that Lizzie was the one who visited twice a week, bringing him soup and bread and fresh vegetables from the farm stand in the summer; who helped him pick out new clothes when all his shirts were threadbare; who played cribbage with him during long gray Sunday afternoons in the winter—despite all this, Ruth just had to come up and as the oldest, she assumed that she knew better, and it made Lizzie burn inside to be made to feel like the clueless, impulsive little sister again, the one who went around making excuses for pouring hot water on people's laptops, which only further reinforced Ruth's idea that the world was going to fall apart unless she, Ruth, *took charge.*

For how Ruth loved to take charge! Ruth had been a lawyer from the age of five, basically—at least, that was the story Lizzie always heard. As a child she had organized the neighborhood games and spelled out the rules. Even at Thanksgiving she came up with an efficient plan to serve the dishes going clockwise so that there was a constant parade of options in front of you, the turkey and stuffing followed by the mashed potatoes and the pureed squash and the creamed onions and the cranberry sauce, a meal designed (in Lizzie's view) to make you feel guilty for not appreciating the bounty that lay before you, since Lizzie basically hated everything except pumpkin pie.

Once, Lizzie had visited Ruth's home in Bethesda (yes, it was true, only once in fifteen-plus years), and arrived to find all the shades pulled exactly halfway down, and the mail in a neat stack in the entryway, and the kids with their Container Store bins lining the walls of their rooms, each with its own label, Art Supplies and Sports Equipment and Dirty Laundry—a place for everything and everything in its place, even in Ruth's own room where every night her husband hung his clothes on one of those wooden valets with hangers and hooks and a little square shelf for change and keys; and Ruth herself had a miniature highboy for her jewelry, and all her shoes lined up by color on racks in their walk-in closet, her library of purses upright in their slots, her wardrobe arranged by category. ("It's like goddamn Macy's," Lizzie exclaimed, and Ruth blushed and said it helped her get dressed quickly in the morning, something Lizzie wouldn't understand, this said not in snide comparison but nevertheless with a hint of condescension that made Lizzie feel like people who worked in Washington, DC, law firms were somehow superior to those who taught literature at northern state colleges.)

Oh, Ruth, Lizzie thought. *If you could just let other people* take charge.

She glanced at the house again, but the sun had come back out, and with its reflection, she couldn't see into the kitchen anymore. She began to feel paranoid. They were discussing her shortcomings, no doubt. Lizzie the baby of the family who didn't have any impulse control. Lizzie the scatterbrained, emotional one. She felt herself grow defensive again. Excuse me, she wanted to say to them; if she was so scatterbrained, how had she gotten tenure? How had she published all those scholarly articles on William Faulkner? Still, again, she wished she'd counted to ten before picking up the teakettle, and she wished she'd shown a little more contrition in front of her family, instead of getting so defensive. Having her family all together brought out the worst in her.

At that moment the screen door slapped shut, and Ruth stepped off the back porch, hugging one of Lillian's old sweaters closely around her. One embarrassing fact about their family was that even after thirty-two years, they still held on to their mother's clothes. What kind of a family were they, anyway, that couldn't get rid of the dead?

She flashed on her mother, boxing up Grammy Holmes's clothes, a week after that old lady died. Lillian had driven Lizzie down to Boston with her to clean out the house. Lizzie at five felt useful, important. She thought she would get a lot of clothes for her dress-up box. But Lillian was relentless with Grammy Holmes's old dresses and suits: she went through the closet garment by garment with a shrug, a quick balling up, a yank of the masking tape: one more box added to the stack going to the thrift shop. So much for dress-up and make-believe. Sentimental, Lillian was not.

It would have been nice to have had a little more guidance along those lines, Lizzie thought now, recalling her mother's efficiency. Would have been nice to have learned how to just let things go.

"Don't run away on me," Ruth said. "I didn't mean to sound like I wasn't on your side back there. I am. We all are. I just hope the burn isn't too bad."

"Me, too."

"Are you really okay with the breakup?"

"Separate ways, Ruth," said Lizzie. "Not breakup."

Ruth waited, as though expecting a confession.

"He was a friend with benefits," Lizzie said with a sigh. "What can I say?"

"Even so," said Ruth.

It was as though her sister wanted to believe that there was something more. Over ten years separated the two of them: Ruth, happily married, mother of two, straight and narrow, high-powered attorney in the bright lights, big city; and Lizzie, single, childless, still a bit of a hippie. They had their issues. But Ruth also had a lease on Lizzie's heart, which, hard as she tried, Lizzie could never quite break.

And which Ruth was waving in front of her right now.

3.

For Company, Add Shrimp

OF ALL THE ITEMS ON RUTH'S AGENDA FOR THE WEEKEND, dealing with a lovers' spat that put someone in the hospital was not one of them.

She'd come prepared, first of all, to convince Lizzie, at her father's behest, that Gavin was not the right man for her; and second, to argue for more help for Murray—possibly even convincing him that he should start visiting a few retirement homes. She'd accounted for schedule-changing contingencies: the possibility that the tropical storm that had been brewing off the North Carolina coast could speed north and prevent the plane from taking off out of Manchester on Monday, for instance; or that—God forbid—Murray might have some kind of medical crisis. Why, her husband's mother had passed out on the sofa, right out of the blue, due to what they later learned was a sudden drop in blood sugar. These things happened to otherwise healthy people in their eighties, and Ruth was aware it could happen to Murray at any time. She was nothing if not a very good worrier.

But Lizzie and Gavin having this kind of a blowup? Not in the picture.

While Lizzie was out raking leaves, Ruth, George, and Murray stayed at the kitchen table and discussed the situation. Murray was of the opinion that a ruined cookbook—even a family heirloom—was a small price to pay for the termination of a bad relationship. George was mostly concerned with keeping Lizzie from feeling alienated from everybody (which was *so* George, when it came to Lizzie).

Ruth, on the other hand, suspected they weren't getting the whole story. She couldn't put her finger on it, but she was afraid Lizzie was omitting some essential details that might have complicated matters.

"You're saying she's lying?"

"Don't polarize, George. I'm just saying she might be leaving out some information. Something else might have ticked her off."

"You're such a gloomy Gus," said George.

"I'm a lawyer, George," Ruth reminded him. "That's my job." She finished her coffee and rose from her chair. "I'm going to go talk to her."

Heading across the lawn, she'd looked up and saw clouds building up over Mount Lafayette. The weather could change so quickly here in northern New Hampshire, and she pictured the inevitable news reports of stranded hikers. She'd been one of those hikers one August long ago, finding herself in a sudden storm on Mount Washington with only sneakers and a lightweight rain jacket. Luckily she and her friends had been able to take refuge in the Lake of the Clouds hut, but they awoke the next morning to find the trail had vanished under six inches of fresh snow. Her father had been livid—that she'd been so unprepared, of course, but mainly that she'd told him she was going up Lafayette and then changed her mind at the last minute. Ruth had cringed under her father's anger, and felt reduced for an entire month.

The clouds were moving fast, and Ruth felt the ionized tug in the air of a coming storm. She pulled her mother's old cardigan close against her chest.

"Hey," she said.

"Hey," said Lizzie, poking at the leaves.

Ruth apologized for sounding like she was taking Gavin's side back in the kitchen, and tried to get Lizzie to open up a little more, but again Lizzie simply insisted that she was glad the relationship was over. Hearing her sister characterize Gavin as a friend with benefits made Ruth feel sad and old-fashioned; she had had her own casual relationships back in the day, but this contemporary phrase was just so blatantly unromantic. "You weren't angry about something else?"

"No, Ruth."

"I'm your sister," Ruth reminded her.

"So cut me some slack," Lizzie said. "It is what it is. The guy's a douchebag. I should have ended things a long time ago."

Ruth decided to stop pushing.

"What do you want to do this afternoon?" she asked. "You want to go for a hike? You want to just hang out?"

"I don't want to sit around talking about Gavin, that's for sure."

"Okay. No Gavin. But why don't you stay overnight?" she suggested. "You and me and George haven't spent the night in Dad's house in I don't know how long."

"I've got to feed the neighbor's cats."

"They can't go one night? Besides, I don't want you driving late."

"What, you think I'm going to drink too much at dinner and then drive home drunk?"

"Don't be so defensive. I just want your company."

"I'll think about it," said Lizzie.

"Where's the cookbook?"

"In my car."

Ruth hugged her chest. "I'm so pissed at him. How could he be so clumsy?"

"Gavin takes very good care of his own personal property," said Lizzie. "When it comes to other peoples' stuff, not so much."

Ruth thought that, knowing this trait, Lizzie might have foreseen the risks and opted not to leave an irreplaceable cookbook at his house. But she didn't say this.

"Come on. Spend the night. It'll make Dad happy. We'll bend over backward not to fight."

"We always fight," said Lizzie. "He expects too much."

Ruth, whose two boys fought all the time, didn't think it was too much to expect a few adult siblings to get together for a short weekend without fighting. But she saw the Catch-22 in arguing this very point with Lizzie right now, so again, she kept the thought to herself.

She wondered if she was going to be keeping thoughts to herself all weekend.

Lizzie was inclined to relent, however, because she said, "I don't want anyone counting how many beers I've had."

"I'll close my eyes. Maybe we can find some time to go through stuff."

"Like Mom's sweaters?" Lizzie nodded at the one Ruth was wearing, a navy blue cardigan with little cables up the front and knobby yarn buttons.

"I like Mom's sweaters," protested Ruth. "I always wear them when I come home."

"Don't you think it's a little weird that we've kept her clothes all these years? Even throughout Dad's move?"

"We didn't keep all of them. And Mom would think it was practical," said Ruth, "given the fact that I still get some use out of them. Besides, they make me feel close to her. Anyway, I'm glad you're staying. It'll give us time to talk about Dad."

Lizzie expelled a puff of irritation.

"Well, am I the only one who worries about him living alone?" said Ruth. "What if he burns the house down? What if he falls? What if he has a heart attack? He's eighty-one."

"I think Dad's in pretty good shape," said Lizzie. "I keep an eye on him."

"Well, I notice things. He didn't shave this morning, did you see that? He left the bathroom heater on. And last night he was using paint thinner to clean his hairbrush! I know everybody thinks it's premature, but I really think it's time we started checking out retirement communities."

"That'll go over like a lead balloon."

"But we have to start talking about it, at the very least! We can't just stick our heads in the sand." Ruth looked at her watch. "Whatever. Right now, come to the grocery store with me. We're low on milk and I'll get stuff for dinner."

"Fine," said Lizzie. "But first I want some coffee cake. Goes great with beer, you know."

"George ate it all," said Ruth glumly.

GAVIN HAD RUINED IT, all right.

Ruth held the worn, familiar cookbook in her hands. Its tan cover had been oil-splotched to begin with, its frayed spine reinforced with brittle, amber-colored tape; but now because of Gavin's carelessness, the cover had curled up as well. The yellowed pages clung together in thick, ruffled wads. Where her mother had once penciled in notes, the writing was now smudged. Ruth worked at the pages and pried them apart to find the recipe for macaroni and cheese. She knew this one by heart. *Use Velveeta*, her mother had written long ago. *For company, add shrimp.*

A blurry mess, now.

A red ribbon attached to the book's spine took her to the recipe for popovers, which sent a shudder through her chest. She recalled that last morning in early November so many years ago, the day of her father's final rally, when her mother had insisted on teaching her how to make them. She vaguely remembered saying something cruel to get out of the cooking lesson—something about not wanting to be just a housewife, like Lillian. And Lillian making some wry comment about ironing underwear, or something like that. She'd felt terrible, but did she apologize? Of course not; she was seventeen. And she'd never had another chance, something that continually ate at her—a good woman scorned, a crime unconfessed. For which Ruth was always trying to atone, in a variety of ways. There was the little shrine she kept in the guest room, with photos and Lillian's wooden jewelry box, her silver comb and brush set on the otherwise empty bureau. The poppy-seed cake she baked every year on Lillian's birthday. The favored brands of soap. A houseful of lilacs every May. If Murray remarked, as he did during one of his visits, that Ruth was idealizing her mother, Ruth cut him off. If Lillian had had flaws, Ruth didn't want to hear about them.

The popovers had turned out perfectly, she remembered now.

Of course, she never made them again.

She continued to pry apart the pages. She found the oddly named recipe for Littleton Spider Cornbread, made in a cast-iron skillet. Rumor had it that Lillian's great-grandmother—a Littleton native—had known Fannie Farmer and was the source for that recipe; Lillian had often made it for the family, and at some point, it must have inspired an idea for a story because beside it, she'd scribbled (in notes now blurred because of Gavin): *Husband keeps asking when she's going to start painting again. Shut up! she finally screams, eyeing the skillet.* Ruth smiled. She would have liked to read *that* story!

She went on, and came across several pages of aspics. How they'd all hated those congealed excuses for salads—hard-boiled eggs in a congealed beef jelly, for instance, with a dash of sherry that Lillian insisted lent the dish an international flair. There was the recipe for American Chop Suey, a crowd-pleaser—nothing of the Chinese variety but rather a bland concoction of macaroni and hamburger and—in Lillian's version—Campbell's tomato soup. The recipe for meat loaf, with the word "Imagine:" penciled in. Beef Doves, Oyster Pie, Chicken à la King—dishes only George liked but ones she served nonetheless. ("You have a no-thank-you helping," she ordered the rest of them—including Murray. Why did she bother? Oysters were on sale or something? Ruth herself didn't cook anything unless she got three thumbs up.)

Salmon Wiggle. Oh, dear.

The best fare was in the dessert section, and Ruth came across the recipe for apple crunch, a family staple made with apples and butter and sugar and either flour or cornflakes. (Lillian had always used cornflakes.) In the margins was one of Lillian's notes, smudged enough now that Ruth could only make out the words "Virginia/plumber." Ruth decided right then that she would make the dish tonight. George would be ecstatic.

Back inside, she wordlessly showed the cookbook to Murray and George, still at the kitchen table.

"Oh man," said George.

"Kids," Murray protested, "it's a cookbook. I think you're all being overly sentimental, don't you?"

"No," said Ruth.

"No," said George. They bumped fists, in agreement for once.

"Lizzie's spending the night," said Ruth. "I talked her into it. She has to feed the neighbor's cats at some point, but we'll all be here tonight. I'm making pesto and apple crunch."

"That's nice," said Murray. "Sox are playing at six."

"Who's pitching?" George asked.

"Don't know."

"Ugh, baseball," said Ruth, starting a list.

Murray looked up. "You do this to Morgan?"

"Do what?"

"Rain on his parade?"

Ruth felt the color rise in her cheeks. She never felt smaller than when her father scolded her.

"If you don't like it, don't watch it," said Murray with a shrug.

She felt, like, ten.

THEY DIDN'T GO through any boxes of "stuff" that afternoon; Lizzie fell into a deep sleep on the sofa, and George went into town. And Murray, too, was napping, so Ruth took the time to check in with her office.

Ruth's practice centered on large antitrust suits, defending Fortune 500 companies against governmental allegations of price fixing and such. She didn't particularly like representing large corporations, but her practice had evolved in this direction over the years, one case leading to another, so that she woke up these mornings and realized she had slid into a groove that was not going to let her out easily, not with everyone in the firm depending on her expertise.

Not that she wanted out. Ruth made a very handsome salary, as partner—more than three times that of her husband, Morgan, who was a lawyer for the National Resource Defense Council. Much of their double income went to the private school where they sent their two children in Bethesda, Maryland, as well as the hefty mortgage they carried on their four-bedroom house, and the second mortgage on a condo on the Delaware shore. They had just spent the month of August there, as a matter of fact, getting the boys, now in their early teens, to concede to beach volleyball and bike rides and card games in the evening with their parents, instead of sneaking off to plug into social media. Okay, maybe the boys were squeezing WhatsApp in between Pamper the Parents, but they'd all had a good month together and came back with no fistfights in the car, something Ruth considered a major accomplishment.

Having checked in with the firm, she called home, only to learn that Morgan had agreed to let the boys spend the night with friends—kids Ruth didn't much approve of, given that one had gotten caught with some pot and the other had recently been embroiled in a cheating scandal. News travels fast among parents, and Ruth had heard of both incidents from her own friend Alison, whose children told her everything, unlike Kyle and Caleb, who with each passing day grew more and more tight-lipped about anything that might shed light on their social and emotional development.

It seemed to Ruth that Morgan grew more lax when she was gone, since being more lax meant less work for him.

Morgan, however, defended his decision because he wasn't feeling so great, and just wanted to veg out that night. It seemed to Ruth that he could "veg out" just as well with two teenage boys playing video games upstairs—it wasn't like he had to change diapers or give baths—but she let it go and told herself not to pat herself on the shoulder too much for how, when Morgan went away, *she* took the boys out for ice cream instead of shipping them off to someone else's house.

"You do sound tired," said Ruth. "Busy day?"

"Not that busy."

"What'd you do?"

"Wrote some comments."

"All day?"

"No, just in the morning."

"Okay," said Ruth. She was getting a weird feeling about this. "What'd you do in the afternoon?"

Morgan fell silent for a moment. "I had a meeting."

"Oh? Where?"

"Up on the Hill."

Now it was Ruth's turn to not say anything. "Up on the Hill" to Ruth meant a woman named Charlene, with whom Morgan had had an affair several years ago. It was short-lived, but as any affair will do, it threw a wrench of doubt into their relationship.

"Oh," said Ruth.

"I didn't see her."

"I didn't ask."

"You don't trust me, though."

No, Morgan, after you fuck a Southern ditz in a fleabag hotel for two months and then tell me about it after you've ended it, leaving me in the cuckolded dark for sixty days and counting, no, I don't completely trust you.

"Never mind," said Ruth. "But I can see how you're tired." This was how it was with them these days: a lot of "never minds" and "it's nothings."

Morgan cleared his throat. "How's the visit going?"

"Oh, Lizzie had some big fight with her boyfriend, or rather her ex-boyfriend, or rather I shouldn't say boyfriend at all," Ruth said, closing the door to the twin bedroom, because George had gotten

back and she'd heard Lizzie's footsteps on the stairs. "It's complicated. Things got messy. And now Gavin's in the hospital."

"What'd she do, deck him?"

Through the walls, Ruth could hear George and Lizzie in the
next room, laughing over something. She felt left out. She briefly
sketched out the scenario for Morgan, but in doing so, the whole
incident sounded silly. A cookbook was a cookbook. They sounded
like the sappiest family around. Indeed, Morgan found it hard to
grasp the level of outrage.

"Aren't there other cookbooks?"

There were, actually. Lillian had liked to watch *The French Chef*
on television, and she'd bought *Mastering the Art of French Cooking,
Volumes I and II*, and taken notes in the margins while watching
Julia Child, and when Julia swigged wine, Lillian did as well. But
Lillian's French dinners—her *pot au feu*, her *boeuf bourguignon*—
had never evolved into family favorites.

She grew defensive. "You don't treat a borrowed book with a
mother's notes like some paperback from the used bookstore," she
said. "I've got to go start dinner. I'll call you later."

Morgan coughed delicately. "Not too late," he said. "I'm going to
bed early. I want to nip this thing in the bud."

Morgan was frequently "nipping things in the bud," and he took
very good care of himself when doing so.

She wondered if Charlene had lost that silly Southern accent
by now.

In the room next door, George and Lizzie were slouching side by
side on the four-poster double bed, cracking up as they watched videos

on George's phone. When Ruth tried to join them, George closed out the app.

"Not really your kind of humor, Ruth," he said.

That hurt.

"Come on," said Ruth, wiggling between them. She noticed a water stain on the wallpaper. Did the house have a leak? Maybe there was black mold everywhere, not just in the bathroom. "Show me something funny."

George reloaded the video, which was an old *Saturday Night Live* clip with John Belushi and Laraine Newman. Ruth laughed loudly. George and Lizzie, who'd already seen it, didn't laugh so hard this time around.

That hurt, too.

Chalk it up to a difference of age, Ruth told herself. There were four years between her and George, and almost eleven between her and Lizzie; Daniel had bridged the upper gap, being a year and a half younger than Ruth. In many of their childhood photos, they were all lined up, oldest to youngest, pretty evenly spaced until you got to little Lizzie. Ruth sometimes wondered if Lizzie had been a surprise. She wished she could ask her mother. She wished she could ask her mother a lot of things. *Did you ever go through a rough patch with Dad? What would you have done, if he'd had an affair? Was Daniel really the most difficult one? And what did you write about up there in the guest room?*

There were no answers to these questions (Lillian and Daniel gone, the stories lost or thrown away), and there never would be. At times like this Ruth resented her mother for dying so early. *Who's going to tell me what to expect with menopause?* she wanted to ask. *Who's going to help me deal with a sixteen-year-old boy?*

And, in the end: *Why couldn't you have gone straight home that night? Why'd you have to drive up School Street hill?*

What Ruth remembered most about Daniel was that he was the family comedian. At the dinner table, in the car, or over dessert, Daniel told jokes and did imitations—of teachers, the mailman, the family physician. Ruth, as his older sister, always felt like he stole her spotlight, but she loved his antics, the way he could simply stand up and make them all laugh. One Thanksgiving, just as they were about to all sing the Doxology for grace (per Grammy Holmes's pious insistence), Daniel tapped his spoon against his water glass. "Ahem," he said. He had his own grace to sing, he said. Warily Lillian cocked her head. Daniel stood up. Holding an imaginary mike to his mouth, he began to croon: "*Danke schoen*, darling, *danke schoen*," on key and resonant, with enough syrupy inflection to make Ruth suspect, three years later while watching *Ferris Bueller's Day Off*, that Matthew Broderick had somehow been listening in that day and taking his cue from Daniel.

"Go Dutch treat, you were sweet—"

"All right," said Grammy Holmes. "That's enough."

Lillian ostensibly agreed with her mother, and tried to look stern, but everyone could see the stars in her eyes.

"You heard Grammy," she said, giving Daniel a hug.

Daniel was even able to find humor in Murray's campaign. This was notable, since after a long day in the Blaire-Mobile it was easy for them to all find themselves in a piqued state. Murray dragged them to a lot of church suppers that fall, which the children hated (baked beans and coleslaw *again*?), but it was Daniel who invoked images of reverent, bosomy old ladies slumbering in happy flatulence later that night.

"Stop that," Lillian scolded them, but she, too, would laugh, stubbing out her cigarette in the little ashtray as they pulled into the church parking lot in the Blaire-Mobile.

"Behave yourselves," said Murray. He'd be neatly dressed for the evening in a pressed pair of khakis and a light blue button-down shirt. "You're potentially members of a congressman's family."

"Afterward can we go to McDonald's?" asked George, twelve at the time.

"No," said Lillian, always cost-conscious. "You eat those beans and hot dogs."

Murray cut the engine, which ticked and wheezed before falling silent.

"Look, Channel Nine is here," Daniel said.

"Will we be on TV tonight?" asked Ruth anxiously. She'd just turned seventeen, and her face was all broken out.

Lillian took a moment to brush dandruff from Murray's lapels. "I will remind everyone to use their napkins. You don't want food on your face if you're going to be on TV."

"Beans, beans, the energy fruit," Daniel began.

"No bean jokes in the church, please," said Murray. "Okay, men, let's get this show on the road. What do we want?"

"Equal rights!" the children groaned. "Health care!"

"And when do we want it?"

"Now!"

Afterward they *would* stop at McDonald's, Murray's pumped-up optimism trumping Lillian's budgetary protests, and they would divvy up the fries and burgers, no longer concerned about napkins, arriving back at the big house in Concord with greasy fingers and ketchup in the corners of their mouths.

Ruth didn't mind these campaign events. She was certain her father was going to win, and she liked to picture herself living in Washington, DC, visiting the White House, the Capitol, the stone memorials dedicated to men she'd read about in history books. She liked imagining a school filled with the children of other congressmen (and they were, at the time, mostly men), girls in plaid skirts and boys in preppy blue blazers who would all take an active interest in civic engagement. She pictured herself visiting the White House and asking questions that might catch the attention of someone important, who would then take her back into the Oval Office to meet the president himself—Ronald Reagan or Walter Mondale, depending on how the election turned out.

So she was crestfallen when, one night, her father made an offhand reference to the studio apartment he would rent if elected.

"Studio?" Ruth said blankly.

"Or a one-bedroom."

"We're not going?"

Murray, who was leaning over the dining room table with a mess of newspapers spread out before him, looked up with surprise. "You weren't expecting me to uproot the family, were you? Pull you kids out of school halfway through the year? No, you'll stay here in the house with your mother. I'll come home on the weekends. It's better that way. You can keep your friends, keep your after-school activities."

Ruth didn't want to keep her friends. She was already at that point where she wanted nothing but to get the hell out of Concord, New Hampshire, where half the kids didn't even know that each state had two senators and an apportioned number of representatives. She wanted to live in Washington, DC, where people would talk about something besides hockey or baseball.

But the most she could hope for, she realized that evening, was that her father would get a one-bedroom with a pullout sofa, maybe, so that she could visit him over school breaks. Quickly she amended her fantasy. She would take the train down; she would spend her Christmas money on a soft-sided suitcase instead of the clunky gray Samsonites her parents kept in the attic. She would buy a leather purse that slung over her shoulder, and a nice trench coat for spring that would coordinate with a new pair of shoes. And she would stop in New York and buy some good makeup, to cover the pimples.

She was all set to tell her father that if he won, she would be more than happy to go apartment hunting with him, when Daniel came in.

"Looking kind of glum, Ruth," he said.

"Don't you have homework?"

"Don't you?"

"Kids," said Murray, folding up the paper.

Daniel was eating peanuts. "So knock-knock."

"Who's there?" said Murray.

"Impatient cow."

Ruth rolled her eyes, but Murray grinned. "Im——"

"MOOOOO!" yelled Daniel, right in Ruth's ear, which made her jump. She pursed her lips, partly out of irritation but partly to keep herself from laughing.

"You are, like, in first grade," she told Daniel.

"Yeah, but people love me," he replied, tossing a peanut in the air to catch in his mouth.

The next day Ruth tried to retell the joke to her own friends. She waited too long for the punch line, though, and then yelled too loud, and the joke fell flat.

THE LAST CAMPAIGN EVENT they all attended that fall occurred in early November, a Saturday rally in front of the State House. Although most of the leaves had fallen, the weather started out warm, the sun strong enough that Ruth knew she would be squinting in all the pictures. First she gave her own well-prepared speech, her voice trembling ever so slightly but then evening out, allowing her to use the inflection techniques she'd learned in English class. Then her father took the podium. He spoke of health care, of course, along with government aid for pregnant women and children, more preschool education, tax increases on the rich—lofty ideas that floated in Ruth's mind like dreams of Christmas morning. Clouds began to gather, but Ruth nevertheless took off her sweater and draped it neatly over her shoulders, trying to casually tie the sleeves together like she'd seen in the Georgetown catalog. Her father kept speaking. The sun vanished. The crowd cheered.

Nobody knew that temperatures were about to plummet into the thirties, icing the roads and sending shivers down the trunks of fruit trees; the next spring there would be no apple blossoms as a result. Not even the weatherman had predicted it—though later George would claim that he sensed the imminent cold snap from the lack of birds in the sky.

"I knew something bad was coming," he said.

HAVING BEEN ABANDONED by Lizzie and George after the YouTube videos, Ruth sprawled on one of the twin beds and killed time on Facebook. Ruth had ninety-seven friends, a relatively paltry number that included a lot of those high school classmates she'd disparaged in her teens, but who now curiously seemed to have grown into decent people, which made her ashamed of her previous snobbery.

Unbeknownst to Morgan, Ruth was in touch with several old boyfriends on Facebook. The friend requests had come from them, not her, and she'd felt it would have been rude not to accept them. She learned that one of them had had cancer. Another was a right-wing Republican. Yet another had continued the personal Messenger thing a little too long, and she stopped responding.

Today there was a recent post from Abe, the one with cancer. He still lived in the Concord area, and Ruth had actually run into him a few years ago in Target. He'd looked as healthy as a pumpkin back then and she was glad for him. She'd tried to remember why they'd broken up. Some of it had to do with his lack of direction, which stood in such sharp contrast to her type-A drive as she started law school. But was that all?

Oh. Right. Morgan.

She read Abe's post, which accompanied a photo of the mountains.

"Spectacular early-morning ride through Franconia Notch," he wrote. "Moose, eagle, apple orchards laden with fruit. I love the Granite State!"

On a whim, Ruth fired off a message. "Am home for the weekend. Any time to connect?" What the heck. It wasn't like she was interested in starting something up with him again. She'd just like to catch up.

Okay, and so maybe she was a little irked at Morgan.

Three hovering dots, and a quick reply. "Camping at Lafayette," he wrote. "Coffee tomorrow? The Grind?"

She didn't know the place, but she'd find out. "10?"

"👍"

Of course, instantly she regretted making the date. Her words were too eager, she thought. She came off as sneaky. She should cancel.

Then she saw that it would look even worse to cancel. *Oh, just see him*, she told herself; *it's nothing but a get-together with an old friend.*

"Ruth!" George called from downstairs.

She went to the top of the stairs.

"Can you iron paper?" he asked.

"How am I supposed to know?!"

"We're thinking of ironing the pages in the cookbook," George said. "We thought you'd know if it was a good idea or not."

"I'm not Martha Stewart," said Ruth. This happened to her at home a lot. People thought she was a walking encyclopedia of homemaking tricks. "Where's Dad?"

"Still sleeping," said George.

Ruth glanced in the hall mirror. Straightened up. Fluffed her hair out. Grinned to see if her teeth looked yellow.

Downstairs she found George and Lizzie with the cookbook open on the kitchen table, the iron plugged in.

"I don't think it's normal, for someone Dad's age to sleep so much," she said.

"You really are a worrywart," said George.

"Yes, I am," she said. "And don't burn those pages."

4.

An Ideal Marriage

GEORGE HAD, IN FACT, ALWAYS BEEN SOMEWHAT OF A WORRY-
wart himself—but mainly when it came to his little sister, Lizzie,
whom he thought of as in need of protection: from monsters and
bogeymen, from boys in general, from his roommates in college
who arrived uninvited over holiday breaks. Lizzie had been born
four weeks early, weighing in at just over five pounds, and she was
slow enough in growing that the pediatrician advised Lillian to stop
nursing and switch to formula, something Lillian—breastfeeding
before it became so popular—did with great reluctance. George remembered bottle-feeding Lizzie and learning to burp her as well.
He took this job very seriously, holding his bobble-headed sister
over his shoulder and patting her to get the air up.

Lizzie began to grow a little faster, but she was never what their
mother called a sturdy child—"sturdy" used more often to describe

George, who according to the notes in his baby book weighed a hefty nine pounds and three ounces at birth and remained in the 98th percentile throughout childhood. Which made sense, for George loved to eat. He loved buttered noodles and cinnamon toast, bloody roast beef, any raw vegetable his mother cut up. He loved milk. He loved pie. Lillian said he was going to eat them out of house and home.

"You're going to eat us out of house and home," she scolded, wrapping him in her arms.

But his little sister: she was petite, and since George was just that much older (by six years) and that much bigger (by sixty pounds, when Lizzie was born), he felt the need to take care of her. Daniel, three years older than George, was off with his own friends and didn't want George tagging along, and Ruth had piano lessons and dance, and when she wasn't pursuing the arts, she had her nose in a book.

And so George, taking Lizzie under his wing, taught her how to tie her shoes. How to whistle. How to turn a somersault, ride a bike, jump on a pogo stick, dive—every step of the way making sure there were no rocks in her path, no spiders in her bed, no throat-swelling peanuts in her Cracker Jack.

In the schoolyard, there were some boys in his sixth-grade class who, during recess, liked to kick the ball straight at the younger girls. Lizzie didn't really need protecting, even as a kindergartner—she kicked it right back, and nearly as hard—but George met up with those boys after school and threatened to beat them up if they ever took aim at his sister again. In high school, with Daniel gone, George grew even more intensely protective, and anatomically specific as well: when one of his classmates referred to the girls in junior high as a ripe crop of cherries just waiting to be popped, George shoved the boy up against a row of lockers and told him that if he looked at his sister in that way, George would cut his dick off.

Which is what Daniel would have said, he told himself.

The older she got, the less Lizzie appreciated George's protective bent. She just wished he would let things take their course. If boys were talking about popping her cherry, let them talk all they wanted; *she* was the one who would decide when and where her cherry would be popped. At one point she told George to stop messing with her life.

"I don't want you to get hurt," said George.

"Fat chance of that, with you hanging over my shoulder!"

George himself was hurt that Lizzie didn't want his help. He thought he was doing the right thing, and he sometimes resented Lizzie for not appreciating it. During Lizzie's sophomore year at UNH, she happened to mention to George that she was going to do some ecstasy before a concert, and George, newly employed as a nurse in nearby Portsmouth, became convinced that she would do something dumb like drink a bathtub full of water. To ensure her safety, he enlisted the help of a buddy to hang out with her, but the buddy hit it off with Lizzie's friend and they vanished, leaving Lizzie alone; and it was while walking home that she was knocked down by a serial assailant the police had been after for two months, and the fact that she *wasn't* raped (no doubt due to her use of the shrieking alarm device George had given her) was of small consolation once she was called to testify against the assailant in court, an ordeal that cut into finals' study-time and resulted in Lizzie getting a C-minus in her course on the Romantic poets.

Which made her glum enough to begin with. But when she

learned from George's buddy of George's role in the evening's plans, she became livid.

"I was afraid you'd overhydrate," George said meekly.

"Get a life, George."

He felt she could have been a little more understanding.

AS FOR GAVIN: George had only met the guy a few times, but he'd had a distinctly negative impression, due in large part to Gavin's name-dropping tendencies (Paul Simon, for fuck's sake!) and the fact that Gavin kept slipping up and calling him Greg. This started the first time they met, at Lizzie's house one afternoon when George had shown up to deliver an old kayak he was passing onto Lizzie (and it was written all over the wall what the two of them had been up to before George arrived), and Gavin, perhaps in some sort of postcoital distraction, kept saying Greg this and Greg that. *Do you like to hunt, Greg? Do you like to fly-fish, Greg?* Gimme a break. The man's shortcomings kept piling up, one on top of another: he didn't offer to help George carry the kayak around to the backyard, nor when George got the pruning saw from his truck did Gavin show any interest in just which tree George planned to prune, but rather whipped out his iPhone and wandered off, shaking his head at some amusing text. Probably from Paul Simon.

But at least it gave him some time alone with his sister.

"How long have you been . . ." he began, when he and Lizzie were surveying the limb that needed to come down.

"He's not really a boyfriend, if that's what you're wondering," Lizzie said.

"Then what is he?"

"A friend," she said. "With benefits, I guess you'd say."

"Oh great." George squinted upward to maneuver the curved blade into the crotch of the limb. "Don't get hurt."

"If we're talking about hurt, we should be talking about Bruce."

"I'm not sure a geriatric friend with benefits is the answer."

"Buzz off, George."

"Does he have Alzheimer's? Just wondering, because he can't remember my name, apparently."

"He's sixty-five. He's not a geriatric, and he doesn't have Alzheimer's."

"Still: you're seeing someone who's on Medicare," George observed. He gave a final yank and the branch came down with a splintering crack.

"I'm going," Gavin called from the back door. "See you, Greg," he said with a little salute.

"Later, Dick," George replied, tossing the branch aside.

After that, George had little interaction with Gavin, as Lizzie made it clear this was not a man she expected to be welcomed into any kind of a family get-together. Gavin didn't join them for a canoe trip on Memorial Day, nor did he show up for Murray's eighty-first birthday that July, when George drove up with a German chocolate cake from Murray's favorite bakery in Concord and Lizzie brought all the fixings for a hamburger cookout. It troubled George that his sister was spending valuable (read: childbearing) time with a man so ill-suited to her long-range needs, but what could an older brother do, at this point in life?

Not much, George thought glumly.

. . .

AFTER LUNCH on this warm September afternoon, George drove into town to see an old friend, hoping he could talk him into a Sunday morning run. He knew it might be seen as antisocial, especially by Ruth, and especially given Lizzie's crisis with Gavin, but George believed that during family get-togethers, you needed to get away for sanity's sake. A Sunday morning run would do everyone good.

But his friend wasn't home, which discouraged him, because escaping on his own tomorrow without the excuse of a partner would be difficult. He foresaw a morning with Ruth bossing everyone around during some group activity that would have him climbing the walls before she was finished. God love her, but he could only take so much.

He'd just have to go running on his own. His spirits lifted, he started back to his father's house. He was about to get on the interstate when he saw the sign for the local hospital. He checked the time: two o'clock. His first thought was that they would have sent Gavin home by now, but maybe the ER was busy. Things could take forever, sometimes.

George sensed he should probably stay out of things, but he couldn't shake the feeling that maybe there was something he could do to help defuse a brewing controversy. Stop by. Put his two cents in. Let the guy know that a simple heartfelt apology would buy him some valuable goodwill with a family who knew exactly what he was up to all this time: taking advantage of a younger woman who was going through her own midlife crisis at the moment. As George saw it.

What the heck.

In the parking lot, he cut the engine and then just sat there for a moment, weighing what he would say to Gavin if he was in fact still there. *Hear you ruined our family cookbook.* Or: *This is what you get for messing around with my sister's feelings for the past year.* He had no idea.

Usually George was Mr. Mellow when it came to confrontations— he'd had to deal with many an aggressive family member outside the ICU and knew how to stay calm—but right now he realized he was clenching his fists. He took a deep breath. From his glove compartment he found a half-smoked joint. One long, deep toke: just enough to keep the lid on his anger while with Gavin. He stubbed it out on a piece of slate, then tucked it back into the glove compartment and got out of his truck.

Lizzie would throw a fit, but fuck it.

GAVIN WAS IN FACT STILL in the emergency room, but this being a small hospital, George simply walked by the front desk and found the older man in a half-curtained-off area, propped up on a hospital bed and hooked up to an IV. He was wearing shorts and Velcro sandals with four-wheel treads; his right hand was bandaged in gauze and tractioned up above his chest. His dark eyebrows were bushy and unkempt, tufted like a set of horns. There was a young woman with him in a filmy white blouse, whom George presumed to be the daughter because she didn't look even old enough to vote.

Gavin looked up.

"Get out of here," he growled.

George felt the back of his neck prickle. He held up his palms. "I come in peace. How's your hand?"

"I said get out."

"Not until you tell me how you managed to drop our cookbook into your sink."

"Your sister's crazy," said Gavin. "I was using it and had it propped up and I reached for something. A few corners got wet. Big deal. But your sister? Did she tell you what she did?"

"To your laptop?"

"Completely ruined."

"Sauce for the gander," said George with a shrug. "Really. How's your hand doing?"

"Terrible. Second-degree burn," said Gavin. "And I'm right-handed, too."

"How come the IV?" He nodded at the bag, at the tube that snaked down to his lower arm, just above his wrist. Not typical for a second-degree burn in itself, at least in George's experience.

"Because I'm a bad diabetic. Haven't been monitoring my blood sugar apparently and they're mad at me. What if I need a skin graft?"

"I doubt you will, but I'm sorry this happened."

Gavin gave out a little humph. "I bet you are. You know she's been stalking me?"

The notion that he didn't have all the facts bothered George tremendously.

"I don't like you," he told Gavin. "I never did. You've had this uncommitted thing with my sister. Why buy when you can rent, isn't that what they used to say? But you've been preying on her at a very vulnerable time."

The girl's phone dinged and she glanced at it languidly.

"And do you think it's right for your daughter to be smack-dab in the middle of this little domestic dispute?" George said, nodding toward her.

"Fuck you," said the girl without looking up.

"Run out and get me some coffee, Sweets," Gavin said to her, digging a bill out of his wallet.

The girl sidled past George, glaring at him. She was tall and very thin, with wispy brown hair pulled back in an untidy ponytail. George could see her nipples through her shirt. She vanished with a swish of the curtain.

With her gone, Gavin rotated his bandaged hand on display for George, who stood at the foot of the bed with his arms crossed. "Ever had a second-degree burn?" Gavin asked.

"No, actually."

"Well, guess what. It hurts like hell. I'd take the bandage off and show you the mess, but they'd get mad at me. It looks like a piece of liver. Let me tell you something about your sister. She's the one who took the initiative in this whole affair. I'm not saying I haven't been to blame, and I've certainly known my fair share of women outside the confines of my marriage, but your sister was one of the more aggressive ones."

"No need to elaborate."

"I just want you to know that she wasn't the innocent victim you probably think she was. She's a thirty-eight-year-old woman who threw herself at me. And speaking of throwing things, I hope she has a good attorney."

George hooted. "For what?"

"She didn't tell you she *tried* to pour hot water on me? It wasn't any accident, you know. First she pours it on the laptop and then she hurls it at me. I shouldn't have reached up to stop her; if I'd moved away, I wouldn't be sitting here in the fucking ER."

"Are you saying she assaulted you? Because that's bullshit."

"Were you there? Ask Jessica. She saw the whole thing."

"That's the biggest crock I've ever heard."

"Your choice, dude, whether to believe me or not. But I'm pressing criminal charges. I talked to the police already. And I don't know what the stalking laws are in this state, but I'll file a complaint for that, too. Calling me at all hours. Showing up on my doorstep in tears. Calling *Jessica*, even. God damn it," he said. "God damn it all. I'm supposed to hike the Inca Trail next month. You think my hand will be healed up for that?"

George ignored the question. "You know, if you press charges, this'll be all over social media," he said. "Do you want that?"

Gavin shrugged. "Might have to see justice done."

"Tell me something," said George. "Your wife really know about your affairs?"

"Don't you second-guess my marriage. My wife couldn't give a shit," said Gavin. "She's got her own boyfriend down in New York. Though I guess you wouldn't know what it's like to be married for thirty years."

"No, but I'm glad I don't have your kind of marriage."

"And what kind of marriage would you have?"

It shocked George, how forcefully this stunned him into silence. How quickly it brought to mind car rides back from the lake on a hot night in August, his father whistling softly, his mother humming along in her low voice. Lillian straightening his lapels, just before a speech. Murray bringing Lillian her Winstons when she was out back gardening, hushing the children so she could have some quiet time amid the zinnias.

His parents' marriage, he would have said to Gavin, if he didn't dislike the man so much. And he realized how far away from that ideal he was. Being a runner meant that George ran from a lot of things, including relationships. He thought of Samantha, whom he'd been seeing this summer. Given the way he'd treated her a month ago, he was light-years away.

"Just don't presume you have all the answers to everybody else's problems," Gavin said. "What goes on between me and Joanna is between me and Joanna. Hey, Sweets," he said, and George looked over his shoulder to see Jessica with coffee for Gavin and a Vitaminwater for herself. Again she glared at George. It was time to go.

"If you press charges," he said, "I will tweet it before you can blink."

"Like I care?"

"If you didn't care, you would have taken my sister out to a few restaurants in the last six months. You wouldn't have been afraid to be seen in public."

Gavin closed his eyes. "Will you please just go about minding your own business?"

"My sister is my business," George said.

"The fuck she is," said Gavin.

. . .

THE BACK ROAD to his father's house was curvy and full of frost heaves, and George drove slowly. He was pissed. Was Gavin telling the truth? A new branch of anger sprouted as he pictured himself having to confront Lizzie about the possibility that she assaulted him. George could argue up a storm with Ruth, but Lizzie brought out his soft side.

A little domestic dispute: But what actually happened? There were two sides to the story, *he said* and *she said*, but Gavin had the witness and Lizzie didn't. He didn't like to admit it, given the circumstances, but Lizzie was known to act without thinking sometimes. He remembered her locking the bus driver out when he was putting chains on the tires in subzero weather; stealing a box of donuts destined for the school bake sale. "Did you honestly think you weren't going to get caught?" an angry Murray said that night at the family dinner table—more disappointed, it seemed, with Lizzie's lack of planning than with the fact of the crime itself.

She could very well have decided to attack Gavin, on a whim; he wouldn't put it past her. Good thing she didn't go for his face.

George headed up his father's long sloping driveway. He noticed that a few limbs had come down in a recent storm and he stopped to clear them. Things were in fact slipping here at the house, and he knew it, and he knew Ruth was going to find a time to bark about it because Ruth liked to bark about things very openly. George did not. George preferred nuance and implication. And he hated the idea of his father going into a place for seniors. Maybe if he were another five years down the pike . . . but eighty-one was just too early for a man who tilled the soil and still had a lot of plans for the fields that currently lay fallow on this small farm.

He should come up more often. He should get up early on Sunday mornings and arrive for breakfast. Bring him the Sunday *Times*. Pick up a pint of Ben and Jerry's. Stay for the day and help out around the house and play a game of cribbage or two. He'd had this very thought many times and never did anything about it, and was angry at himself for that.

He pledged to do better.

At the house he found his father sleeping and Ruth on the phone, behind the closed door of the twin bedroom. Instead of confronting Lizzie, as he knew he should, he killed some time with her watching videos on YouTube. Tried to accommodate Ruth when she barged in on them. Wished he'd taken another toke on that joint before coming in the house.

Although when the police car pulled up, he was very, very glad that he didn't smell like a dispensary.

5.

Riot Act

MURRAY WAS DOZING, HAVING FALLEN ASLEEP WITH A library book on his chest. He was dreaming he was at a campaign event and a brass band materialized out of nowhere, and all the people followed the band instead of staying to listen to him. Lillian was about to take the stage and read one of her stories, when he heard a light knock on his bedroom door.

"The police are here," George said.

Murray tasted something bad in his mouth, something bitter, like acorn meat. He moved his tongue around and his teeth were furry and he wanted five minutes to pull himself together. It wasn't the cops' fault, but he wished he'd had a little warning.

"I'll be right there," he replied.

"Do I let them in?"

"Of course you do," said Murray. "You be polite."

He glanced in the mirror and ran a comb through his thinning hair and wiped the dried spittle from the corners of his mouth. There were times, and this was one of them, when he couldn't reconcile the face he knew with the face he saw in the mirror. It was in fact his own father looking back at him today, with the long nose, the deep vertical lines in his cheeks and the wobbly jowls that hung below his chin. The face of an old, old man. Where did it come from? And what happened to the real Murray?

He tucked his shirt into his pants and tightened his belt. He'd been afraid the police might get involved. He hadn't said anything, but he'd suspected another side to Lizzie's story, one that might not sound so accidental; things could look awfully different from the other party's point of view. He wished he'd had time to talk to her privately and raise his concerns, so she would know what to expect when the police questioned her.

Downstairs he found two police officers from the Sugar Hill Police Department waiting in the front hallway.

"Hullo, Murray," the taller one said.

"Austin," said Murray, nodding. "Bob." He knew them both. They were a comical team, Austin tall and skinny as a telephone pole, Bob short and built like a brick. Austin had a surgically repaired cleft lip and had trouble with his S's, which sounded like they were coming out of both sides of his mouth.

"We're actually looking for your daughter," Austin said. "We tried her house and one of the neighbors told us to check here. Seems there was a little incident with a friend of hers that put him in the hospital."

Murray cleared his throat. He wasn't in the habit of lying to the law, but he had a sudden urge to tell these two that Lizzie wasn't here.

But as if reading his mind, Bob said, "That her car in the driveway?"

Murray excused himself and went upstairs, where he found Lizzie and Ruth sitting side by side on one of the twin beds, like two children waiting to be spanked. A golden band of light slanted across the bare wood floor. Both beds were made, their popcorn spreads pulled taut; Ruth was a tidy guest.

"They want to ask you a few questions about Gavin," he told Lizzie.

"What for?"

"Vandalism," Ruth pointed out. "You poured hot water on his laptop, remember?"

Lizzie rolled her eyes.

"Plus it's possible that Gavin gave them a different version of the events," Murray said. "Anything we need to know?"

"Screw that," said Lizzie, standing up. "What I told you is what happened. I don't know what Gavin said, but if it's anything different from what I said, he's lying."

Ruth reclipped her hair back up in its claw. "So give a statement," she said, "but if I tell you not to answer a question, don't answer it."

"Don't play hardball," Murray cautioned his older daughter. "It'll set the wrong tone for things to come." In the afternoon light, he saw that twin parentheses had formed around Ruth's mouth. Lillian had had them as well, but Ruth's were deeper. It always startled him to remember that his daughter was older than his wife had ever been.

His mind went back to the dream again. A brass band? He

remembered Ruth playing her flute in the high school marching band as part of the Fourth of July parade, the day he announced his candidacy. Lillian was wearing a light blue shift, he recalled. It was hotter than Hades and he'd worn a long-sleeved white shirt with the cuffs rolled up. The kids were dressed neatly as well. No shorts. No tennies. He'd been so proud of his family up on the dais with him, even if Daniel and George had to be separated lest they duke out some unspecified conflict that had erupted that morning—over firecrackers, he now believed it was, which were forbidden anyway; Murray knew his torts, if anything. And later that night, when the older kids were still out, after Lizzie had finally fallen into a damp, sweaty sleep in just her underwear, he and Lillian made love on top of their sheets, cooled by the old oscillating fan. Lillian had—

"Dad?" said Ruth. "Are you coming?"

Downstairs again, he motioned for the policemen to sit on the sofa. Lizzie took the rocking chair, and Ruth positioned herself on a stumpy hassock beside her. She was still in her sweats and Murray wished she looked a little more professional. He decided to remain standing. He pretended to scratch his ear and adjusted his hearing aid.

"Elizabeth," said Austin with a nod. "Looks like you and your friend Mr. Langley had some kind of a dispute this morning. Could you tell us what happened?"

"I can." Lizzie cleared her throat. "I went to his house to get a book back. It wasn't just any book, it was an old cookbook that had belonged to my mother, so it has a lot of sentimental value, and he'd had it for a long time. Maybe four months. So he went into his office and got it. Well, it was completely water damaged! Like he'd dropped it in the bathtub! I can show you the book," she offered. "It's all warped now and the pages are all stuck together. Do you want to see it?"

"At some point," said Bob.

"Not right now," said Austin.

Murray glanced at George, who had appeared in the doorway from the kitchen. He was glad to see that George wasn't eating at the moment, that he looked as somber and focused as the rest of them.

"Okay then," Lizzie said. "So I was pretty upset when I saw the book. I admit it. I wanted to get back at him and there was an electric teakettle on the island and I picked it up and poured hot water on his laptop. Which was wrong, and I'll replace it. Even though he can't replace our *cookbook*," she added darkly.

It was true, Murray thought; there was a complete lack of equivalence here between the cookbook and the laptop. Sentiment being inversely proportional to monetary value.

Lizzie went on: "Anyway, Gavin got really upset when I did that, no surprise, and he lunged at me and tried to grab the teakettle, and hot water spilled all over his hand. He did it to himself," she said.

"Mr. Langley says you *tried* to pour hot water on him."

At which point Lizzie straightened up indignantly. "Excuse me? He came at me and tried to grab it! If he'd left well enough alone, he wouldn't be hurt now!"

"So you're saying you never tried to pour hot water on his hand?"

Ruth said, "She just said that."

Murray laid a hand on Ruth's shoulder. This wasn't court.

"Mr. Langley has given a very different account, you see," said Bob. "We're just trying to sort out the facts."

"Well, I didn't try and attack him," said Lizzie haughtily, as though she'd been accused of murder. "That's completely absurd."

Austin and Bob exchanged glances.

"How's his hand?" Lizzie asked.

"We're not authorized to go into that," said Austin. "But it's a pretty good burn, is what I've been told."

Murray didn't see any need for the two policemen to remain in his house any longer. "Gentlemen," he said, and he showed the two policemen to the door. When they had left, he rejoined his children in the kitchen, where George was opening a bag of chips. Murray turned on the small kitchen TV set, anticipating his news programs, but kept the volume on low.

"I swear," Lizzie said. "He's making this all up. I did not go after him with the hot water. That is total bullshit."

"Are you sure?" said Ruth.

Murray added, "Because if you did, we ought to know."

"He's turning this into some kind of Lifetime movie!" Lizzie exclaimed. "Look, he tried to grab it out of my hands, and hot water spilled out. That's something he should have foreseen. I didn't go after him."

"If you did, it would be an assault," said Ruth. "An attempted assault at least."

"So it's my word against his?" said Lizzie. "I'll take one of those," she said to George, who had gotten one of her beers.

"He's got his daughter as a witness, though," Ruth pointed out.

"And that makes her an authority?" Lizzie cried. "She's going to say anything her father wants her to say!"

Murray went to the liquor cupboard and got out the bottle of gin, filled a glass with ice, and poured some gin without measuring. He added some tonic water and wished he had some lime, but he'd used it up the night before while waiting for the kids.

Ruth looked surprised. "You're drinking gin these days?"

"Yes, I am," Murray replied. He found a lemon in the refrigerator and cut a slice. "Would you like a gin and tonic, Ruth?"

"I hate gin," said Ruth.

"Since when have you started drinking gin again?" asked George, curious as well.

"I keep it in the house," said Murray. "Nothing wrong with that."

"It's just kind of funny," said Ruth.

Gin was Lillian's drink.

"Are you sure you don't want one?" Murray asked.

"Yes, I'm sure," said Ruth. "Why is everyone drinking? It's four o'clock in the afternoon."

"It's five o'clock somewhere," said George.

"Well, one of us should stay sober," Ruth said.

Lizzie and George clinked bottlenecks.

"Fuck it," said Ruth. "A little wine won't hurt."

"So am I going to have to go to jail for this, just because Gavin says one thing and I say another?" said Lizzie.

"Possibly," said Ruth.

"He can just make up a story and get me arrested?"

"If the police believe him," said Ruth. Suddenly she turned on Lizzie. "Why'd you have to go and do this? I come up for the weekend and we're supposed to have a nice time together and you have to go and get in a big fight with your boyfriend that puts him in the hospital and you maybe in jail?"

"Come on, Ruth," said George. "What's done is done."

"But she always has to create a drama, whenever we get together! Last time I was up, she got into a bike accident and we spent most of our time in the ER. The time before that, there was the chimney fire. And remember the meth dealers who blew up the house next door?"

"The meth dealers weren't her fault," George pointed out.

Ruth closed her eyes for a moment. "I know," she said. "I'm sorry. But this was supposed to be a weekend where the biggest drama was me trying to get Lizzie to end things with Gavin."

The room fell silent, only to be broken when Murray cleared his throat. "Uh, Ruth."

Lizzie's face had gone flat. "That's why you came up? To read me the riot act?"

Murray finished his drink.

"Dad just wanted me to talk to you," Ruth explained. "Gavin hasn't been the best match."

"Then I'm sure you're all happy it's over."

Murray rattled his ice cubes. He felt betrayed by Ruth. She could have exercised a little discretion here, he thought. Though it did occur to him that maybe she'd been waiting for an occasion to drop this little bomb, to make Lizzie think that Murray was closer to Ruth than to her. It wasn't a very nice thought, but then sometimes Ruth wasn't a very nice person.

It's true, he told Lillian. *You know it's true.*

At some point he felt Lizzie's eyes upon him.

"What?" he said.

"Do you think I'm, like, twenty?" Lizzie demanded.

"I just thought Ruth might be able to shed some light on things that I couldn't. I've already told you I wished he wasn't a part of your life."

"You never said that!"

Murray was about to snap back with a retort, but it occurred to him: maybe he'd merely had the thought without articulating it. That happened to him a lot these days.

"Well, I know George has tried to talk to you," he said. "And I thought if it came from your sister, you might listen a little more closely."

Ruth crossed her arms, sulking. "Like anyone ever listens to me?"

"Oh, Ruth, cut it out," said George.

"All of you, cut it out!" Murray exclaimed. "I think we need to settle down and just wait and see what happens. Gavin might be overreacting, wanting to get back at you, Lizzie. Maybe once he knows that you fully intend to replace his laptop, he won't be so angry. He'll realize his hand will heal and life will get back to normal. In the meantime let's try to enjoy our time together. No more fighting! Seems like we should be able to get together for one brief weekend without you children arguing up a storm."

He couldn't remember the last time he'd lectured them like this. He hated lecturing. When Lillian was alive, it had been her role; she was the bad cop who scolded, Murray the good cop who later explained the rationale. They made a good team. Of course, it was Daniel who needed scolding the most. After the accident Lizzie stepped into that role, acting up as a teenager, and with Lillian gone, Murray had been forced to perform in a new capacity. *What were you thinking, stealing road cones and setting up a bogus detour? Running naked across the football field?*

"Don't put me in this position," he said. "You're all adults. We've got an adult situation on our hands. Let's act like adults."

"You sound like Mom," said George quietly.

"You do," Ruth agreed. "Especially during the campaign. She was always lecturing us during the campaign."

"And sending us to our rooms," said George.

"If I did that, there'd be no one here," said Murray. "I'd be the loneliest man in the world."

Just then an ad came on for Clinton, followed by one for Trump. It was the season.

"Baboon," said Murray.

"Fascist," said Ruth.

"He'll never win," George scoffed. "Have you seen Nate Silver?"

"You never know," said Murray. "Don't be too sure."

"Please no October surprise," said Lizzie.

"Please no Brexit," said Ruth.

Then came an ad for New Hampshire's incumbent congresswoman, a Democrat. Murray and his children watched a clip that showed her talking with the parents of a child who'd died from an opioid overdose. Murray felt that old familiar pang of regret.

"What are her numbers like?" Ruth asked.

"They're good," said Murray. "A four-point lead at least, I think."

A silence fell over the group. A four-point lead was what Murray had had, way back when.

"But hey," Murray said, shutting off the television. "Anything could happen."

PART TWO

1984

6.

Team Blaire

IT WAS ONE OF THE HOTTEST, MOST HUMID JULY FOURTHS on record, and Lillian Blaire, dressed in a pale blue shift, stood on the dais beside her husband and wondered if people in the audience could see the dark crescents under her arms as she sweltered in the bright noonday sun.

Here on the makeshift stage stood the entire family as Murray announced his candidacy for Congress: Ruth in her band uniform, Daniel whose pants had grass stains, knock-kneed George in a pair of Daniel's castoffs that were too big, and little Lizzie the most comfortable of all in a loose-fitting sleeveless frock that caught the breeze from below. As for Lillian, her feet throbbed in high heels, and her ash-blond hair hung bone-straight despite her attempts with a curling iron that morning.

"And we have to stop increasing our obscene military budget,"

Murray was saying, sleeves rolled up as he squinted into the crowd, "and put that money to good use educating our children, and feeding the poor, and making sure our bridges don't crumble while we're driving over them!"

Suddenly, out of the blue, Lillian heard the first line to a new story: *Julie Ann was reading five cases ahead in Constitutional Law when her husband interrupted to ask what was for dinner.*

The line was so crisp that she found herself mouthing the words without thinking, and she had to force herself to stop, lest Murray's supporters think she was loony up there, talking to herself. It wasn't unusual for her to hear first lines. After a long dry spell (commencing when Ruth was born), Lillian found them coming fast and furious these days, often at inconvenient times, requiring her to jot them down wherever she could: napkins, the backs of receipts, sometimes in the margins of the cookbook she used every day, as though annotating her way through the daily drudgery of hard-boiling enough eggs for potato salad for six. If the children weren't pestering her, sometimes she could sneak up to the third-floor guest bedroom, where she kept her Smith Corona on a rickety table; there, with a cigarette dangling between her lips, she would manage to type out a full draft, if she were lucky. It was golden time.

But right now, despite the beginning to a new story, she had a different role to play, a different hat to wear. She beamed at the crowd as Murray drew her close. "Thank you!" he boomed into the mike. "Thank you all very much!"

"This is so lame," said Daniel, who'd turned fifteen a few months ago.

"Can I wave?" Lizzie asked, tugging at Lillian's dress. At six, she was hoping to be in a parade.

Lillian hoisted her up and together they waved to the crowd.

"We look like a bunch of dorks," said Daniel.

"Zip it, Daniel," said Lillian, waving still.

Then Daniel nudged George, who slapped his hand away. There was a scuffle. Lillian rearranged the boys, one on each side of her, and kept smiling.

"How was I?" Murray asked, after the applause died down and the crowd began to disperse.

"You were great," Lillian said.

"What's for dinner?" asked George.

"Dad's got a barbeque to go to," Lillian replied. "And we expect everyone to be there."

"I've got plans at six," Ruth said, smoothing her band pants. They were made from a heavy polyester and had a wayward crease that wouldn't go away.

"And I've got plans right now," Daniel announced.

"Both of you show up at five," Murray warned. "Half an hour is all. How are ya?" he exclaimed, moving away from his family to greet a cluster of well-wishers. "Thanks for coming! Bobby D.! Where ya been hiding out? Gotta do lunch one of these days, right?"

Lillian found his use of the vernacular annoying. He didn't talk like that at home, so why should he do it with his supporters? It sounded forced. She would say something about it tonight. They had four months ahead of them, speeches and fish fries and coffees and factory shift changes, and she wanted Murray to present his real self, not some cooked-up version of Yankee Joe Voter.

Meanwhile she hustled the children—minus Daniel, who'd already vanished on his bike—toward the Chevy van that she'd parked right in the sun. When she opened the side door, a thick wave of heat blasted her face, laced with the smell of dirty socks, sour milk, and the hammy remains of a half-eaten sub. She thought to herself, *Do I really have the nerve to make the kids clean the van on this Fourth of July when most families are headed to the beach or the lake or the city pools?*

She sure did.

"You're mean," George sniffled, carrying a bag of trash to the garage, later that afternoon.

"Yeah, and what about Daniel?" Ruth said, wiping her brow. "What are you going to make *him* do? Because it isn't fair that he just took off before you decided to make us do this."

"Daniel will get his fair share of work," Lillian assured her, though she dreaded giving Daniel any task, because she knew he would complain to the point where she would just want to do it herself. Her funny, good-humored son had turned so unpleasant in the last year. Just fifteen he was, and he thought the world owed him a big giant favor. Lillian suspected there was a girl involved in this most recent mood swing, but Daniel wasn't volunteering anything and Lillian certainly wasn't going to ask.

"Thank you," said Lillian to the three sour faces when the van was done. "Who wants a Popsicle?!"

The original idea had been to view the fireworks as a family; but with Ruth leaving at six to meet friends, and Daniel having failed to show up for the barbeque for even a minute, it was just George and Lizzie who accompanied the parents to Memorial Field, and even George, who'd promised to take Lizzie to get some cotton candy, spotted some friends and took off.

Lillian spread out an old quilt. The mosquitos were biting and she fumigated Lizzie with bug spray. Lizzie was not happy at being abandoned by her siblings.

"Look what I have," Murray said, and he brought out a box of sparklers. Cradling Lizzie from behind, he struck a match to a sparkler, and, placing his large broad hand over her small plump one, he guided her in spelling out her name with light. When the fireworks began, the three of them lay back and watched the spectacle, standard red and blue chrysanthemums but also the towering rockets that sizzled and popped, and spiral-tailed bursts, and the silent ones with a flash of light followed by a loud sonic boom.

In the darkness, Lillian felt Murray's warm hand close over hers.

"Don't ditch me now," he murmured.

"Don't blow it," she whispered back.

"I'd be home on weekends," he said.

Counting chickens, Lillian thought. *Crossing bridges.*

A pop, and a boom, and curlicues of smoke spun dizzily toward earth.

"It hurts my ears," cried little Lizzie, wriggling with delight.

LILLIAN HOLMES WAS just twenty-three when she married Murray Blaire in front of a justice of the peace in Boston. Lillian's father, a banker, didn't bring a shotgun to the ceremony, but he might as well have; John Holmes had taken the news of Lillian's pregnancy with the harsh disappointment of the Puritan that he was. By contrast, Murray's parents, liberal Democrats from conservative New Hampshire, were simply thrilled that their thirty-one-year-old son was finally settling down and producing a grandchild for them to fawn over.

At the time, Murray was in his second year of law school in Boston. He'd met Lillian the summer before, when he'd been working as a summer associate at the downtown law firm where Lillian was a secretary. He'd wasted no time in asking her out, and soon they were officially dating.

Lillian hated her job. She'd graduated from Smith with a degree in English and considered herself a writer before anything else. In fact she was working on a novel, and she could sometimes be seen at her desk after hours, taking full advantage of the firm's IBM Selectric with its busy little ball. At one point she received a stern reprimand from the head of the secretarial pool; Lillian refrained from using the typewriter, but stole paper and other supplies as often as she could, rationalizing that a big corporate law firm should be happy to subsidize a struggling artist like herself.

She and Murray had been seeing each other for almost six months when she skipped a period. "I can't be!" she gasped, when the doctor at the clinic gave her the news. She and Murray had diligently used protection. "Condoms aren't foolproof," the doctor told her. "I'm sorry."

This was right before Christmas, and Murray had already gone up to his parents' house in New Hampshire. That night she called him with the news.

"What do you want to do?" he asked.

Lillian knew her options were limited. This was 1966, when a girl who didn't want to be pregnant had two choices: get a back-alley abortion in the United States, or fly to Puerto Rico. Well, three, actually: she could do it herself. For Lillian, the notion of a back-alley abortion was daunting; one friend had gotten an infection that left her sterile; another had almost bled to death. And she didn't have the money to go to Puerto Rico, or the guts to attempt something herself.

Besides, she wasn't sure she even wanted an abortion. It had occurred to her that this could be her ticket out of a stifling situation. Not that she was trying to scam Murray, not at all—she truly did love him—but she thought that motherhood would be more compatible with novel-writing than a nine-to-five job typing up other people's legalese. She figured she could write while the baby napped.

"I've got money," Murray offered.

"I don't want an abortion," she said. "Marry me instead."

"Marry you!" Murray thought about it for a moment. "Well, I guess I could do that. I was going to ask you after law school, anyway."

"I proposed to *him*," Lillian would later tell her children, whenever they clamored for the details of their parents' courtship. It was a story they never tired of hearing. "No getting down on one knee, either. I asked him over the phone. We got a marriage license. We stood before a judge. I wore a green dress."

"I want to be a *real* bride," Lizzie would declare. "I want a *real* gown."

"Don't make Mom feel bad," said George.

"Nothing can make me feel bad about my marriage to your father," Lillian said. "And I look good in green."

In any case, after the quick civil ceremony, the newlyweds and their parents all went out to dinner in downtown Boston. Murray's parents were appropriately celebratory, but John Holmes was grumpy the whole time.

"Study hard," he told Murray as he paid the bill. "You've got a family to support now."

"I couldn't be happier," said Murray.

"I hope you mean that," said John Holmes.

"Sir," said Murray, "I've never been more sure of anything in my life."

AFTER MURRAY GRADUATED from law school, they moved up to Concord, New Hampshire, where in the state capital Murray joined his father's law firm. For the first few months they lived on the top floor of an overheated duplex with a long, narrow sagging porch. Lillian was always on the lookout for a real home. One bright fall day, after a harrowing excursion at the supermarket with thirteen-month-old Ruth trying to climb out of the grocery cart, she was driving through a tree-lined neighborhood when she happened to spot a For Sale sign. She pulled over and stopped the car.

Set back from the street with a large yard on all sides, the house stood three stories tall, with a wide, wrap-around porch and leaded windows and a rounded Old World tower that clung to one of the corners on the second floor. Rhododendrons flanked the front of the house, and the yellow leaves of a droopy catalpa tree shaded the double swing on the front porch.

Back at the duplex she called Murray. "Come quick," she told him. Murray was able to get off at four; and at five o'clock, standing in the sunlit master bedroom, the young couple shook hands with the real estate agent on the full purchase price of $32,000.

The house was made for a big family—five bedrooms, a big yard, and a basement rec room made for tumbling around when the weather was bad. Lillian had recently found out she was pregnant again, and the next April Daniel was born, followed by hungry George and then, after a six-year respite, tiny Lizzie, after which Lillian finally prevailed upon Murray to get a vasectomy.

The Blaire children: theirs was a childhood of open lawns and unlocked bicycles, of neighborhood games of Kick the Can and Capture the Flag and touch football on those flaming October days. If Murray didn't get home too late, during the languid June evenings he could be seen with his sleeves rolled up, pitching a whiffle ball to young batters out on the back lawn, while Lillian enjoyed an after-dinner gin and tonic on the back porch.

Lillian, meanwhile, hadn't written a word since Ruth was born. Her novel lay packed away in a box in the garage. Motherhood was not in fact compatible with writing, she had found, especially with the arrival of more children. Nobody really napped, and there was always a skirmish to deal with. Besides, even if she had the time, what would she have written about? Diaper rash? Her fear of failure, in truth, was epic.

And so instead of trying to write during this time—and failing— Lillian became a model mother. She joined the Junior Service League and worked every Wednesday at the thrift shop, where she economized by buying good-quality coats for the children. She served on the PTA and baked mountains of cookies for their bake sales. On Saturdays during the winter she drove a carload of kids to nearby Mount Sunapee to ski; in the dog days of summer, when they weren't vacationing at Murray's beach house or the Holmes's lake house up in northern Vermont, she drove them to Newfound Lake for the day.

"Very happy," she wrote on her Smith alumnae questionnaire. "Couldn't ask for more."

BUT IF PRESSED, Lillian would probably have admitted to a sizeable hole in her life when her children were young. Every once in a while, she climbed the stairs to the third-floor guest bedroom, which had become a catchall for the unwanted. There she surveyed the random boxes and broken chairs, the trunks and suitcases and a rack full of clothes for the thrift shop, and she imagined it as her own writing space. Cleared of junk. Painted white. A lone table up against the wall, with the Smith Corona that had gotten her through many a term paper in college.

One night she mentioned it to Murray. He jumped on the idea. He said he'd always felt bad she didn't have a place to write, and all that junk could be moved to the garage. He encouraged her; he said the room could be ready in a weekend.

Lillian knew she should be falling over backward with gratitude. But she wasn't.

"I meant *sometime*," she said hastily, draining her gin. "Not necessarily right now."

"Well, I'm ready when you are," Murray said.

She told herself to be glad that her husband was so gung ho. But his enthusiasm tickled another nerve, one she generally tried to ignore, which was the way Murray often had of prevailing on things, of orchestrating their lives. He was a good man, but he had strong opinions. Especially on matters of finance—for instance, if they disagreed on how to spend some extra money, Lillian more often than not found herself giving in, vaguely conscious of an unchallenged assumption that since Murray earned the income, Murray got the ultimate say. Hence new gutters instead of new drapes, the ski vacations up north instead of a week in the sun.

And it was not just Murray but his family as well. Lillian loved her in-laws, but they, too, could steal the show. Take vacations. Usually they split their two weeks during the summer, with one week at the Holmes's lake house in northern Vermont, and another at the Blaire family's beach house on New Hampshire's small stretch of seacoast. It was clear which place the children preferred. John Holmes ran an austere summer cottage at the lake, with oatmeal for breakfast and Edgar Allan Poe before bed. By contrast, Murray's parents lived with one goal in mind: to cram as much good food and fun as possible into each twenty-four-hour cycle. Hence the clambakes, the boogie boarding, badminton, volleyball, and silly parlor games every night.

"Why can't we just spend both weeks at the beach house?" Daniel often complained.

"Oh! I just *love* the beach," Lizzie declared, removing a lollipop from her mouth.

"It's just more fun with Nana and Bumpy," Ruth admitted.

"Mom?" said George. "Are you crying?"

Nobody said anything. Outside a blue jay screeched. A lawn

mower started up. Lizzie was staring at her, fascinated. Lillian wished everyone would just go away.

"Knock-knock," said Daniel.

Ruth bit. "Who's there?"

"Euripides," said Daniel.

Lillian blew her nose. "Euripides who?"

"Euripides jeans, you pay for them," Daniel said.

And Lillian burst out laughing. Everyone laughed, relieved. A sad and awkward moment had been averted. Daniel told more knock-knock jokes. He had them in stitches. Lillian could laugh just looking at Daniel.

And yet when the children finally left the room (in search of food), despite all the welcome jollity, Lillian couldn't shake the unease she was feeling, a sense of disquiet. Her tears weren't about the beach house, she knew; they were about the fact that these days she just felt swallowed up as Mrs. Blaire. Even if Murray fixed up the guest room, it would be for Mrs. Blaire. Wasn't she something more?

She thought of her novel, packed away in the garage. Was she a writer, if she wasn't writing? When was she going to get over her fear of facing the blank page with nothing to say? When was she going to give Murray the go-ahead to fix up the writing room, and actually *write*?

Sometime. Just not right now.

BUT NATURE ABHORS A VACUUM, especially one involving any version of ambition. One summer night, after a long day at the lake and a hot ride home, Lillian and Murray were sitting on the back porch. Lillian had fed the family a slice of boloney, a scoop of cottage cheese, and fruit cocktail for dinner, then put Lizzie, three at the time, to bed. Now Murray had made them each a Tom Collins and they were watching the older children and a bunch of neighborhood kids horsing around in the Geesons' plastic swimming pool next door—at four feet above ground and twelve feet in diameter, it was not really built for a gang of nine—and Murray was worrying about property damage with all the water that was getting slopped onto the lawn. Lillian was going through the day's mail.

"I've been thinking," said Murray.

"Oh great," said Lillian. "Another dentist's bill. That Chuck! Charges you to remove a piece of popcorn."

"I had lunch with Robert today," said Murray. "He was down for a doctor's appointment."

Robert was a friend of Murray's father who lived up north.

"He said it was time I thought about running for Congress," said Murray.

"You'll never win," she said bluntly. "You're a Democrat." At the time, New Hampshire was overwhelmingly Republican; since the Civil War, it had elected only a handful of Democrats to Congress.

"That's what I said." Murray chuckled. "Robert said I should give it a try someday."

"I don't want to move to Washington."

"You wouldn't have to. I'd get myself an apartment and come home on weekends."

"And leave me with the kids."

"Well, yes," said Murray.

"Why don't you just run for the state legislature? It was good enough for your father."

There must have been something petulant in her voice, because Murray asked, "What's the matter?"

"What's the matter? What about my plans?"

"For writing? I've told you, I'll fix up that room for you any time. You keep putting me off."

"Well, maybe I'm ready now."

"Then let's do it!" Murray exclaimed, growing impatient.

"But you'll still leave me with the kids. How am I going to do anything, if you're jetting back and forth to Washington every week?" She stood up. "Ruth!" she shouted. "Daniel! George! Time for bed!"

"I just thought I'd put it out there," said Murray. "You knew something like this was coming at some point."

He was right; she'd known all along that he had political ambitions.

"But not now," she said, definitely grumpy at this point. "I don't want to be a candidate's wife right now. I feel enough like Suzy Homemaker as it is."

"You don't have to get mad," said Murray.

"I'm not mad."

"You seem mad."

"I've had a long hot day. I've driven home with sand in my crotch and a car full of screaming kids. And I'm sorry if nobody was happy with dinner tonight, but it was too damn hot to cook."

"I was happy with dinner," said Murray.

"You would have been happier with a steak."

Murray was silent.

"You see? Nothing I do is right these days! Everyone complains all the time! You try taking care of the kids and getting dinner on the table every night and scheduling all the doctors' appointments and filling out the school forms and making sure Ruth isn't ruining her eyes by reading in bad light and Daniel actually goes to his swim lesson and George isn't eating all the leftover chicken and Lizzie isn't running away to feed the ducks at the park. You try it."

"I'm not saying it's easy," Murray said hastily. "You work your tail off."

Lillian stubbed out her cigarette. "I could use another one of these," she said, handing Murray her glass. "No you don't," she said to the children, who were tromping up the steps sopping wet. She went and got towels from the dryer and tossed them out. "And wipe your feet, I don't want the Geesons' fresh-cut grass all over my house."

IT WAS MAYBE A FEW MONTHS after that discussion that Lillian awoke in the middle of the night, drenched in a cold sweat. The dream had been so vivid! Swimming at night, a neighbor's pool, the sound of crickets . . . For the first time since before she had children, words and images were spilling from her head. Quietly she got out of bed. She removed her nightgown and rubbed herself dry with a towel, then slipped into a fresh gown and tiptoed downstairs to the kitchen. A magical moment: if this had happened while she was cooking dinner, she might have only been able to scribble a note to herself. But no: tonight, with nobody to distract her, she found one of Murray's legal pads and immediately wrote, *The night after her neighbors went on vacation, Mrs. Klarner went skinny-dipping in their pool.* She paused, and reread the sentence. Who was Mrs. Klarner? What possessed her to sneak into the neighbor's pool? Was there a Mr. Klarner? *Her husband found out,* she continued, *but instead of chastising her for trespassing, the next night he joined her for a swim, and afterward they made love on the neighbors' chaise longue. It was the first time they'd ever had sex out of doors, and Mrs. Klarner climaxed to the sound of crickets whirring noisily in the dark, close by.*

"I could get used to this," she said to Mr. Klarner.

Suddenly Lillian wanted to work on a real draft, wanted the feel of her fingers typing at ninety words per minute. She found a flashlight and went out to the garage—a small detached garage, just another repository of junk. They hadn't parked a car in there since they moved in. She beamed the flashlight about, searching amid the clutter of garden tools, skis, bikes, Christmas decorations, and trash cans. Ah! There it was, the gray plastic case, under a utility shelf.

Back in the kitchen, she set the dusty case on the table and opened it up. Inside was her Smith Corona—powder blue, with creamy white keys. She ran her hands over it and recalled hunkering down in her tiny overheated room at Smith, pounding out term papers on Eaton's Corrasable Bond.

Lillian unfastened the holding clips, lifted the typewriter out, and set it with a clunk on the table in front of her. She found a sheet of blue-lined notebook paper and rolled it into the platen, feeling that satisfying catch with each incremental turn. To her amazement the keys did not stick; the ribbon was low on ink, the a's and o's solid black due to gunk, but it was good enough for now. She began to type, slowly at first, then faster and faster. The words fell from her fingertips. No, they flew, with the little bell dinging as she neared the end of each line, prompting her to whisk the carriage back for a new line.

They began to make a regular practice of it, bringing a bottle of wine and slipping naked into the cool water, making love on a blanket, or even up on the neighbors' settee on the back porch. Mrs. Klarner envied the porch furniture and sometimes felt a wash of anger that Mr. Klarner didn't make enough money for them to afford nice porch furniture and a swimming pool, but the sex was so good that she didn't say anything.

Then one night, when they were lying spent on an old sleeping bag, they heard a car pull into the driveway—

She heard a noise, and looked up and noticed little Lizzie standing in the doorway in her plastic-footed pajamas.

"Oh!" she said. "You scared me."

"What are you doing?" Lizzie asked.

"I'm writing," Lillian said.

"What are you writing?"

"A story," Lillian admitted.

"Will you read it to me?"

"Go back to bed," Lillian said. "It's the middle of the night."

"But you're up."

"Yes, but I don't have school tomorrow."

Lizzie padded over and tried to climb up into Lillian's lap, but Lillian was firm. Couldn't she be off duty at three a.m.? "Back to bed," she said, standing, but Lizzie reached up and tried to push a key, which stuck. Lillian debated letting Lizzie type a line or so of letters, but she didn't want to set a precedent. "This is Mom's typewriter," she said sternly. "You don't touch, do you understand? It's not a toy. Now off you go!" In the end she had to carry Lizzie upstairs and tuck her back into bed, which she suspected Lizzie wanted all along. Then she returned to the kitchen and picked up where she had left off.

Mr. Klarner grabbed his pants. Mrs. Klarner picked up a towel and fled, stubbing her toe on a garden gnome. "Call the police, Bill!" she heard her neighbor say. "Somebody's in the backyard!"

By dawn she had written a dozen pages. The Klarners' marriage was now in shambles. The neighbors sued. All sorts of bad shit was happening, and Lillian was thrilled.

AND IT WAS, indeed, the start of a new phase of Lillian's life. She and Murray finally cleared out the third-floor guest room and gave it a fresh coat of paint. She moved an old sewing table up there as a desk, where she set up her typewriter, along with a box of Corrasable Bond and a cup of pencils. She moved her books up as well, arranging them by course offering: the Modern American Novel, James Joyce, the Russians. She bought herself an electric teakettle so she wouldn't be tempted to go downstairs. A heavy glass ashtray that she wouldn't have to empty every time she turned around.

Every morning, as soon as the kids went off to school—Lizzie was in kindergarten now—Lillian climbed the stairs to her office and wrote. There was no phone extension up there, so if the phone rang downstairs she let it go. Whoever it was, they would call back. She chain-smoked. She talked to herself. Sometimes she typed fast and furiously. Other times she did not in fact have anything to say and found herself standing murderously in the middle of the room with a fly swatter. Regardless, she worked until eleven thirty, at which point she went to pick up Lizzie. Her three hours of golden time were over.

The children weren't allowed in the room unless there was an emergency. Once Daniel raided her paper supply and she felt vandalized. "Do I have to put a Keep Out! sign on the door?!" she shrieked.

"Respect your mother," said Murray.

Lillian wasn't too keen on showing the family members her work, because she felt like she was starting at square one again as a writer. Plus there was sex in her stories. As a result of this secrecy, everyone had a different attitude toward her writing. "Mom's little writing projects," Ruth sniffed to friends, covering up a sense of injustice over her mother's refusal to share her work with a daughter who routinely got A's in English. "Whatever she does up there," Daniel mumbled, because he couldn't conceive of what she was doing and had little interest in trying. "Mom's work," said George, with respect. "Mom's special alone time" was how Lizzie characterized it, a note of fear in her voice.

"Just don't write about me," Murray joked.

AS FOR MURRAY'S CONGRESSIONAL AMBITIONS, after that first discussion they hadn't gone very far; Republicans continued to control the state, and Murray kept toiling away at his law firm. But in

February of the year Lizzie was in kindergarten, one of the state's representatives got embroiled in a sex scandal, and Murray's friends told him that his time was now or never. Based on a rudimentary poll, Murray determined that the people of New Hampshire's second congressional district might, just *might*, be ready to elect a Democrat. He thought he had a good shot.

Lillian was wary. She knew she was never going to be a good Candidate's Wife. And she didn't want anything to cut into her golden time. It was hard enough as things stood; there was still cooking and cleaning and laundry to be done outside her writing time, and if a child was sick in the night, it was Lillian who stayed up and fell asleep at her desk the next day. So many of the great women writers had opted out of children completely, she remembered from her literature classes, and of those who had children, many had had just one. Was she doomed, with her brood of four?

Well, all she could do was try. Be stern, be selfish for those three hours a day, she told herself. And if Murray wants to run for Congress, let him. They'd figure it out.

"Okay," she said. "As long as I get three hours a day in my room to myself."

"Six hours," Murray corrected her, "starting next fall, when Lizzie'll be in first grade."

Six hours of writing time! She could hardly believe it. Maybe she would even dig her novel out of the box in the garage.

It was going to be a very careful balance for Lillian.

And so Murray registered his candidacy. They had a long talk with the kids one night about the importance of remaining on good behavior while Murray was running for office. "You don't have to be perfect," Murray told them. "But no arrests, okay? No drug dealerships? No babies out of wedlock?"

"Dad!" exclaimed Ruth, turning red.

"Just being clear," said Murray.

On the night of the Fourth, Murray and Lillian returned from the fireworks to a stifling house. After putting a crabby Lizzie to bed, they turned on the oscillating fan in their bedroom and lay on top of the sheets, feeling the cool, silky air glide across their tired limbs. They made love and were still wide awake. As they waited for their other children to get home, they strategized for the upcoming campaign. Despite the heat, and in a good mood that she attributed to her writing the day before, Lillian felt magnanimous and open-minded. They would tour the district in their van during weekends, they agreed, with everyone dressed in matching blue-and-white T-shirts. ("We'll call it the Blaire-Mobile," Lillian decided.) They would saturate the bean suppers, the county fairs, the Friday night football games in the fall. They would work as a team to get Murray elected.

Team Blaire.

7.

Zipper

THE MORE IMMEDIATE QUESTION AFTER THE FOURTH OF July was where to take their vacation that August, and since Murray planned a campaign blitz for his two weeks off, it made the most sense to go to the beach house for the entire time. Lillian couldn't really argue with this; it was only an hour from Concord, after all, as opposed to the lake house up in Vermont.

As she didn't expect to get much writing done during those two weeks of raucous family activity, she agreed to spend much of her time campaigning with Murray. The idea was for Murray's fun-loving parents to supervise the children while Murray and Lillian traveled across the state. And so during those two weeks, they rose at six to shower and gulp down some coffee. At seven they got picked up by two aides in a humble Ford and were driven perhaps to Concord to meet with the public employees, to a rally on the town common in Keene, up to Claremont to keep Murray's face alive in the Connecticut River Valley, and back to Concord for an early evening fish fry with the electrical workers. The scheduled day over, Murray and Lillian and his two aides drove back to the beach house and retired to the living room to talk strategy over pizza. Murray's numbers showed a good solid lead over his opponent, who managed to keep putting his foot in his mouth with the sex scandal.

"Speaking of which," said Murray.

"What?" Lillian said warily. She didn't like sentences that began with "Speaking of which . . ."

"Martin here thinks you ought to start making your own appearances." Martin Tobin was Murray's chief aide.

Lillian didn't like the idea. She'd never been comfortable speaking in front of groups; she was much more comfortable putting words on a piece of paper. But she was conscious of feeling a little like Pat Nixon these days, always smiling by Murray's side. *Take one for the team*, she told herself. Martin suggested that she start with a coffee, something informal, and the second week in August, Lillian found herself on the schedule with a meet and greet down in Salem. The teachers' union would welcome her.

"Try and keep the focus on education," Murray said the night before. "Maybe talk about Head Start and WIC. Keep it light. And don't get into gun control. Same with abortion—stay away from those kooks."

He was referring to a couple that had been protesting at an abortion clinic the week before. They had been carrying graphic signs, and at one point they blocked the way of a young woman who had shown some hesitation upon seeing the photographs—a possible convert, they might have thought. In any case, the office manager came out to shoo them away, at which point the couple barged into the clinic and started shouting at the people in the waiting room— girls with their boyfriends, girls with their mothers; girls alone. A scuffle ensued between the man and one of the boyfriends, and the police had to be called in to extricate the couple from what was, of course, private property.

Murray's feelings about the right to choose were pretty black and white. Occasionally he thought back to that evening in December when Lillian had called to tell him she was pregnant, and although he couldn't imagine life without Ruth, and had no regrets about marrying Lillian, how nice it would have been if they'd had a real, safe, and legal choice. And these days, with four children who might find themselves in the same predicament someday, he often gave a silent prayer of thanks to Justice Blackmun for his opinion in *Roe v. Wade*.

But Murray was also courting the Catholic vote in his district, and while he was firmly pro-choice, he didn't want to go out on a limb to emphasize this. Lillian thought it was cowardly of him.

"Those 'kooks' you're referring to ought to go to jail," she said, cracking an egg on top of some ground beef in a mixing bowl. She was making meat loaf tonight. Too much pizza. "They started the fight. You should say that. If people are antiabortion to begin with, you're never going to get their vote, anyway." She heard the beginning of an essay in her head. *Imagine: You're sixteen and pregnant . . .* With the cookbook open before her, she wiped her hands and simply wrote down one word at the top of the page: "Imagine:"—the colon being essential to the clue prompt.

"All I'm saying is try to avoid the issue," said Murray. "I need to be pragmatic. I don't want a huge blaring headline."

The next morning Lillian was ready at seven, dressed in khakis and a longish white sweater that covered up the little pooch she'd developed after four children. Meanwhile, Murray's parents had come down with some kind of summer bug, so Ruth was going to drive the children up the coast to Old Orchard Beach for the day.

Lillian gave them their last-minute instructions. "No cotton candy, unless you want to pay the dentist bills," she said. "And remember: your father's running for public office. Don't do anything that'll embarrass him."

"I'll make sure," Ruth vowed.

"Oh, thank you, Ruth," said Daniel, in his best falsetto.

"What's for dinner tonight?" George asked.

"I don't know; go ask Fannie," Lillian replied absently. Actually, maybe they'd just get Chinese.

"Am I tall enough for the Zipper, do you think?" little Lizzie asked.

"Absolutely not," said Lillian.

"You're tall enough for the kiddie cars," said Daniel.

Lizzie stuck out her tongue at him.

"Nobody goes on the Zipper," Lillian declared. "It makes everyone throw up. Here," and she handed them each a five-dollar bill. "Have fun, and I'll see you for dinner."

The coffee in Salem was held at the local high school, with about thirty teachers in attendance. To her dismay, Lillian got stage fright; her voice cracked as she began, and she found it difficult to breathe. But she quickly recovered and thanked them for all they were doing to shape the next generation of thinkers. She talked about the need for early childhood education and cited figures that showed the success of programs like Head Start. She talked about all the budget cuts President Reagan had proposed, and stressed that Murray would fight for more education funding.

But she quickly moved on to Q and A, thinking it would be easier than speechifying. Someone asked about merit pay, and Lillian explained that without standards, it promoted cronyism. Someone else wanted her to talk about the Seabrook nuclear plant, and she deftly noted the risks of nuclear power and the need to start investigating alternative sources of energy that wouldn't give us another Three Mile Island.

It was all going well until someone from the back raised his hand.

"This is perhaps off topic," said the young man, "but I understand that Mr. Blaire thinks it's okay to kill innocent children."

Lillian took a sip of coffee. It was burned and bitter. She set the Styrofoam cup down.

"If you're talking about abortion, you're talking about a fetus," she said calmly. "Let's get our terms straight."

The man held up a photo. "This is a fetus?" The photo showed a seven-month old . . . well, call it a fetus, call it a baby; whatever. It had arms and legs and a big alien head and was sucking its thumb.

Lillian felt her neck burn. These people loved showing photos that blurred the lines. She wished she had a comparable photo of a six-week embryo.

"How can your husband condone the murder of a child like this?" he asked.

Lillian tucked back a loose strand of hair. "What he condones, and supports," she said carefully, "is a woman's right to make the very difficult decision when and if to bear a child. As articulated by the Supreme Court."

"But this is a child," the man said. "How can you deny that? And an abortion would have killed that child. Therefore abortion is murder. How can you refute that?"

"Come on, Richard," protested a teacher from another table. "Write her husband a letter if you want him to know how you feel."

"No," said Lillian. She felt fueled by the *Imagine:* essay she was planning to scratch out on one of Murray's legal pads later that night. "It's okay. I'll tell you what's wrong here. What's wrong is men like you telling women like me what we can and can't do with our bodies. Are you trying to tell me that if my daughter is raped and becomes pregnant, she has to spend the next nine months of her life in a state of incubation—and then feeding, clothing, and educating a real child for the next eighteen years? I don't think so. I don't see your people stepping forward with a tax plan to help women in that position," she said. "You're pro-birth, is what you are. You're not pro-life. So quit giving me that bullshit abortion-is-murder argument and vote for my husband who will at least try to allocate more money for all those innocent little children who have *already* been born."

An uncomfortable silence filled the room, punctuated only by the clearing of throats. Her heart was racing. In the back of the room, a reporter scribbled furiously.

Murray was going to kill her.

She looked at the group before her. They were expecting something. An apology? Well, she wasn't going to apologize for her views.

What she did apologize for was swearing. "Maybe I got a little too emotional. Maybe we can move on to another topic."

There was shuffling, more throat-clearing. Nobody had another question. She took another sip of coffee.

"Well then," she said brightly.

As she collected her notes, she turned to a somber-looking Martin, who handed her purse to her. The group began to disperse but several people came forward, including the man who had stuck up for her.

"Richard's like that whenever we have a staff meeting," he explained. "He likes to make trouble."

"I shouldn't have sworn," Lillian sighed.

"You're human," said the man.

That's right, Lillian told herself as they headed north to Concord, where she was going to meet Murray for lunch at a senior center. *Buck up,* she thought. *You're human. So you got a little emotional. So what?*

"How'd it go?" asked Murray, when she joined up with him.

"Well . . ." Lillian began.

Murray looked at Martin, who explained that someone had pressed her about abortion.

"He was an asshole," Lillian said defiantly. "He was looking for a fight."

"Did you give him one?"

"Well . . ."

"How bad was it?" Murray asked Martin. "And was the press there?"

Oh, the press was there, all right. The next morning the *Man-*

chester *Union Leader*, the state's ultra-conservative newspaper, would publish a photo of Lillian with her mouth in an awkward snarl, with the caption "Candidate's Wife Attacks Pro-Lifer." The story opened with a summary of her "dramatic outburst," describing her as "prickly," and portraying Richard the Pro-Lifer as steady and measured.

But by the next morning, this story wouldn't upset them as much as expected—because upon arriving back at the beach house after Lillian's outburst, they had something else to deal with. Apparently, during their day at Old Orchard, Daniel had snuck off with some friends and spent his five dollars on a quart of vodka, and not only vomited on the Zipper but stumbled as he was getting off and did a face-plant on the cement, knocking out his two front teeth. The press, who had been following the four Blaire children from ride to ride (this being a human interest story; "The Candidate's Children Have Some Fun" was the editor's idea), got a photo of a bloody-faced Daniel being dragged off by Ruth and George with Lizzie trotting behind carrying Daniel's two front teeth in a giant cup of Coke, and followed them to Maine Medical in Portland, where the Blaire children were met by a police officer, who promptly ticketed Daniel for underage drinking, even before the ER technicians had hooked him up to an IV.

And now they were all back at the beach house, gathered in the living room. Daniel lay on the sofa with a mouth full of gauze; the dentist who showed up at the ER had simply stuck his teeth back into his gums. Murray's parents emerged from their bedroom, looking dazed and rumpled from their summer bug—and probably from the Pernod that Murray's father insisted was a cure-all.

Murray paced back and forth on the worn braided rug. "How could you?" he demanded.

"Ih wah ust a ew hots," Daniel mumbled.

"Enough to give you a blood alcohol level of point one three!"

"Ho?"

"So that's pretty goddamned drunk," Murray said. "Do you do this on a regular basis?"

"It was me who found his teeth," Lizzie whispered to Lillian.

"Very good, dear," said Lillian.

"I put them in my Coke," said Lizzie proudly.

"Very good, dear," said Lillian. She was wondering which story would draw more attention: Daniel getting soused, or her blowing her cool with Mr. Fetus.

"Can someone explain what happened?" Murray's mother pleaded.

"Ruth, where were you?" Murray asked. "You were supposed to keep everyone together."

"Daniel said he was going to the bathroom. What was I supposed to do, follow him into the men's room?" Ruth's tone flared with righteous indignation; she perceived her role in the day's events as one of supreme responsibility for being there when Daniel stumbled off the Zipper, and for getting him to Maine Medical without herself getting a speeding ticket on Route 1. She was quite pleased with herself, really.

Lillian wanted a drink, but didn't want to drink in front of Daniel, so she went into the kitchen and poured an inch of vodka (gin would smell too much) into a mug and carried it back in, cupping her hands around it and blowing as though it were hot tea.

"You realize this will be all over the news," Murray told Daniel.

"How do you think it's going to make me look? Like my family's out of control, that's how."

Lillian didn't think it was a requirement of public office that a candidate have a perfect family. Look at those Kennedy kids. She thought back to her outburst, though, and found it unfortunate that her outburst and Daniel's drinking had coincided on the same day.

"Can we eat?" asked George.

"It's bad enough to go off and get drunk like that," Murray went on, pacing. "Do you realize how many brain cells you killed today? It was a stupid thing to do. But it was selfish as well. Were you thinking of anybody besides yourself when you did this?"

"I'n horry!" cried Daniel. "Okay? I didn't know how drunk I ould get!"

"Well, now you know, don't you?" Murray shook his head. Lillian thought he was rubbing it in a little too thick. She felt sorry for Daniel. He was, after all, only fifteen. His mouth was a mess. His head was a mess. Murray didn't need to make it worse.

Lillian lit a cigarette and waved out the match. "Beating a dead horse . . ." she murmured.

Murray turned to her. "It's an opportunity to learn a good lesson, Lillian," he said sternly. "He's got to understand that he's not the only person in the universe."

"I'm just saying you don't need to be so hard," Lillian said. "I think he's already learned his lesson."

"Can I try some vodka?" Lizzie asked. "Does it really taste like water?"

Murray glared at her. Things were getting out of control. Everyone had had a long day.

"I think dinner would be a good idea," said Lillian, although she noticed Daniel looking queasy at the mere mention of food. Still, dinner would distract everyone, would give them time to cool down. She went into the kitchen and opened up the boxes of Chinese food and called everybody in.

"No pot stickers?" Murray's father asked.

"I just remembered our teacher telling us that if we lost a tooth, put it in Coke," Lizzie was telling Murray's mother. "And I had a Coke, so I put Daniel's teeth in it."

"You're a smart little girl," Nana Blaire said. "Though I think it was milk, not Coke."

Lillian made herself a moo shu pork pancake and helped herself to some of the fried rice, though she didn't have much of an appetite herself. She followed her family into the living room, where they sat with plates on their laps, and Murray began to calm down, and there was just the clink of forks on plates as everyone ate. *I wish the press could photograph* this, she thought. "The Blaire Family Survives a Crisis." "Blaire Teen Learns a Valuable Life Lesson." Murray's numbers would rise, not fall. They would be seen as a regular *family*. They would go on to sweep their district.

"What happens tomorrow?" she asked Murray. "What's on our schedule?"

Murray sighed. Lillian could see a cynical response forming on his lips, *Noon rally at Fuck-Up Plaza* or something like that, but instead he said he thought they'd take a day off. It wouldn't hurt them. Besides, Daniel had to see an endodontist, and Murray wanted to be there.

Lying in bed that night, she found herself thinking back upon her outburst. She was glad she'd stuck up for herself, glad she didn't let herself get bullied into silence. If it hurt Murray's numbers with the Catholic vote, so be it. And Daniel's problem would blow over. Team Blaire did not have to be perfect all the time.

The rest of the house was still. Next door Murray's parents snored off their bug. Down the hall Ruth was probably reading with a flashlight while Lizzie lay with limbs splayed on the bed next to her. Farther on down in the boys' room, Daniel would be tossing fit-fully, and George would be dreaming of breakfast. The only noise came from outside, the sounds of the Atlantic Ocean, waves break-ing gently, lulling all the summer people to sleep.

All but Lillian, that is. She slipped out of bed and went into the kitchen and found a legal pad. *Imagine: You're sixteen and pregnant*, she wrote, continuing the idea from the night before. *You're nau-seous. Your boyfriend is a child. You have no money, no diploma, no support from your parents* . . . She paused and reread her words. She didn't like them. There was something self-righteous about the tone. And it was going to be too abstract.

She poured herself some gin and thought back to her own experi-ence, learning she was pregnant back in 1966, and about her friend who had almost bled to death. What if she hadn't loved Murray enough to want to marry him? And as she began to write, she be-came that girl in her essay, and followed her up some dimly lit stairs to a second-floor apartment with the linoleum floor, the wind-rattled windows, the threadbare sheet laid across the dining room table. She clenched her teeth throughout the procedure and barely made it home on the T before collapsing into her own bed, and when, two days later she ended up in the emergency room at Mass

General and got a scolding from both the nurse and the doctor, she refused to give the name and address, because if he didn't do it, who would?

There, she thought, setting down her pen. Much better as a piece of fiction, first-person point of view. She stepped outside into the cool, salty night air and lit a cigarette. She planned to quit after the campaign, but right now it was the most satisfying cigarette she'd ever had.

It was three o'clock when she went back and climbed into bed beside Murray, who lay curled away from her. He slept in a T-shirt these days, not the old-man pajamas Lillian's mother gave him every Christmas. She wanted to tell him about the piece she was writing but didn't want to jinx things. So she merely spooned up against him and smelled his sweet, peppery smell.

He sighed, and settled more deeply into sleep.

8.

Fidel-ity

THE IDEA FOR THE BLAIRE-MOBILE, BORN AFTER LOVE-making on the Fourth of July, blossomed into reality after Daniel's incident. Murray wanted the people of New Hampshire to see that they were a normal family, one that did things together on the weekend. A family that explored the state together, and stopped for pie and coffee now and then, and took a swim at one of the state's many pristine lakes—as opposed to, say, a family with a wayward teen who went off and got himself drunk as a skunk at an amusement park while his mother was out yelling at antiabortionists.

Ruth, at sixteen, was excited to have an official role. Daniel, however, saw this compulsory togetherness as punishment and couldn't believe his parents were going to make him drive around with them on a perfectly good Saturday. George wanted to paint a peace sign on the old blue van; Murray vetoed that idea, but allowed him to plaster the bumpers with Murray's blue-and-white stickers. Lizzie just wanted to bring her Barbie.

Despite the underlying discord, they were a photogenic bunch, packed into the van with Murray at the wheel. Lillian agreed not to smoke in the car, and the children perfected the art of the white-toothed smile that showed off years of budget-busting orthodontia.

The problem was that, even though it was a van, it was a very small space for a family of six to confine themselves for a long day full of campaign stops, and things could get touchy. Squabbles usually broke out within the first hour. Daniel's feet stank. *Daniel* stank. George wanted to make the A Band this year (rather than the dreaded B Band), so he brought his trumpet along. Ruth cried that it was blasting her eardrums. Lizzie kept singing the same song over and over again, right in Murray's ear. Ruth was getting carsick from Daniel's feet. Lillian broke down and had a cigarette.

Murray wondered if every family fought as much as his did.

"You and your brothers fought," Lillian reminded him. "Your mother said she had to break up fistfights. At least we don't have fistfights."

"Not yet," Murray grumbled. "Wait until George's testosterone kicks in."

"If they get into fistfights, I will spray them with the garden hose," Lillian vowed.

The short-term solution—at least as far as travel in the Blaire-Mobile went—was obvious. Daniel had to shower and keep his shoes on. No smelly bags of popcorn. No cigarettes. No trumpet. Books were allowed, a Walkman, too; general conversation was allowed unless it veered toward the argumentative, in which case Lillian called a Quaker Meeting. *Quaker Meeting has begun, no more laughing, no more fun.* With these restrictions, the day on the road could be tolerated by everyone.

All through September they spent their Saturdays tooling around New Hampshire's second congressional district. Sometimes Murray allowed Ruth to drive. They visited Hanover, the White Mountains, the Great North Woods. They visited a shoe factory and a woolen mill. They toured a meat processing facility, where they got free baloney roll-ups with frilly toothpicks. Leaves changed color and they got stuck in traffic jams with leaf-peepers from New York.

"I gave up football for this?" said Daniel.

"You didn't make the football team," Ruth reminded him.

"Because I have a bum knee," Daniel shot back.

"Poor cripple," said Ruth.

"Quaker Meeting," said Lillian.

Meanwhile, they were constantly having to deal with the press. It amazed Lillian how much they could dig up. They found out that Murray had been a member of Students for a Democratic Society for a brief time in college. That Lillian had dated a Black Panther one summer in Boston, before she met Murray. "It was just one date," she protested, but nonetheless the story ran in large part focusing on her wealthy childhood and speculating that her association with student radicals in college was simply a way of rebelling against her privileged background.

Murray slammed the newspaper down.

"This isn't reporting; it's total conjecture," he fumed. "Who cares who you hung out with back then?!"

"What's a Black Panther?" Lizzie asked. She had shaved her

Barbie with Murray's electric razor the day before, and was now trying to fix matters by scotch-taping the hair back on. "Are there any in New Hampshire?"

"You dated a Black Panther?" Ruth asked. It being 1984, she was learning about the sixties in her U.S. History class.

"Once," Lillian said. "It was never serious."

"Was he really black?" Lizzie asked.

"No, he was lime green," Ruth said.

"Ruth," Lillian said. "Really."

"I'll bet Grandfather didn't like that," Daniel declared, always titillated by a little family discord.

"No," said Lillian, "he didn't." She didn't tell them how her father refused to shake the young man's hand. It still mortified her.

Suddenly Lizzie whapped her Barbie on the table. "It's not working!"

"Let me try," said Lillian, taking the doll. "You need to think before you act, Lizzie dear."

"I wish I'd never been born!" Lizzie cried, burying her head in Lillian's lap.

George came out of the pantry holding a jar of Skippy. "We're out."

"That's because you eat it like ice cream," said Ruth.

"I'm a growing boy," said George.

"You're a Neanderthal is what you are," said Ruth.

"What's that on your chin, Ruth?" said Daniel, who sensed his plump younger brother at a disadvantage. "Is that another zit?"

Ruth touched her chin.

"Leave it alone," said Lillian. "You'll just make it worse."

"It's growing as I watch," said Daniel. "Oh my God, it's turning white on top."

Ruth burst into tears and fled the room.

Lillian sighed. "Really, Daniel, was that necessary?"

"She called George a Neanderthal," said Daniel. "Watch this." He began juggling three tangerines. Lizzie tried and promptly dropped them.

"Nobody answered me," she said, scrambling to pick them up.

"I forgot what you asked, dear," said Lillian.

"What's a Black Panther?"

"A radical," said Ruth, back now wearing cakey orange makeup.

"What's a radical?" asked Lizzie.

And so Ruth proceeded to explain the different political factions in the United States, going on about liberals and conservatives and the radical right and left, SDS, SNCC, the antiwar movement, the John Birch Society, and Patty Hearst, so engrossed in her didactic role that she barely noticed that everyone had left the room except George, who, having located a new jar of Skippy, had made himself a mountain of toast and was going through the stack, piece by piece, annihilating the jar of peanut butter that Lillian had allocated for the next week's sandwiches.

MEANWHILE, THE POLLS were tightening as voters stopped worrying so much about a sex scandal as about the collectively horrific prospect of electing a Democrat. In an effort to discredit Murray's qualifications for public office, his opponent was relentless. Murray missed a tax payment on the house one year. (True.) He represented the Mafia. (Ridiculous.) He represented drug addicts. (Half true; he'd once defended a junkie and gotten him into a methadone clinic down in Boston.) He comingled his clients' funds. (False.) Each charge required some kind of rebuttal, which took away from Murray's dwindling time to talk about the issues that mattered.

On Lillian they dug up more dirt. The *Union Leader* made a big deal of the fact that she'd been seen leaving the new Copley Place in Boston laden with bags from expensive stores, implying extravagance, implying in turn a lack of connection with Murray's more blue-collar base. This was unfair; Lillian's mother had simply taken her shopping for her birthday—and they bought from the *sale* rack, for heaven's sake. Another reporter, following up on the story, noted that she'd claimed a home office deduction on her taxes one year. What was her business? She was a writer, she replied. Did he want to come and see her office? Did he want to see her stack of rejection letters?

But nothing prepared her for the next big question. Lillian and the reporter were sitting at a booth in a coffee shop on Main Street in Concord. The reporter opened a manila envelope and slid a folded, yellowed newspaper across the tabletop. It was a copy of the *Daily Hampshire Gazette*, whose front page showed a black-and-white picture of an amateur but very convincing mural of Fidel Castro, complete with cigar, that had been painted on the southern wall of the Northampton Chamber of Commerce in Massachusetts. "Smith Seniors Arrested in Act of Vandalism," the accompanying headline read, and the article went on to describe how Lillian Holmes and two other students had been apprehended by the police just as they were filling in the man's scruffy beard.

"Do you care to comment on this?" asked the reporter.

"Oh for heaven's sake," said Lillian. "I was twenty-two. It was our senior prank. Why don't you ask me where my husband stands on aid to dependent children? Or about my volunteer work at the soup kitchen?"

"My, my," said the reporter.

"Go to hell," said Lillian, and she reached for the newspaper, but he took it back.

"Did you plead guilty?" he asked.

With her father's attorney by her side, Lillian had in fact pleaded guilty to vandalism, and she had been sentenced to a month of community service, plus the cost of sandblasting the besmirched wall.

"This interview is over," Lillian said. "Write what you want. Here's my statement. 'As a college student I was exposed to a variety of ideas, some of which can be attributed to youthful idealism. I do not support, nor have I ever supported, the Communist regime in Cuba.' There. Are you happy?"

The reporter was scribbling furiously.

"I have what I need," he said.

"Good," said Lillian, standing up. "Now go fuck yourself."

She stormed out of the coffee shop. By the time she arrived home she'd calmed down, but she got upset all over again when she saw Murray, because she'd never told him about the vandalism charge. Murray himself had just gotten home and was upstairs in the bedroom, changing out of his work clothes. Lillian sat on the window seat.

"How'd the interview go?" he asked, loosening his tie.

She told him about her confrontation with the reporter.

"Wait—you're saying you painted a picture of Castro on the Chamber of Commerce building?"

"Mural, actually." She tried to keep the note of pride out of her voice. Because it had been a very good mural, in her opinion. For someone who didn't think of herself as an artist.

"And you got arrested?"

"I paid a fine," said Lillian. "And got the wall cleaned."

"How come you never told me about this?"

"I should have," said Lillian. "I'm sorry."

Murray had had a bad day. A new poll had come out. "Sorry's not going to save my ass in the polls," he said. "Not when people find out I married a Communist sympathizer."

"I'm not a sympathizer!" Lillian exclaimed. "And I never was! Look, I was taking a course on the politics of the Caribbean. And I just thought it would be funny. I was young. I wasn't really thinking."

"Still, it'll look bad," said Murray. "Joe McCarthy is alive and well in some circles in this state. God damn it."

He had a way of curling up the corners of his mouth when he was mad, in a grade-school teacher way, and she found it unattractive. She reminded herself that nobody looked very attractive when they were angry, but this went deeper; it was as if a switch had been turned off and she couldn't remember how she'd *ever* found him attractive.

(Though she was probably no great shakes to him right now, either.)

Just then there was a knock at the door. Murray opened it a crack. Lizzie reported that George was throwing up hot dogs.

"We're having a discussion, Lizzie," said Murray. "Your mother will be out soon."

"He missed the toilet," Lizzie said.

"Give us a minute," Murray said crossly.

When Lizzie had left, Lillian went and sat down on the bed and hugged her arms around herself. "I should have told you," she said again. "I should have told you way back in the beginning."

"So why didn't you?"

She tried to go back in time, to her frame of mind at age twenty-three, when she'd met Murray that summer at the law firm. She must have thought that this young law student would have thought poorly of her. She'd certainly never thought about the ramifications of her arrest record coming back to haunt them in a far-into-the-future political campaign.

"I don't know," she said.

Murray glared at her, but then his look softened. "I guess it wasn't like we had a confession marathon," he said. "Still. You should have known that someone would have dug this up. We'll have to tell the children, since it'll come out in the papers. You can do it. God damn it."

Chastised, and now in a very bad mood, she left him in the bedroom and went downstairs to fix dinner. They had just had the floor redone in faux-brick linoleum; her whole work routine had gotten messed up, with workers in the house. She turned on the oven, put the pot pies onto a baking sheet, and started making an apple crunch for dessert.

But she was not a happy cook tonight, even making a good dessert. She was mad at Murray and mad at herself and scared that the reporter was going to report how she told him to go fuck himself. Between that and the event with the teachers down in Salem, people were going to think she had a mouth.

She *did* have a mouth. And to tell the truth, she was proud of it these days. She should have *more* of a mouth, she thought.

She poured another smidgeon of gin into her tonic and got an idea for a story. *Virginia/sex with plumber,* she wrote in the margins, next to the recipe for apple crunch.

When everyone was seated around the table, when they had all been served and were intent on tipping their pot pies out of their little aluminum holders without breaking them, she told the children about the escapade.

"Way to go, Mom," said Daniel.

"You mean you have a criminal record?" Ruth asked anxiously, and then: "Will I have to disclose this when I apply to college?"

"Certainly not," said Murray. "And don't let this give any of you children ideas," he grumped.

"I'm feeling better," said George, who had been sentenced to chicken bouillon. "Can I have a pot pie?"

"Absolutely not," said Lillian. She had cleaned up George's one mess and had no intention of cleaning up another later tonight.

The words of the old nursery rhyme came to mind: *She whipped them all soundly and put them to bed.*

As it turned out, the *Union Leader* did its very best indeed to link Murray himself with Fidel Castro the next day. They did this by publishing the photo of Lillian's mural with Murray's name in large bold type, and if you skimmed the article you might even have come to the conclusion that Murray himself had painted the mural just recently. Murray slammed the newspaper down; Lillian got huffy again; Daniel bought an extra copy to bring into Social Studies class; and Ruth wrote an editorial for the school newspaper that focused on how what you did as a young adult could come back to haunt you years later. Contributions to Murray's campaign dipped, as did his numbers in the somewhat primitive polling that went on in a small-state congressional campaign in 1984. Lillian, who'd been scouring her memory for other things she might have done that (as Ruth pointed out) could come back to haunt her, was too preoccupied to write, and indeed, when she made it up to her office that day, she decided that everything she'd written that past month was garbage. Her characters were all one-dimensional. Her stories were too descriptive; there was no *story* to them. She cursed the campaign and found herself making no bones about the fact that she wished Murray would lose, so their lives could return to normal.

BACK TO THE NIGHT BEFORE, THOUGH: Lillian didn't forget about the note she'd made in the cookbook about Virginia and the plumber. As with Mr. and Mrs. Klarner, she wanted to know what was going on. Just give me half an hour, she told the family, and strung the rope across the stairwell to the third floor so Lizzie wouldn't be inclined to follow. Then she went upstairs, sat down at her desk, and rolled a new sheet of paper into the typewriter.

Once Virginia realized that she could sleep with the plumber and get away with it, she scheduled all sorts of household repairs.

She hesitated. Good lord! What if Murray read this? He would think she wanted to sleep with the plumber!

Nevertheless she kept going. *She got the gutters cleaned; the gutter-man wasn't quite as good in bed as the plumber, but he sufficed for one afternoon. Then she got the tile repaired on the front steps, and slept with her first black man.* (Lillian wondered if the story was going to be set in a place like Concord. There weren't a lot of black people in Concord.) *She scheduled an appointment to get the chimney swept, but feared at the last minute that the chimney sweep's soot would rub off on her, and he flounced out of the house a disappointed man.*

She sat back, reread what she'd written. Who was Virginia married to? How would he figure in the story? She lit a cigarette.

Hubert, on the other hand, was happy, she wrote. *Unbeknownst to Virginia, he had plans to sell the house, and he wanted everything in working order. He gave her a list of more repairs . . .*

"Ahem," said Murray, and she jumped in her chair.

"Don't sneak up on me like that!" she exclaimed. Involuntarily she cupped her hand over the page.

"George is throwing up again," he said from the doorway.

"And you can't deal with it?"

"Lizzie says she doesn't feel so good either," he said. "If we've got two kids throwing up, then no, I can't deal with both of them at once."

Lillian sighed. "I'll be right down."

"I'm sorry," said Murray.

"Don't be," she replied. "I never get any good work done in the evening, anyway." But this wasn't one hundred percent true. She was rolling right now. She was cooking. Nevertheless she pulled out the page, wrote "Home Repair" at the top, and placed it in the desk drawer.

"How do *you* feel?" she asked Murray, following him down the stairs.

"Not so hot," he admitted.

ON THE FIRST Saturday in November, four days before Election Day, Murray's aides scheduled a large rally on the State House lawn. Murray said he expected everyone in the family to attend. "The campaign's almost over," he promised them. "Nobody wants to look back and wonder if there was something else we could have done."

"I don't see what having me up there on the stage with you will do to influence voters," Daniel grumbled. He was so touchy these days. Lillian missed the clown.

"We're a family," Murray said. "We stick together."

"Can I talk into the microphone?" Lizzie asked.

"If anyone gets to speak, it should be me," said Ruth. "I at least know what the issues are in this campaign."

"You want to speak?" said Murray. "You can speak if you want to."

"I can?" Having gotten what she asked for, Ruth allowed a nervous smile.

"Sure," said Murray. "You write up a little speech and run it by me. No more than five minutes."

And so Ruth began to draft a speech, practicing it in the bathroom every night. Two days before the rally, she tried it out on the family.

"No comments from the peanut gallery," Murray warned the other children as they gathered in their cluttered living room. "Respect your sister. She's worked hard on this, and she's got to look professional."

"This is so stupid," said Daniel, slumping on the sofa.

"What's eating you, son?" Murray demanded. "Every time we do something now, you act like the wise guy. Something wrong at school?"

Daniel crossed his arms and glared. George came into the living room with a big bowl of popcorn, as though it were movie night. Lillian sat in a rocking chair. She never could relax on the sofa because she always noticed how shabby the chintz fabric was, and felt overwhelmed about choosing something new. It was a sore point.

"Okay, Ruth," said Murray. "Let's hear it."

Ruth stood in front of the fireplace. She was still dressed in her school clothes—a pleated plaid skirt, a white blouse, and a cardigan sweater. Suddenly self-conscious with her family, she splayed her index cards, closed her eyes, mouthed some words, and then began.

"I'm up here because I believe in my father," she said, addressing the seascape above the sofa. "I believe in the things he stands for." She went on to touch on all of Murray's talking points, and it struck Lillian that Ruth had a flair for oratory, something she hadn't realized. Her mind leapt ahead and she saw Ruth becoming a lawyer in her time, maybe even running for public office herself someday, and she imagined the pride she would feel, watching Ruth speak with the moral convictions that Lillian and Murray had instilled in her since the beginning. She looked at all of her children and despite her sour attitude toward the campaign these days, she suddenly felt such love for them: Ruth up there looking poised and unruffled and so sure of herself; Daniel going through this awful phase but coming out a man who could make people laugh, take them out of their bad moods and inject them with a sillier view of life; George taking care of others, the same way he'd always taken care of Lizzie; and jumpy little Lizzie living outside the mold, doing whatever she chose to do. Her love was visceral; it rose from her gut up through her chest and into her throat, like smoke, and with it came a terrifying sense of loss, because there was so much at stake in the very fact of their lives. She had the sudden conviction that despite all the normal day-to-day discord, her children would one day be as tightly aligned as a jigsaw; that after she and Murray were long gone, the four of them would turn to each other, lean on each other, love each other to the ends of the earth; and that she had had a hand in this, and could give herself a pat on the shoulder for a job well done.

9.

Snow

ON THE DAY OF THE LAST RALLY, THE SATURDAY BEFORE the election, Lillian rose early to find the lawn frosted over from a cold snap in the night. Her zinnias had turned brown, but the hardy chrysanthemums stood strong, their red and gold blooms tipped in white. She made a pot of strong coffee and stood by the window, appreciating this last bit of color before the long gray New Hampshire winter set in.

She had about half an hour before Murray and the children got up, so she climbed the stairs to the third-floor guest room and sat down at her desk. She picked up the envelope that had arrived in yesterday's mail: a thin, cream-colored envelope, not one of the 9-by-12 manila ones she was accustomed to getting back, those malevolent packets that contained the story itself along with a rejection letter. This one contained a personal letter on matching heavy-stock stationery from the editor of *The Northern Review*, one of the many small presses she had been sending her stories to on a regular basis. Lillian unfolded the letter and read it for the fifth, possibly the sixth time.

Dear Ms. Holmes,

We very much enjoyed your short story "Whose Business Is It, Anyway?" and would like to publish it in The Northern Review.

However, there are certain changes that we believe would make the story much stronger overall. I've outlined these changes in the enclosure. Please look them over and let us know if you would be willing to consider them.

In any event, we are delighted that you sent us the story and look forward to working with you.

Very truly yours,
Marshall Vaughn
Editor

She reread his enclosure: such simple changes! And they would in fact make the story stronger—so who in their right mind would object?! She picked up her copy of the story and reread the first line. *Lucy wanted egg salad but Eleanor was saving the hard-boiled eggs . . .* At that point she wanted nothing more than to take up her red pencil and spend the entire morning up in that third-story guest room, producing a clean and much-improved manuscript. But it would have to wait until Monday, when she had the house to herself again.

She slid the letter and the enclosure back into the envelope and tucked it beneath a stack of drafts. She hadn't told Murray about it yet; when he was preoccupied with a speech, anything she said would go in one ear and out the other. She would tell him tonight, after the rally. He probably hadn't ever heard of the magazine, but he would see how excited she was and be happy for her.

By now it was seven thirty, and she went back downstairs to the kitchen and poured herself a second cup of coffee. She heard stirrings upstairs; in a moment Ruth came wandering into the kitchen in her long flannel nightgown, barefoot, hair uncombed. She opened the cereal cupboard.

"We're out of Life," she announced, like Lillian could just snap her fingers and produce an unopened box.

"Pick something else, then," Lillian told her, pouring the last of the orange juice into the fourth of six glasses. Shit.

Ruth made a face, then brightened. "I know! Will you make popovers?"

"Oh, Ruth," said Lillian, as she evened out the orange juice among all six glasses. Lillian was very good at stretching things. "We have such a busy day ahead of us," she protested.

"Please?"

Lillian was going to say no, but really: What was the big deal? She'd made them dozens of times. You stirred together a few eggs, some milk, and some flour in a bowl and greased a bunch of muffin cups. You poured the batter in and put them in the oven and thirty minutes later you pulled out a pan of golden pillows. Everybody loved them—Daniel especially. They might put him in a good mood today.

Plus: learning opportunity for Ruth.

She reached for Fannie Farmer and opened it to the page for popovers, stained from use. Alongside the original list of ingredients ran a list of doubled amounts. There was George to think about, after all.

Do NOT use cold oven method, she'd noted.

Do NOT sift flour!

An idea came to her suddenly. *Make Eleanor more exasperated w/ Lucy*, she wrote in the margin.

"What's that mean?" Ruth asked, peering over her shoulder.

"Nothing," said Lillian. "Get a bowl."

Ruth looked dubious. "I was going to go shower."

"Oh no you don't. You can shower while they're baking," Lillian said. "You should learn how to make these."

"I don't want to learn how to make popovers," grumbled Ruth.

"Oh *please*."

"I hate cooking," said Ruth. "When I grow up I'm going to hire somebody to do all my kitchen work. No offense, Mom, but I don't want to be just a housewife, like you."

Lillian caught her breath. Just a housewife? Were all seventeen-year-old daughters so cruel? She struggled to gather herself together. "If you want the popovers, you make them yourself," she said with a shrug, and Ruth must have realized how awful she'd sounded, because she hung her head and didn't snap back at Lillian. "Start with the eggs." She walked Ruth through the recipe, looking on. "Don't mind the little lumps." Meanwhile she greased two muffin pans with a wad of waxed paper. "Oh, add more—fill them two-thirds full," she said as Ruth began spooning out scant amounts. "You want them big."

After Ruth had placed the pans in the oven, Lillian told her to go shower. "Take the timer with you, though. I need to mop the floor and grind some more flour and iron your father's underwear in the meantime."

Ruth slunk out of the kitchen.

Within the hour, everybody was at the kitchen table, eating warm popovers.

"Thanks, Mom," Daniel grunted, his mouth full.

"Don't thank me, thank Ruth," said Lillian, sitting back and lighting a cigarette.

Daniel grinned. "Little Suzy Housewife."

"Screw you," said Ruth.

"What time is the rally today?" asked Murray.

"Three o'clock," said Lillian. "And I want everyone looking spiffy. Clean pants. No tennies. Ruth, how's your speech? Do you want to run through it one more time?"

Ruth shook her head.

"I'll coach you," Daniel said.

"Like that'll help," said Ruth.

"I try to be nice," Daniel complained. "Look what happens."

Ruth turned to Murray. "Do I go before or after you?"

"Before," he said. "You're my warm-up. Remember to speak into the mike. I really wish you didn't smoke at the table, Lillian."

She stubbed out her cigarette. "Everybody clear their plates," she said. "And put them in the dishwasher."

Daniel looked at George, who was filling the last popover with jam. "Jesus, George," he said. "You could have at least asked if anyone else wanted it."

THEY ENDED UP DRIVING two cars down to the State House, because George at the last moment dribbled Hershey's syrup on his shirt, and Murray was getting anxious. Lillian thought this was a waste of gas, taking two cars, but if getting there early made Murray fret just a little bit less, so be it.

Never had the weather changed so quickly as it did that afternoon. It had been sunny all morning, but as the rally began, clouds could be seen gathering in the north. Lillian looked out at the crowd. The last event! Not as many people had turned out as they'd hoped, but there were still a lot of blue-and-white signs bobbing about. She was aware that the Blaire family still presented an attractive lineup on the platform: Lillian and Murray, flanked by Lizzie and Daniel on one side, Ruth and George on the other—Daniel with his feet planted apart, Lizzie clutching her hairless Barbie, Ruth with her index cards, and George not knowing what to do with his big hands and feet.

It was while Ruth was giving her speech that the temperature began to drop—quickly. When Murray took the mike, a drizzle had begun, and by the time he finished his speech, it was spitting snow. Despite their enthusiasm for their candidate, supporters hurried off to their cars.

Including the Blaire family themselves. Ruth and George wanted to stay in town, and Murray had to meet with the VFW, so Daniel and Lizzie joined Lillian in the van.

"Can I drive?" Daniel asked. He'd turned fifteen and a half a week ago, and had just gotten his learner's permit.

"Not today," Lillian said. Slush was already collecting on the roads, and she climbed into the driver's seat. "Hurry up," she told the children.

"Remember I need to stop at Jennifer's," Daniel said.

"What for?"

"My bio lab."

"Can't it wait until tomorrow? The roads are terrible." That, and Jennifer lived at the top of School Street hill—a steep climb, not one Lillian wished to make when the weather was bad.

"No, it can't wait," Daniel said irritably.

After Ruth made popovers this morning, you still have to be a pill? "Why?"

"Because!" he groaned.

Lillian rolled her eyes. She reminded herself there was more at stake here than a biology lab. And did she want to deal with Daniel being in a bad mood the rest of the night, just because she was afraid to drive up School Street hill? It was just a little slush.

"Okay," she said. "But make it snappy."

And actually, she made it up the hill just fine, pulling up in front of the Whites' house to find its windows lit up, golden in the blue light of a late snowy afternoon. On the lawn were two campaign signs, one for Murray and one for Mondale-Ferraro. The Whites were part of a new wave of Democrats in Concord, former liberal Republicans who had despaired during the Nixon administration and finally changed parties and voted for the peanut farmer in 1976. The Whites themselves had contributed generously to Murray's campaign.

Barbara White, a friend of Lillian's from the thrift shop, greeted Daniel at the door, then frantically waved Lillian in.

Lillian rolled down the window to a blast of cold air. "I can't!" she called out. "I've got a half-frozen kid in the car and I have to get home and fix dinner!"

"Oh, bring her inside. We've got a big fire going!" Barbara cried. "The Carlsons are here!"

"Do you mind?" Lillian asked Lizzie.

"I don't mind," Lizzie said, eager to please.

"Oh bless you, child," Lillian said, giving her daughter a hug. "Just ten minutes," she promised. "No longer than that."

"Where's Murray?" Barbara asked at the door.

"Meeting with the VFW," Lillian explained. "We had our last rally this afternoon. Thank God this campaign is almost over."

"Lillian, my dear," said Chuck White, greeting her with a dry kiss on the cheek. He was the family dentist and had teeth to show for it, straight and white, with no pointy canines. He gave out toothbrushes on Halloween. "You look like you could use a Manhattan."

Lillian and Lizzie stamped their shoes on the entry rug. The Whites' living room was decorated in a more formal style than the Blaires', with tightly upholstered furniture and a glass-topped coffee table, on which sat a basket of crackers and a chafing dish of something greenish-yellow. Lillian took a seat in a wing chair by the fireplace. Behind her, Lizzie twined herself around the chair's bone structure, hiding. At some point Chuck gave Lizzie a glass of ginger ale with a maraschino cherry in it.

"Say thank you," said Lillian.

"Thank you," said Lizzie. She went and climbed into the matching wing chair.

There were pleasantries, talk of kids, and then the discussion turned to the presidential election. Glumly people made note of Mondale's numbers. "I can't believe we're looking at four more years of the Gipper," Chuck said. Joe Carlson said that Murray might be the only good thing to come of the election. "You send him down to Washington and tell him to give 'em hell," he told Lillian.

"Can we go?" Lizzie whispered.

"Soon," said Lillian.

There was talk of the weather. How much snow was forecast. How bad the roads would be. How hair-raising, teaching kids to drive.

"Can we go now?" Lizzie asked.

"Why don't you go find Daniel and Jennifer?" Barbara White suggested.

"Yes, interrupt whatever they're doing," Chuck drawled.

Lizzie trotted off. Chuck winked at Lillian. "Always good to have a little sister around to interrupt things."

It surprised Lillian that Chuck might be so cavalier about whatever his daughter might be doing with Daniel upstairs; she was sure Murray wouldn't be so lighthearted if it were Ruth.

And in fact, when Lizzie returned to report that the door was locked, Chuck didn't look so jocular. He went and stood at the bottom of the stairs. "Jennifer! Unlock that door!"

"I'm so sorry," said Lillian.

"It's not your fault," said Chuck. "Boys will be boys. Problem is,

I know what I was wanting at that age. Jennifer!" he shouted again. "Do I have to come up there myself?"

"I'll go," said Barbara, standing.

"No, I'll go," said Chuck. "Excuse me." He mounted the stairs two at a time, for despite his earlier effort to make light of the situation, his little girl's reputation was at stake here, and Lillian and Murray might have been very good friends and very prompt bill payers, but their son Daniel had the apparatus with which to ruin that reputation.

She heard him knocking, rattling the knob; the sound of footsteps, and then the door opening. Lillian could only hope that Daniel had his pants on, because the thought of him being dragged bare-assed down the stairs made her cringe.

But there was no dragging of young, unclothed teenagers down the stairs in front of the older generation. Lillian smelled something vaguely sweet, faintly pungent. She looked up and saw Chuck making his way down the stairs with Daniel by the scruff of his neck, Daniel's big teenage feet tripping over each other. He wore a startled, goofy expression.

"I don't think this would look very good in the press," Chuck said. "Correct me if I'm wrong."

Lillian didn't like Chuck's implicit threat that this might come out in the paper. She stood up and put her hands on her hips. Part of her wanted to light into Daniel right then and there, and another part wanted to make a quick exit with dignity and then give it to him full blast out in the van.

"What smells funny?" Lizzie asked.

"Ask Daniel," Lillian replied, keeping her gaze fixed on her son, who was avoiding her eyes.

"Where's Jennifer?" Barbara demanded.

"I told her to stay upstairs and worry about the consequences," said Chuck. "Let her sweat it out."

Lillian was furious. Did those two really think that they could get stoned upstairs in the White household with five adults downstairs? "What in God's name were you thinking, Daniel?" she said in a low voice.

"I don't see what the big deal is," said Daniel. He reached for a cracker but Lillian stopped him.

"The big deal is it's illegal," said Chuck. "Tell me. Was it yours, or Jennifer's?"

"I take the Fifth," said Daniel, chortling, and Lillian wanted to smack him.

"Do you realize you could get us all arrested?" Chuck demanded. "That as a homeowner I'm legally responsible for whatever the police might find in my house?"

Lillian wasn't sure that Chuck—who was after all a dentist, not a lawyer—was correct in his analysis. She thought she would run this by Murray. In the meantime, she felt that her idea of a quick exit was advisable.

"Get your coat," she told Lizzie.

"What's wrong with Daniel?" Lizzie asked.

"Ask Daniel," Lillian said again.

"Booga booga," Daniel said to Lizzie, making starbursts with his fingers.

"You have less maturity than your six-year-old sister," Chuck told him.

Lillian stood up from zipping Lizzie's coat. "Excuse me?"

"I don't want your son coming around here anymore," said Chuck.

"Who says it was Daniel's?" Lillian said.

"It certainly wasn't Jennifer's," said Chuck.

"You don't know that," said Lillian. "They're all smoking pot these days." Indeed, she knew for a fact that Joe and Nancy Carlson's twin daughters had been caught under similar circumstances.

"Not my daughter," said Chuck.

"Oh good lord," sighed Lillian. "What a clueless imbecile you are, Chuck. And your office charges are ridiculous, by the way."

"I could sue you," said Chuck.

"Go right ahead," said Lillian. "Sue the shit out of me. You won't get past go. Come on, you two." She hurried the kids out, fuming at Chuck but berating herself for (again) mouthing off. The walkway had iced over by now and frozen slush crunched underfoot. They reached the van without anyone falling and Lillian was thankful for that. "In you go."

Daniel climbed into the front seat, Lizzie in back. The windshield had iced over and Lillian had to stand outside in the cold to scrape it clean, but she was freezing in her light jacket and she skimped, clearing just two ragged ovals.

"Regardless of who had it, your father is not going to be happy about this," she told Daniel, settling herself in her cold seat. "First vodka, now pot—what's next, Daniel? LSD?"

"Is there anything to eat in here?" Daniel asked.

"I have licorice," said Lizzie, and she handed Daniel a Red Vine, covered in lint.

Lillian started the engine and turned on the wipers, which smeared the windshield. "God damn it," she said. "We never should have made this detour. Now I have to drive home in the snow and ice. Did you even get the lab notes?"

"Huh?" said Daniel.

"Oh, you are so screwed, buster," said Lillian. "Sit down, Lizzie."

"Is Jennifer your girlfriend?" Lizzie asked Daniel.

"Daniel's in time-out," Lillian told Lizzie over her shoulder. "Don't talk to him, please. And sit down, I said." She put the van in gear and the tires crunched against the frozen slush. "I don't even have my snow tires on," she said. "And I make an effort to help you with your homework and this is how you thank me? By getting high? Lizzie, how many times do I have to tell you? Sit *down*!"

But Lizzie perhaps thought that since Daniel had misbehaved, she could as well, for she remained behind Daniel's seat, on her knees, whispering in his ear.

"Shut up and go back and sit down," said Daniel. "You heard Mom."

They were approaching the top of School Street hill. Lillian tested her brakes. The car skidded a little, and she downshifted into low gear as they headed down the hill. Another car was on its way up, spinning its wheels.

Suddenly there was a violent scuffle, both kids swatting each other, and Lillian broke into a fury, thinking, *Why can't my children behave in the car? Why can't they do something for* me? and she flung her right arm back to separate the two of them, an act of twisting that brought with it a quarter turn of the steering wheel so that the van slid toward a row of maple trees that lined the street, and in this moment of fury she forgot all the things you're supposed to do when losing control of a car on a slippery hill, which is to say, don't slam on the brakes, don't overcorrect; because that's exactly what she did, panicking over those maple trees on one side and the oncoming car on the other, sending her own vehicle into a wide, slow spin; and the harder she pressed on the brakes, the more weightless she felt as the back of the van swung around to the side.

Like skiing on velvet, she thought.

PART THREE

2016

10.

Gravity

FOR A LONG TIME AFTER THE ACCIDENT, LIZZIE LEANED on Ruth for just about everything. And Ruth obliged. She was there to help Lizzie choose her outfits each morning. To make her school lunch. She supervised Lizzie's homework and forged the requisite permission slips. After graduating from high school, Ruth left for college and couldn't help with these things, but she was only two hours away, so she came home for Lizzie's frilly ballet performances, for her piano recitals, and when Lizzie got her first period, it was Ruth who advised her what to buy—Murray not having thought to stock up on feminine hygiene products.

But it was around that time that Lizzie began to feel the loss of her mother most acutely. At twelve she missed having a mother who yelled at her for wearing too much eye makeup or too short a skirt. She missed having someone to wait outside the bathroom door while she struggled with her first tampon. "Tilt it a little," Lillian could have suggested, saving Lizzie the discomfort of walking around with it half in, half out. She missed having someone to bitch about with her friends. She even missed the cigarette smoke. It's true. She did.

Murray himself didn't know quite what to do with a house full of estrogen. Come to think of it, he'd barely noticed Ruth's adolescence. But Lizzie stomped around like a tyrant some mornings. She burst into tears over a haircut. She screamed at George when he ate the last piece of Sara Lee. She mouthed off to teachers (still). Bewildered, Murray took to fining her; and when that didn't work, he grounded her; and when that didn't work, he forced her to accompany him to the beach house for a weekend of home repairs. He feared the hammer in her hands.

Basically, Lizzie hated her mother for dying, and she wasn't about to make things easy for Murray. Oh, she gave it to him. Shoplifting. Drugs. She learned how to hotwire a car and pick a lock. Murray got an ulcer. It wasn't until her midtwenties that her rage began to cool, after George and Ruth read her the riot act one Christmas and persuaded Murray to cut off funding unless she shaped up. Lizzie felt chagrined. She dug a hole and filled it with all her anger and tamped down the dirt. She enrolled in a PhD program. She met Bruce. She pledged to make things up to Murray, and when the job came through at the state university in northern New Hampshire, near where Murray had just bought a farmhouse for his retirement, she took it, glad that she could be around to help him in the coming years, to cook the dishes her mother had made, to spell him during the sunflower harvest. She felt like the daughter she'd never been and was happy for it, and the only thing she cursed was the passage of time as the years ticked by, one after the other.

ON THAT SATURDAY NIGHT, after Austin and Bob had made their dour appearance, the three Blaire siblings managed to cook dinner with minimal discord (fresh pesto, at Ruth's insistence—*not* from Fannie Farmer), which brightened Murray's day, Lizzie could tell, which in turn both saddened and shamed her, to know that his spirits could be lifted by something so trifling.

"Here's to my children," he said, raising his drink.

"Here's to you, Dad," said Ruth, raising her wineglass in turn. "Best father on earth."

In the middle of dinner Lizzie suddenly remembered the neighbor's cats. She stood up from the table and gathered her purse and keys. "I have to pick up my overnight things, anyway."

"What about dessert?" said Ruth. "I made apple crunch."

"This isn't an excuse to go and see Gavin, is it?" Murray said. "Because I would hate to think . . ."

"How about if I go with you?" said George.

"How about not," said Lizzie, "seeing as you're all making me feel like a nutcase. I'll be back in an hour and we can have dessert then."

Once in the car, she opened all the windows and breathed in the cool autumn air to settle her nerves. But as she drove back to Sugar Hill, her mood began to darken again. Away from the family, away from the happy clatter of dishes, she wondered whom the police were talking to, whether they'd cornered Jessica to get her version of the story. Which would of course favor Gavin. Lizzie had had little interaction with the girl, but during those few instances, Jessica, who went to a private school in Manhattan, had been sullen and snobby, dismissive of the hinterlands, wedded to her iPhone and little pink packets of vitamin C. Lizzie didn't trust her not to make up a big story that portrayed Lizzie as an out-of-control lunatic, hell-bent on destroying person and property.

You can't control what she says, Lizzie reminded herself. *So there's no point in worrying.*

The cats were yowling when she unlocked the door to her neighbor's house. Quickly she spooned some food into their dishes, checked their water, and made sure they were using the litter box. Then she drove to her own house, where she collected her sleep clothes and toiletries. She had papers to read by Monday and—

Jesus Christ, she thought. *What if I'm in jail?*

Lizzie had never really been in trouble with the law and she didn't know much about police procedure except from television shows, and she pictured herself sitting in a cold cement cell wearing an orange jumpsuit. Would they let her out on bail? And what would she tell her students if they didn't?

Overcome with dread, she stuffed the papers into a tote bag and turned out the lights. In the car she reminded herself again that it was pointless to worry. Who knew what was going to happen? Gavin could be as unpredictable as she. She wondered what he was doing tonight, a thought that made her hesitate at the end of the driveway. What if she stopped at his house? Showed some concern for his injury? It wouldn't be much of an olive branch, but it might be enough to get him off her case.

No, she told herself firmly. *Stay away. You're still too emotional. Turn right and get on the interstate. Do not turn left. Do not under any circumstances turn left. Do not turn left even if your life depends upon it.*

She cranked the wheel and turned left.

Two miles down the road, Gavin's house was tucked back behind some large spruce trees. Instead of pulling into the driveway and announcing her presence, Lizzie found a place to park along the side of the road so she could plan what to say to him. She cut the engine and turned off her headlights. The entire downstairs was lit up, and she could see Jessica moving about in the kitchen. She imagined the girl microwaving some frozen dinners, serving Gavin his red wine in the bowl-shaped glass that he favored so that he could swirl the wine and appreciate its bouquet, something Lizzie never bothered to do and which used to drive Gavin mad. She imagined Jessica sliding a cushion underneath his bandaged hand, bringing him his pain meds, a glass of water.

Just then her phone dinged.

Where are you? Ruth wrote.

On my way, she wrote back.

Hurry up.

Fine but why the rush?

Dessert. Plus I want to talk about
some things while everyone's here.

Because I might be in jail tomorrow?

Stop. Dad's tired. He wants to go to
bed right after the game.

Then stop texting me so I can drive.

Ruth didn't answer back. Lizzie stared at her phone. She found herself growing angry again, and imagined what she would say in a text to Gavin.

Quit making stuff up to the police. I never assaulted you. And I'm not sorry about your hand. You brought it on yourself.

That's what Gavin needed, more people saying things like that to him.

His wife certainly did. Such a strange marriage they had! No love lost, but no divorce after all these years, either. Lizzie had met her once, during the summer, when Joanna had driven up from New York to retrieve a cane-seated chair that Gavin had been storing out in the barn. Gavin made no effort to get Lizzie out of the house before Joanna arrived, so Lizzie had to endure the woman's bemused gaze when she stepped out of her Prius to find Lizzie leaving after their Thursday afternoon tryst.

"And which one are you?" Joanna asked. She wore her dark hair pulled tightly back from her face, severely so, like an aged ballerina. Heavy earrings weighed down her wattly earlobes.

"I'm Lizzie." Lizzie the Slut.

"Well, Lizzie, aren't you the lucky one. Tell me: Does Gavin still say I try to rob him blind? Because it's not true. He's a cheap son of a bitch, isn't he? Throwing around money where it shows and then skimping on the basics. So he opens very nice bottles of wine and then when it's Jessica's tuition time, suddenly he doesn't seem to have any royalties coming in. So you enjoy that wine, *chica*!" she said, punching air with vigor. "Oh, hello, Gavin."

Lizzie looked over her shoulder to see Gavin standing in the doorway, daintily holding an espresso cup, even though it was late afternoon.

"Joanna my love," he said. "You met my friend Elizabeth?"

"Your fuckbuddy?"

Gavin made his way down the wide, unpolished slate steps. Lizzie liked to sit on those steps on sunny days, liked to feel the warm, flat stone against her bare thighs. She didn't want to sit there now.

"Where's your dude?" Gavin asked.

"My *dude*, whose name is Colin, has other things to do today than drive up into the sticks to pick up a chair that you were supposed to bring down to me last Thanksgiving. I don't know why you didn't choose Vermont when you decided to move up to New England," she said. "There are Trump signs all over the place in this state. At least Vermont has Bernie."

"Live free or die," said Gavin. "Don't insult Elizabeth; she's a native."

"Look, I should go," said Lizzie.

"Oh, don't go!" Joanna exclaimed. "Then Gavin and I will just have to talk about my upcoming hysterectomy. Not that I care about losing my uterus, but for some reason the insurance company refuses to say I need surgery and so Gavin, dear, I'm going to need you to cough up some extra money next month and don't tell me you don't have it because I saw on our credit card statement a hefty deposit with a tour guide in Peru and a man who has money to take a ten-thousand-dollar trip to Machu Picchu certainly has the money to help his wife take care of her health, isn't that right, Lizzie?"

"So sorry to hear that you need a hysterectomy, dear," said Gavin. "Though you've been saying you needed one ever since Jessica was born, and why you need to have it now is something I can only view with suspicion, since it coincides nicely with the kitchen remodel you're doing—in the apartment for which I still pay the co-op fees."

"Aren't you glad you're not married to this man?" Joanna said to Lizzie.

"I have a lot of papers to grade," Lizzie said. She was teaching summer school. "So if you'll excuse me."

"Oh, go, little one, Gavin and I can survive half an hour on our own, I guess." Joanna gave a sigh. "Just promise me you won't believe him when he tells you stories about me, because he's a pathological liar."

What a toxic conversation it had been! Now, sitting in her car outside Gavin's house, Lizzie tried to neutralize the poisonous memory—and the anger that was still simmering. She reminded herself of Gavin's better side—obviously he had one; she wouldn't have stooped that low. She ticked off a short list: The time he took, the attention he paid to her in bed. The little surprises: a book here, a bottle of champagne there; a piece of art for her house, some laugh-inducing weed that had them watching *South Park* one afternoon. Contrary to what Joanna said, he was very generous with her.

They'd even ventured into the personal, of late. One day after sex, Gavin lay on his back amid the tangle of sheets, legs splayed, belly slack; she lay on her side and played with the coarse hair on his chest. Outside, crickets twined in the heat; clouds hung heavily, threatening a thunderstorm. Suddenly out of the blue Gavin started telling her about how he'd stuttered as a child. Some teacher had made him use his right hand. (Gavin was left-handed.) He recounted the children at school making fun of him. "I swore at them," he said. "'G-g-g-g-go to hell!' I shouted—the worst possible curse I could come up with at age eight." He chuckled at himself.

"How did you stop?" She found it difficult to match the stuttering child with the giant, confident man surrounded by adoring women at his readings.

"Went back to using my left hand," he said. "Simple as that. Your turn," he said, patting her hip. "Memory lane."

This was unusual for them; rarely did they dig into one another's pasts. But she cautiously began to share some of her own memories, and once she did, she found that she couldn't stop. Her mother, typing fast and furiously. The rope across the stairs, barring access to the third-floor guest room while her mother worked. Her father practicing a closing statement in the backyard. The Blaire-Mobile. Bean suppers. Daniel.

The accident.

"That's a lot of shit to carry around" was all he said when she finished telling him about the scuffle in the car.

Yet the very nature of Gavin's better side was what got them into trouble eventually. Gavin had a motorcycle, and one hot, languid afternoon, instead of spending their time in bed, they rode to a little-known trailhead and hiked the old, overgrown path up to Gravity Falls, where icy-cold water spilled over slabs of granite worn smooth by time and elements. People had stacked loose rocks into artistic cairns, which gave the falls a mystical feel, a place where you could fall asleep and wake twenty years later to the rolling thunder of tenpins.

There were no people around that day, and Lizzie and Gavin shared a picnic of wine and smoked fish. Blue jays cawed, and the sun filtered down through fat summer leaves. Gavin lay back on the warm rock and closed his eyes and let his fingers trace a line up her bare leg. She felt herself stir and, on a whim, she sat up and removed her top and unhooked her bra and lay down, simultaneously feeling the heat of the rock under her back and the cool damp river air on her chest. She closed her eyes. Gavin's fingers reached the hem of her shorts, and she moved her legs, and the next thing she knew, her shorts were off and he was inside her, moving, and when she cried out, her voice sent birds flapping their wings, flying up into the haze above.

Back at his house he gently washed the abrasions on her back. Usually they didn't take risks like this, but she counted the days in her head and figured it was probably safe, what they had done. Safe enough that she didn't remark upon it to Gavin, nor he to her, and they simply let that afternoon at Gravity Falls stand as a reminder of the heat that existed between them, independent of anything they might want to call love; and she wondered if it was safe to feel this way with someone, knowing there were limitations, and told herself that as two consenting adults they had nobody to answer to but themselves.

Lizzie was remembering that afternoon, and cursing Gravity Falls, when suddenly Gavin's house exploded with chemical blue light. Lizzie jolted up. His floodlights. He'd had them installed after a break-in the previous year. Had they heard something?

As if answering her question, the front door opened and Jessica's ghostly figure appeared.

Had she gotten spooked? Lizzie's heart began to pound. Big mistake to come here. Big mistake to think she could talk to Gavin. But if she started her engine now, Jessica would hear it and then you could add Peeping Tom charges to the list of grievances Gavin would file against her. She wished she had her old VW bug because she could have simply put the car in neutral and rolled the car and then popped the clutch when she was out of earshot; but this car, an old Saab, had an automatic transmission and nothing worked unless the engine was running. In horror she watched as Jessica stepped off the porch and headed toward her, a flashlight beaming right and left and then straight ahead, skittering across the hood and then flashing right through the windshield into Lizzie's eyes.

Without waiting she peeled off. Down the dirt road, down from Sugar Hill into the town of Franconia, where at the one blinking light in town she caught her breath. Nobody was following her, thank God. She calculated that Jessica had had maybe a three-second glimpse of the car, which didn't give her a whole lot of time to be able to describe it to anyone—and in fact since it was black, maybe she hadn't even seen it at all.

But if she had seen it, she would tell her father; and who else had a black car who would be sitting outside his house right now?

Her phone dinged.

Dad just forgot Gavin's name. You see?

BY THE TIME she got back to her father's, everyone had moved into the living room, where Murray had turned on the Sox game. George was sitting on the sofa, scrolling through photos. In the kitchen Ruth's dessert sat on top of the stove, rich and crumbly-looking. Quickly Ruth got out bowls and spoons and began dishing it out, adding a scoop of ice cream to each serving.

"Double for me," called George. "I love that stuff."

"Me, too," said Lizzie. "Thanks, Ruth."

Proudly Ruth brought the bowls into the living room. George looked at his. Lizzie looked at hers. Murray began eating his without a glance.

"What's the matter?" Ruth asked George.

"What is this?"

"It's apple crunch, George, are you blind?"

"It looks different. Where's the cornflakey part?"

"I didn't use cornflakes. I used oatmeal."

"Oatmeal!" George exclaimed, peering in his bowl, as though it contained ants.

"It's healthier," said Ruth.

"Oh," said George. "Got it." He took a bite. Lizzie, too.

George got a far-off look in his eyes as he chewed. Lizzie took another bite. It tasted good. Well, pretty good. Well, not as good as their mother's. She thought Ruth may have skimped on the sugar, too.

"What, you don't like it?" Ruth finally said.

"I didn't say that," said George. "It's just that I was expecting what Mom used to make, and she made it with cornflakes. So this is different."

"Oh my God," said Ruth.

"It's great, Ruth," said Lizzie. "It really is." *Say it's great, George,* she prayed. *Please say it's great.*

"You want cornflakes, George?" Ruth said. "I can get you corn-flakes. Wait." She got up and went to the kitchen and came back with a box of Kellogg's. "How much?" She poised the open box over George's bowl.

"Chill," said George. "I merely said it was different. But it's great. Look at me. I'm eating it. I'm loving it."

"Just not as much as Mom's," said Ruth.

"Stop it, you two," said Lizzie, and she went and got a beer, because she really, really wanted it, and didn't care that it wouldn't go so well with apple crunch and ice cream. Now it was Ruth's turn to look surprised, or maybe she just wanted to lash out at someone in revenge; Lizzie wouldn't say that Ruth exactly raised her eyebrows, but she did glance at the bottle, and that was enough for Lizzie. Although she'd been trying to keep the peace, this was too much. Her sister was wearing her down.

"Say it, Ruth."

"Say what?"

"I drink too much."

"I don't necessarily think you drink too much," Ruth allowed. "I'm just surprised that you're drinking after dinner. And beer with dessert?"

"Drinking before dinner's okay, but drinking after dinner makes me an alcoholic?"

"Well, you had a beer this morning. I just think you should maybe keep track and see how it all adds up at the end of the day," said Ruth. "Speaking of which."

"Oh dear God," said George, his face stricken. "What now?"

Ruth set her bowl on the coffee table. "Since we're all here, I suggest it's a good time to talk about Dad's future. Dad? Can you listen? We really need to know what our options are, and then maybe we can come up with a plan."

An uncomfortable silence hung in the air, though Murray seemed oblivious to it; he sat in his chair picking apple skins out of his teeth.

Lillian had always peeled her apples.

"I'm not saying we have to act on any options right now," Ruth went on. "I just think we ought to know what's on the table."

"This is so premature," said Lizzie.

"Hear me out," said Ruth. "Morgan didn't talk to his parents at all about these issues and then Janey died and there was no one to watch out for Herb, and he stopped cooking and was living on cold cereal, and when Morgan's brother suggested he go into a facility, he acted like it was the most absurd thing in the world. They fought for months. Herb lost twenty pounds."

"And didn't he die two months after moving in?" George asked. "Died of grief, I'll bet. That must have been a hefty deposit he lost."

Ruth ignored him. "With Dad, I'm not trying to just yank him out of his house and home. But as he gets older, he may need a little more help and we need to think of how things might end up eventually."

"I'm right here," said Murray, not taking his eyes off the screen. "Haven't gone anywhere."

Ruth looked guilty, which made Lizzie feel smug, which in turn shamed her.

"But Dad, you don't even have a housecleaner," said Ruth.

"Does my house look dirty?"

"Your house looks fine, but at some point you're not going to want to push a vacuum around. You've got the money. Hire someone. And I don't think you should be climbing ladders, either," she went on, gaining confidence. "You could fall and break your hip. I'm serious," she said when Murray rolled his eyes. "Do you know what happens when someone breaks a hip? They're in the hospital for, like, six weeks. They lose muscle mass and it's the beginning of the end. Ask George. Isn't that right, George?"

"Jesus, Ruth," said Lizzie, for she thought her sister was being a little heavy-handed. "Laying it on a little thick, don't you think?"

"It's all in the planning," Ruth returned. "If you plan for it, it won't happen. If you don't plan for it, it will."

"Ruth's law." George chuckled.

"Just because *you* live five hundred miles away doesn't mean *we* do," said Lizzie. "I'm here at least once a week, and George is, too——"

"Not when he's off in Arizona," said Ruth.

"Whoa," said George. "Who goes to Vail every year? Who went to Europe for two weeks last summer?"

"I told you all, I could be on the next flight home if something happened, and I was never without my phone."

"Me, too," said George.

"I for one never get a fly-away vacation," Lizzie pointed out. "I for one don't have the money to leave the state and now I for one might not even have the legal *right* to leave the state."

"Oh my God, we are *so* getting sidetracked!" Ruth cried. "The issue here is Dad. Yes, you, Dad. What if you fall in the shower? You don't even have a grab bar installed!"

Lizzie felt ashamed that she hadn't thought of this.

"I can install one," said George.

"No, *I* can install one!" Murray exclaimed, swiveling his chair around to face them. "Look, I appreciate the concern, but whose business is it, anyway, where I go? It's my business. And I plan on staying here another ten years at least. Don't you kids put me in a home, period. Understood? I don't want to eat with strangers and I don't want to make birdhouses and I don't want to take an exercise class with a bunch of old people! Even when I'm old," he added. "You kids seem to forget sometimes what I've lost in life. I've lost my wife. I've lost my son. I don't want to lose any of you, and I don't want to lose my house. It may seem insignificant to you in the grand scheme of things, but it's significant to me. Okay?"

"Okay," said Ruth eagerly. "Okay. I'm glad you articulated that. What about having help in the house? Someone to cook for you? I worry you might start skipping meals. Wouldn't you like someone to come in and fix dinner a few times a week?"

"I like to cook," Murray said. "I consider it an adventure."

"No one likes to cook every day," said Ruth. "I'm not talking about full-time help, just someone a few days a week."

"When I need it, I'll think about it," said Murray. "You're raising my blood pressure, Ruth. We've got enough on our plates this weekend, with Lizzie's problem, without you bringing this matter up. It's making me grouchy."

"It's not like I'm asking people about their burial preferences," Ruth grumbled.

Without looking up from his laptop, George said, "Actually, I want to be cremated. And I want my ashes to be scattered on Heartbreak Hill in Boston. For the record."

"Oh *Christ*," said Murray, back to watching the ball game.

"Lizzie?" said Ruth. "While we're on the subject?"

"This is too depressing," said Lizzie. "I refuse to talk about it. Dad's made things clear. No nursing home. Now can we talk about something else?"

"Well, we can always talk about a possible assault charge, if you want," said Ruth.

George groaned. "Is that all you can talk about, Ruth? Depressing things? Don't you ever like to sit around telling jokes? Or funny stories? Is the world really just one big danger zone for you?"

Ruth touched her chin, as though George had just told her she had a pimple. She looked hurt. "I laugh on the inside," she said. "Maybe you think I don't see the humor in things, but I do. I just don't get all *haw haw* about it."

"Then work a little harder, Ruth," said George. "I hate to see you go through life misleading people."

Now Ruth looked like she was about to cry. Murray must have sensed this with the silence, because he looked up from the TV screen.

"Don't everyone dump on Ruth, please," he said, and Lizzie

realized that despite his apparent absorption in the ball game, he had heard every word they were saying. Another point for his side of the scoreboard. "She's just trying to be a grown-up about all of this. Ruth, I'm sorry if the rest of us are acting like children. You're doing a good thing, discussing these contingencies. But now that we've discussed them, maybe we can put them all behind us and focus on the problem at hand."

That being me, Lizzie thought glumly.

"It's just that Morgan felt so lost, with his father." Ruth sniffled. "He had no clue how to get beyond all the denial."

"So we cross that bridge when we get to it," Murray said. "We're not there yet. I'm not going into a nursing home. And I don't want help. I've got Boyd. That's enough for right now."

"YEAH BIG PAPI!" George shouted at the television.

Murray whipped around so fast that he almost tipped over his armchair. "God damn I'll miss that guy," he said.

AT TEN O'CLOCK, Murray bade them good night and told them not to stay up too late. "French toast tomorrow morning," he said. "And with that, good night."

The children stayed in the kitchen, where Ruth made tea, George ate more apple crunch, straight out of the serving dish, and Lizzie opened another beer, ignoring any look Ruth might give her.

But she did want Ruth's take on her situation. "This assault thing," she said. "I really didn't try and pour hot water on him. Believe me. But are the police still going to come and arrest me?"

"Gavin has a witness," Ruth reminded her. "That tips the balance."

"And what happens once I get arrested?"

Ruth laid out the process for her: jail, a bond hearing, bail. Then a preliminary hearing. "It would never go to trial, though," she said. "You'd plead out. I don't know Gavin that well, but what if you just offered to pay for his laptop? Would he forget about pressing charges?"

Lizzie exchanged a glance with George.

"Gavin can be pretty stubborn," she said. "He doesn't like it when things don't go his way."

"Then I'd say he's probably likely to dig his heels in and file a complaint against you."

"And it's his word against mine?"

"Like I've said, his and his daughter's word," Ruth reminded her.

George burped loudly. "His daughter doesn't strike me as the most believable witness, frankly."

Lizzie frowned. "How do you know?"

"I met her," said George.

"When?" said Ruth, frowning as well, and Lizzie could tell her sister hated not having command of the facts. Well, so did she, in this case.

"I went to see Gavin after lunch," said George. "He was still in the ER with his hand all bandaged up. And his daughter was there. She's pretty flaky."

"Well, it doesn't matter, for purposes of an arrest," said Ruth. "All she has to do is give a credible statement."

"How was he?" Lizzie asked George.

"Doped up and pissed. Hooked up to an IV because his blood sugar's out of whack. Stop jiggling your foot, Ruth, I can feel it over here."

"Did you tell him Lizzie will pay for a new laptop?"

"Was I supposed to?"

"No," said Ruth, "although it might have helped matters. I'm not meaning to be critical," she added hastily.

"Also not meaning to be critical, but I wish you'd checked with me," Lizzie told George. She didn't like the idea of him talking one-on-one with Gavin.

"It was more spur-of-the-moment than anything," said George. "Don't get pissed."

The three children fell silent. Ruth's foot was going a mile a minute.

"I'm so wired," she said.

"Want to smoke a number?" George asked.

"No, I do not want to 'smoke a number.'"

Laugh lines deepened around George's eyes. "When's the last time you got high, Ruth?"

"I don't know—twenty years ago? I got tired of feeling paranoid."

"Weed is so different these days," said George. "You really ought to try it."

"I'm game," said Lizzie.

"Come on outside, then," said George.

Grabbing her jacket, she followed George out to the driveway. It was a beautiful evening—chilly but not cold enough for a frost, with a sliver of moon. The leaves in the trees rustled and the ground seemed to give off the heat it had been storing up all afternoon. A small animal rooted about in the nearby brush, and the air smelled of woodsmoke; someone was having a fire nearby. Then, suddenly, the flicker of flame and the smell of pot.

She took a hit and held it in her lungs. She and George stood there quietly together. They'd always been able to just *be* together, without talking. After the accident she used to go and sleep in his bed with him, and sometimes they would lie in the darkness, not saying a word. Other times he would tell her stories, made-up tales about boys lost at sea, boys without parents, boys alone in the wilderness. "Put girls in your stories," Lizzie used to say. "And no more orphans."

She let the air out of her lungs; feeling dizzy, she bent over and put her head between her knees, and then on a whim she decided to lie down right there on the hard dirt of the driveway. George joined her, settling his head next to hers but angling his body away, two spokes on a wheel. Lizzie looked up into the sky, and caught the tail of a shooting star.

It didn't help matters that Lizzie's birthday had arrived two days after the procedure. Talk about feeling old: She felt as old as the world. She'd lain in bed that morning, still cramping, and cursed Gavin. But the anger felt stuck in her throat, like dry potato. Nothing could make things better. What was gone was gone.

"Don't fall asleep," George said.

"I'm not," she said. "Did you see that shooting star?"

"I did. Too bad Ruth isn't out here."

"It is."

Silence.

"Do you think Ruth is happy?" George asked.

Lizzie had to think about this for a moment. "I think Ruth has a vast untapped side to her that nobody knows about."

"That's pretty heavy."

"Must be the weed."

"But I think you're right," George said. "I don't think things are so hot with Morgan."

"Why?"

"Stuff she said in the car yesterday. She kept calling Morgan, and then when she hung up, she'd have something snide to say about him. 'Morgan might as well be semiretired these days.' 'If Morgan remembers the boys' soccer games, it'll be a minor miracle.' I would so like to see her ditch him."

"Ditch her job."

"Ditch the whole shebang."

"Maybe not all at once, though," said Lizzie.

"By the way, what's this about Nepal? You're not going to quit your job, are you?"

"No," Lizzie sighed. "I think I'd just had a bad class. Summer school. Note to self: don't think out loud to Dad."

"Especially when it involves going off to live on the other side of the globe. He's pretty fragile, when it comes to us kids."

"Once there were four, and then there were three," Lizzie murmured. "Story of his life."

The kitchen light went out, and a million more stars appeared.

"Have you ever been in jail?" she asked.

"No."

"So I'd be the first of us kids."

"Unless Ruth hasn't told us something."

They both chuckled at the thought of Ruth in jail.

"Daniel would have beat you to it, though, I bet," said George. "Man, he was just headed for trouble. Do you remember the vodka incident?"

Lizzie said, "I remember him puking on me. I don't remember much more, though. But I was only six."

Go sit down, you little brat!

"Do you remember his impersonations?" said George. "He could do Ronald Reagan. Johnny Carson. He was a real hoot." The two fell silent, gazing up, contemplating the enormity of the stars in the context of a brother lost.

"And then there were his science projects. Remember them? Taking up the whole downstairs with his catapult thingy? Breaking the window when it worked too well? I so wanted to be like him," George sighed. "I wanted to be funny. I wanted to make people laugh. But I couldn't tell a joke for the life of me. Mom *loved* Daniel," he added.

"She loved all of us," Lizzie protested. "Wasn't that the party line?"

"Yeah, but she really loved Daniel. I know that's not how it's supposed to be, but I could tell. It didn't bother me, though. I always just wanted her to be happy, and Daniel made her happy."

"I'm envious of your memories," said Lizzie. "I wish I'd had more time with both of them."

"What do you remember about Mom?"

"I remember her reading poetry to me from a big book," Lizzie said. "'Oh the Raggedy Man, he worked for Pa . . .' Remember that one? We'd read while you guys were at school. But then inevitably she'd say she needed her special alone time, that's what she called it, and she'd hook a rope across the bottom of the stairway up to the third floor. 'You stay down here,' she'd tell me. 'Don't touch that rope,' she'd say. I was always afraid it would electrocute me."

"Sad," said George.

"Then one day I touched it and nothing happened. So I went upstairs. I could hear the typewriter clattering away. I peeked into the room. There were crumpled papers all over the floor, and Mom was at her table, and she had a cigarette between her lips and this deep ugly line between her eyebrows as she typed. Then I must have made a noise because she jumped in her chair. 'Don't scare me like that!' she cried. 'Go back downstairs!'"

Lizzie, I said sit down now!

"Do you ever feel sorry for her?" Lizzie asked.

"For Mom? No! Why?"

"She saw herself as a writer. All that work, and nothing to show for it."

"But she was our mother," said George. "She had us to show for who she was."

"That wasn't enough," said Lizzie, who knew firsthand how much the publication of anything—short story, poem, or academic paper— could mean, at a point in time when you didn't think that anyone gave a hoot about the words you set down on paper. "She wrote and wrote and wrote, and never got any credit for it."

"I wish Dad could remember what he did with her stories," said George.

Lizzie gave a hmmph. "He can tell you where every cancelled check is in the basement, but not the stories."

"How about Daniel's box? I haven't seen that lately, come to think of it."

"Oh, it's somewhere down there, I'm sure," said Lizzie. "He moves things around sometimes."

Murray himself had never been able to face cleaning out Daniel's room. It fell to Ruth and George finally, a year after the accident, to box things up and bring them to Goodwill. Before they got rid of everything, though, the three children all chose a few objects to keep. A flannel shirt. A report he'd done in third grade, featuring his annual Little League portraits. His hockey skates and his baseball jersey. His harmonica. These they put in a banker's box, marked it with his initials, and put the box in a back corner of the attic. It wasn't until Murray moved from Concord up to the north country that he discovered the box himself; Lizzie had been with him, helping him clean things out, and she watched as he squatted and quietly placed his hands on the cover and simply held them there for a good minute or so, staring at Daniel's initials. Then he stood up and walked away and left it for Lizzie to carry down to the truck.

George handed her the joint, but she waved it away. The pot was overwhelming her now, and she wished she hadn't smoked so much. She thought again of Lillian. Thirty-two years of living without a mother had made it seem the norm, for the most part—until moments like tonight, when someone like George cut a hole in the fabric of her life and all these memories came spilling out. She remembered her mother at a party, wearing a shimmery dress, hoisting Lizzie up to the smiling faces of the partygoers. She remembered her standing at the counter in one of her A-line skirts, beating eggs, her hips wiggling back and forth with the motion. Blowing smoke rings for Lizzie to poke with her finger. In all of these memories her face was young and pretty; what would she look like now?

"Do you think Dad needs to move?" she asked.

"No way! But I think he could use some more help."

Lizzie agreed. "Did he really forget Gavin's name?"

"Did Ruth say that?"

"Yeah."

"Just for a moment. He called him Calvin."

"Calvin!"

"Close enough. Then he remembered."

"Then I don't think it's something to worry about. Everybody forgets names."

"Even Gavin himself," George said. "He calls me Greg."

"You know what they say," said Lizzie. "Forget a name, that's normal. Forget who they are—well, in you go."

11.

Ar Bishen Fulla Marg

AS THINGS TURNED OUT, LIZZIE'S AND GEORGE'S ALTERED state of mind was nothing compared to what Murray was about to face, for upon waking the next morning, he found himself confused and disoriented, as though emerging from a complicated dream. He couldn't remember dreaming anything, though. He lay in bed and gazed out the window. Where did that maple tree come from? What month was it? What day of the week? Where were his children? Where was Lillian?

Just some momentary confusion, he told himself. *Lillian's gone, of course.* But when he sat up in bed, he realized there were two maples. There were also two windows, two bureaus, two nightstands. He swung his feet over the side of the bed and felt for his slippers and shuffled into the bathroom, steadying himself by holding onto the wall.

It wasn't until he switched on the light and looked into the mirror that he knew something was in fact very wrong. There were two faces, for one thing. The right side drooped like a Dalí painting, and his right eye sagged with excess folds of ash-colored skin. He tried to smile and saw that his smile was lopsided and stupid-looking and his tongue felt like a slab of meat.

He recalled that his daughter Ruth was visiting.

"Moth?" he called.

"Whom!" he shouted, and he banged his fist on the wall.

In a moment Ruth came hurrying into the bathroom, hastily wrapping herself in a shabby rose-colored bathrobe. Lizzie followed, in a long T-shirt.

"Oh, what's wrong?!" Ruth cried. "Lizzie, get George!"

Murray slapped his cheeks, thinking he could wake up dead flesh. George came in and took one look at Murray and told his sisters to call 911.

"Dad," he said calmly. "Do you know what day it is?"

"Ar bishen fulla marg!" Murray exclaimed.

The first thing George did was to make Murray sit down on the little stool he kept by the tub. Then he gave him an aspirin. Murray had trouble swallowing the pill, since only one side of his mouth worked, but after much dribbling he got it down.

"Now, where's your blood pressure monitor?" George asked. Murray pointed to the linen closet. His doctor had told him he should check it daily, but he'd not followed those orders; in fact, he had never learned how to use the damn gadget. George found it and wrapped the small cuff around his wrist and watched the numbers blink. When the device beeped, George took note of the numbers but didn't relay them and Murray was glad because he suspected they were off the charts.

"You having any pain, Dad?" his son asked.

Murray shook his head. He had never seen George on the job. Occasionally Murray would have an appointment at the hospital complex down in Concord and he would meet George for a cup of coffee in the cafeteria, so he'd seen George in his scrubs with his hair neatly banded back in a stubby ponytail. But he'd never been on the receiving end of his son's authority and he was impressed now with how calm and reasonable he sounded.

Meanwhile the paramedics arrived: five men stomping up the stairs like the fire brigade they were, laden down in boots and canvas vests and carrying heavy-duty plastic cases, and they simultaneously asked him a lot of questions and took his blood pressure and hooked him up to an IV. All he could do was nod or shake his head, and as they carried him down the stairs on the gurney, Murray wondered if this was the end of life as he knew it; if this was the Event that would put him in a nursing home, or in need of all that care Ruth had been suggesting he might need at some point down the line—because maybe it wasn't down the line anymore, maybe it was right here and now, and he had the awful feeling that between last night and this morning, he had lost both his autonomy and his authority as patriarch of the family. From now on, he thought with a sinking heart, his children would be his boss.

Soon he was being wheeled outside, down the porch steps, and into the back of the ambulance. From there, he looked out at a box of daylight. There were his three children, huddling together: George in a pair of sweats, Lizzie who'd put on some jeans, and Ruth in that shabby rose bathrobe. It had belonged to Lillian, a Christmas gift from her parents, Murray recalled (at least he had some memory!), and he could picture his wife sitting in the wine-colored armchair in the sunny living room in Concord, opening a large box from Jordan Marsh, a cigarette dangling from her lips. That same Christmas they had outfitted the children with new ski equipment, and when the holidays were over, Murray and Lillian started looking for a vacation home up in the White Mountains, figuring it would be a good place to spend weekends and school vacations; the fresh air and exercise would perhaps keep their adolescent children out of trouble.

You want to make God laugh? Tell him your plans.

Who said that?

Now George leaned into the square of white light. "We'll follow you. You're going to be fine, Dad."

Of course I am, Murray thought, with no small amount of irritation, because he knew this was what you routinely told someone in a medical crisis, that they would be all right, when really what you were thinking was that they would not. He wanted to tell George—all three of them, in fact—not to worry, but he was afraid of the gobbledygook that might come out of his mouth, so he just gave a thumbs-up.

"Are you warm enough, Mr. Blaire?" a paramedic asked.

Murray nodded. He was comfortable. But as soon as the ambulance started down the long driveway, he began to feel woozy and nauseous, so he closed his eyes. He saw the house in Concord in springtime, with the leaves budding and the rhododendron in bloom. They were a distressing shade of purply pink and he'd always wanted to clip them off, but soon they withered and the garden was taken over by the red and yellow tulips—Lillian's lollipop garden, he liked to call it, and indeed, for Lizzie's third or fourth birthday, he couldn't remember which, Lillian went out and planted giant spiral lollipops for the gaggle of girls that came to celebrate in their frilly dresses and black patent leather shoes. He saw his children running through the backyard sprinkler, whooping with delight, on a Saturday afternoon as he sat on the back porch going over trial transcripts. Then it was Christmas in his mind again, with ropes of greenery festooning the banister, a tall balsam tree filling the house with its tingly aroma.

With his good hand he rubbed his chin, wishing he'd had a chance to shave. He was going to look like an old man to anyone who saw him today and he wasn't an old man. Old was drool. Old was cloudy eyeballs. Old was taking out a trash bag of used Depends so the house wouldn't smell. He felt the ambulance slow down, felt it make a big turn, and soon it rocked to a stop, the doors swung open and he was rolled out and the cold air licked his neck and his nose began to run and it became paramount, above all else, that someone bring him a tissue before the little drop of moisture at the tip of his nose crystallized, and froze his veins, and turned him into a slab of blue ice on a white sheet while all around him people called out strings of numbers that never added up.

LYING IN THE MRI TUNNEL, surrounded by jackhammers, he tried to calm himself. He remembered Lillian whispering something vaguely suggestive right before a speech.

He remembered a slip-and-fall case involving Kmart, a jar of tomato sauce, and a 268-pound woman in a pink warm-up suit.

He remembered Ruth calling to tell him she'd gotten into Yale Law School.

George winning an art contest in seventh grade.

Daniel juggling.

He remembered the kitchen in Concord, the refrigerator crowded with snapshots and drawings and permission slips, and wishing for one, just *one* uncluttered place in his house, his castle.

"IT WON'T BE LONG," the technician assured him.

"ANY MINUTE NOW," a nurse said.

AND THEN, STRANGELY, after he'd been wheeled back to the ER, he began to feel different. It was akin to Novocain wearing off: as he lay on the hospital bed, he found himself massaging his dead cheek again—but to his surprise, it wasn't so dead anymore. In fact, when he made a monkey face, he felt all the muscles tighten responsively. He opened his mouth wide. He raised his eyebrows up and down.

"Ruth," he murmured, tentatively. "George. Lizzie. Daniel. Blah blah blah. Blippity blippity blippity. Little Jack Horner. There was an old woman." By God! How could this happen, so magically? He was in the midst of reciting the whole nursery rhyme when the doctor came in, a petite, dark-skinned woman of Indian heritage with a tight bun at the nape of her neck. She couldn't have been more than fifteen, Murray thought.

"I see you're recovering your faculties," she said in her lilting accent. "How about the Gettysburg Address?"

"'Four score and seven years ago,'" said Murray. "You haven't seen three kids, or rather kid-like adults, wandering around, have you?"

She smiled as she checked the monitors and typed some notes into her laptop. Then she examined him, listening to his heart and to a point on the side of his neck. She loomed up close to his face and shined a bright light into his eyes. She tested his knee reflexes and made him struggle against her, hand to hand. She scratched the bottom of his foot.

"What you've had is a mini-stroke, also called a TIA," she finally told him. Murray had heard the term before, but he'd never paid it much attention. The doctor went on to explain that this TIA might or might not be a precursor to a full-blown stroke, and so she wanted to start Murray on an anticlotting medication and keep him in the hospital for twenty-four hours, for observation and possibly further tests.

Murray was about to quip "There goes the weekend," but before he could articulate that rather ungrateful thought, he heard footsteps and in swarmed his children, Ruth carrying a cellophane cone of flowers, Lizzie with a cardboard tray of coffee, and George with a box of donuts.

"I hope I can have coffee," he said to the doctor.

"You're talking!" Ruth exclaimed.

"'Four score and seven years ago,'" said Murray. "Can I have coffee?"

"Why don't you wait on that," the doctor said. "I want to make sure you can swallow safely before you eat or drink anything. I'll get a speech therapist to assess that. If you can swallow okay, you can have coffee and a decent breakfast. But no donuts; they'll send your blood sugar through the roof."

The doctor left, and the children gathered around his bedside. Murray relayed the doctor's diagnosis, including her recommendation that he spend the next twenty-four hours in the hospital.

George frowned. "They don't want to move you down to Concord?"

"No mention of that," said Murray.

"Because we have a stroke unit," said George. He left the room.

"No big deal," Ruth chirped. "We can hang out here just as well as hanging out in the living room back at your house. Can't we, Lizzie?"

"No problem," said Lizzie. "I might have to spend some time grading papers. Unless I get hauled off to jail, that is."

Murray tried to recall what it was about Lizzie and jail. Then it came to him.

"Gavin's laptop," he said. "You poured hot water on it."

"And he's claiming I assaulted him," Lizzie added glumly.

Ruth's phone pinged, and Murray heard her swear under her breath. She typed something, then tucked her phone back in her purse. He appreciated that.

"I have a suggestion," Ruth said. "How about we just put Gavin out of the picture, unless and until he actually does something. We don't need that cloud hanging over us. If he presses charges, we deal with it. But until then, let's just enjoy the time together."

Murray thought this was uncharacteristically calm of Ruth; she was usually so inclined to hype herself up over worst-case scenarios that she rarely enjoyed any time for what it was.

"Good idea," he said.

George returned, and Ruth asked what the doctor said about Concord.

"No transfer, unless he were to need surgery," said George.

"I'm sure they're going to take good care of me here," Murray said. "Don't any of you go second-guessing my doctor. I like her. Ruth," he said after a long moment, looking to change the subject, "why don't you tell me some news from DC."

Ruth had to think. "Well, let's see . . . we're thinking of putting an addition on the house," she finally offered.

"Your house is already huge," said Lizzie.

"Morgan wants an exercise room," said Ruth. "Right now he keeps his rowing machine in the family room, plus all his weights. It's very cluttered. So I wouldn't mind having a place for him to put everything. This would give him space for the NordicTrack, too."

"Don't you belong to a gym?" Lizzie asked.

"We'd quit the gym," said Ruth. "Morgan did the math. We don't really use it very much."

"But you like to swim at the gym," said Murray. "Would you be putting in a pool as well?"

"That's probably out of our budget."

"So the addition is basically for Morgan," said George.

"Oh, I'd use it, too," said Ruth.

"When are you doing this addition?" Murray asked. He didn't like to think that Ruth was going to lose out on her pool access.

He himself regretted all the times he'd insisted on getting his way, at Lillian's expense. Why had he always needed to have the final say? Why hadn't he let her have new drapes, when she'd wanted them? He'd been such a dictatorial poop sometimes.

"Next summer," said Ruth. "We're also thinking about putting a mother-in-law unit in. Not that I'm suggesting it's for you, Dad, but winters up here are so long and gray. DC has a lot going on for seniors. Flowers come out in March."

Murray tried to remember the name of that town in Mexico. Maybe it would not in fact be too touristy. He wondered if he could rent a car there; it might be nice to get out and see some of the countryside. Would he need a different kind of driver's license? Would he need to get shots? Was the water safe to drink? Did he have to worry about the drug cartels? He pictured himself learning enough Spanish to converse with his neighbors. *How do you make that fish soup?* he would ask. *Do you know of an English-speaking doctor in town?*

"You'd have your own bathroom," Ruth was saying.

Murray swam back to the hospital room from the Tropic of Cancer. "Don't do it just for me," he told Ruth.

"Oh, I'd use it as a study, too," she added hastily. "It wouldn't be only for you. Just something to think about."

"Or you could come with me to Chile," George suggested. "I'm running in Santiago in April."

Murray didn't want to go live with Ruth for the winter, nor stand around watching George run by in a flash in Santiago. He wanted to do something by himself, where he wasn't a father, or a lawyer, or a state representative, or even a small-time farmer. Going off and living in a small town in Mexico seemed like the perfect way to do something different. Not that he didn't love his children. He loved them so much it hurt. But he'd always been a son, then a husband, then a father of four. He'd never had time to be just a *guy*.

"Where do you all get the idea that I want to get away for the winter?" he asked, for perhaps he'd spoken his thoughts about Mexico out loud. He didn't want to tell them his plan yet. They would find ways to stop him. *You don't speak Spanish*, would be the main one. True. But he'd get one of those Rosetta Stone courses and then learn the rest on the street. *What if you get sick?* And now: *What if you have a full-blown stroke?*

"We were just talking on the way over," Ruth said.

"I'm not in on it," Lizzie assured him. "I know you want to stay here. I know you don't mind the cold."

It boggled his mind, how far off base they could be sometimes.

AROUND NINE O'CLOCK some orderlies came in and wheeled him out to the elevator and up to the second floor, to a semiprivate room. Nobody else was in the other bed. "It's the last room I can put you in without having to double you up," said the nurse. "Consider yourself lucky." Murray chose the bed by the window, which looked out onto Mount Lafayette. After getting the okay from the speech therapist, an orderly brought him some breakfast—cream of wheat, canned peaches, and tepid coffee. It was pretty bad, but he didn't care. After he ate, he told his children he was tired and he didn't want them to spend the whole day sitting around his hospital bed.

"Go take a hike or something," he said. "Come back after lunch."

After putting in a respectable amount of protest, the children agreed to go, and Murray found himself alone. Aside from the beeping of the heart monitor, the room was quiet. He closed his eyes. He could dream all he wanted about going off to Mexico, but the truth was, he would never be able to get away from worrying about his children. About the very worst, for one thing: for what had happened once could always happen again, such that whenever he watched one of them get behind the wheel, his mind skittered back thirty-two years to a snowy night, the bright lights of the ER, the doctor meeting him with a grim look.

But he also worried about more philosophical matters as well. This could have been the end for him, and where would he have left his children? Were they satisfied with their lives? Were they happy? Had he done enough for them? Too much? He was often slipping Lizzie a hundred dollars here and there, since her salary was so low, and he wondered if she had come to depend on it. Of course, after he was gone there would be his estate at their disposal; they would each inherit a modest sum, but he couldn't help but think that he should make sure Lizzie was standing on her own two feet before he left this world . . .

A shaft of golden sunlight woke him up. He was still hooked up to wires and, to his relief, the other bed remained empty. He looked out the window at the mountain range. As a college student, he'd spent a summer working in Greenleaf Hut on Mount Lafayette. The job involved cooking dinner and breakfast for the overnighters and hiking down once a week for seventy pounds of supplies. A heavy load but doable, when you were twenty.

Once he'd taken Lillian up to the hut. She was never much of a hiker, but she'd braved the steep, rocky trail. This was the summer before she got pregnant. He had to urge her along like a child. When they got to the hut, she stayed out on the deck, smoking. That damn habit! He worried about lung cancer all the time. She was always saying she was going to quit, but there was always an excuse. A new baby. A toddler to run after. Teenagers. Murray had never smoked and couldn't grasp the difficulty of quitting. The day after the accident he threw away every single ashtray in the house.

Well. At least she never got lung cancer, he thought darkly.

Just then the nurse came in and told him that lunch was on its way. She checked Murray's signs and then informed him that he would be getting a roommate.

"Sorry to have to double you up," she said.

Murray didn't really mind. He thought it might be nice to have someone who wasn't family to talk to. His kids! He could see it all now: because of the TIA, they'd be jabbering nonstop about this what're-we-going-to-do-with-Dad business.

He was just finishing his Jell-O when he heard voices in the hall. Someone was protesting that his blood sugar numbers weren't all that wacko. Soon the wide door to his room swung open. From his gurney, the new patient took one look at Murray and closed his eyes.

"You gotta be kidding me," said Gavin.

12.

Two Top Hats on a Bike

RUTH HAD TO KEEP TELLING HERSELF THAT THE DOCTORS at this small hospital in northern New Hampshire were really just as competent, smart, and up-to-date on the latest medical research on transient ischemic attacks as anywhere else, and that she didn't need to insist upon transferring her father down to the stroke center in Concord, or over to Dartmouth Hitchcock, for adequate medical care. It was a difficult role for Ruth, stepping back, but she felt it was the right approach, for if she let herself go down the road of skepticism and paranoia, it would only cause more anxiety for everyone involved, and the outcome would probably not be all that different—that is to say, Murray would probably still be there in his semiprivate room in a small north-country hospital looking out at the peaks of the Franconia Range.

But just to be clear, Ruth had a *lot* of experience dealing with incompetent doctors. When Kyle broke his femur during a soccer match, the first doctor said he didn't need an X-ray because there was no swelling or bruising and Kyle didn't react much when the doctor moved his leg. Well, Kyle didn't react much because the EMTs had pumped him full of painkillers out on the soccer field when Kyle was screaming in agony, so that by the time they got to the ER he was drugged out. Only after Ruth herself pushed for an X-ray did a second doctor order one, which revealed (no surprise to Ruth) a clear break. And this was right in Bethesda, Maryland!

Regarding the situation at hand, she'd gone and Googled Murray's symptoms on her phone and learned all about strokes and TIAs, enough to satisfy herself that the doctor here was taking the right approach. She would have to remain on her toes, though; if Murray had a second incident she would insist on a transfer immediately. But for now, she would go along with the doctor's decision.

Boy, did this bolster her argument for the retirement home, though.

WHILE THEY WERE STILL in the ER with Murray, Ruth tried calling Morgan's cell but got no answer. Before she could try their landline, though, she received a text from Abe, asking if they were still on for ten o'clock. She'd completely forgotten about their coffee date. She texted him back and told him there'd been a family emergency, and felt relieved that she didn't have to meet him.

But now that Murray had a private room and was kicking them all out, she was faced with a decision: to get back in touch with him or to let things slide. She thought about it and decided to let things slide. The whole idea was a foolish one, for a host of reasons: (A) They had only one car and if she asked George and Lizzie to drop her off at a coffee shop, they would ask why and who and read too much into it; (B) She never should have gotten in touch with Abe in the first place, she'd only been upset over Charlene; (C) They had nothing in common anymore, and they'd be hard-pressed to find anything to talk about; and (D) He'd had cancer and she never knew what to say to cancer people.

She took out her phone. "Turns out I have some free time," she wrote. Her arms tingled.

"The Grind at 10:30," Abe wrote back.

"I have a favor," she told Lizzie and George as they headed out of the hospital. "Could you drop me off at a place called the Grind?"

"You're dumping us?" said George.

"Who are you meeting?" asked Lizzie.

She told them.

"Abe!" George exclaimed. He and Lizzie exchanged looks.

"Don't," Ruth warned. "It's just coffee. Don't tell Dad, though. He'll get all weird."

She flashed on Abe's belly, with its long appendicitis scar.

They drove into town in Lizzie's car and pulled up in front of a tiny coffee shop nestled between a tattoo parlor and a Thai restaurant. Ruth told them to pick her up in an hour. Inside it was dark and close and people sat at tables with their laptops open or the Sunday paper spread out before them.

Abe's face lit up when he saw her. His hair had thinned out since she'd last seen him and he was all sinewy in the arms and legs, which were visible as he was wearing a cycling shirt and Lycra shorts and clattery black elflike shoes. With a big grin he told her up front that his cancer was in remission, but he had a new disease. "Muscle wasting!" he marveled. "Zonks me out after four hours of bike riding. I'll be using a walker in five years," he admitted, as matter-of-factly as if he were talking about gum surgery.

Which made Ruth feel positively rotten. She realized she'd actually harbored a tiny hope that they might flirt, maybe share a knowing gaze that lasted a little too long, not so much in vengeful spite toward Morgan but because Morgan's affair with Charlene had crushed a part of her and she wanted to see if it was still there. She was ashamed now at how grossly utilitarian that was; here was a man who was dealing with life-and-death issues and for her to bat her eyes over a latte was about the most callous thing she could do.

"I'm so sorry," she said, for many reasons.

Abe grinned again. "It sucks, but it won't kill me. Putting in the bike miles while I can."

She told him about the boys and her job and the number of hours it consumed.

"And what do you do for fun?" Abe asked.

"For fun? Oh! Well, I read and watch movies . . ." It didn't sound very exciting. "And we travel a lot." But that wasn't exactly fun because she still had to deal with the boys forgetting their ski mitts or Morgan getting antsy because he hadn't gotten his heart rate high enough that day. She wished she could say she painted, or played the piano, or did Masters swimming. She felt him judging her, too, and wanted to take out her phone right now and sign up for a trek in the Himalayas with a group of women friends. Now *that* would be fun.

It was pathetic, really.

"I'm hoping things will slow down," Ruth said, "once the boys go off to college."

"You gotta take care of yourself, Ruth," said Abe.

"Oh, I do, I do!" she protested. But her words rang false as soon as she said them. She took care of everybody *but* herself. She thought back to her mother, scrambling eggs at the stove on those cold winter mornings, getting everyone off to school. But then she had those four, five, or six hours all to herself, up in her third-floor room. Writing. Creating. She never published anything, but was she happier with her lot in life than Ruth?

Another question that would go forever unanswered.

Soon their time was up. They stood from the table and hugged, and she promised to get in touch the next time she came north, and he promised he would call if he was ever in the DC area. "Say hi to the fam," he said, and clattered his way outside to his bicycle.

Watching him ride off, Ruth did the math. Caleb was fourteen, Kyle twelve. Six years until college.

LATER THAT MORNING, they ended up at Lizzie's house, in her kitchen.

"Have a seat, guys," said Lizzie, and she set about tidying up while George checked his messages on his cell phone. Ruth, meanwhile, was looking around the kitchen. Still somewhat shaken by her visit with Abe, she wasn't in the best of moods and found herself feeling judgmental. It didn't bother her that Murray had helped Lizzie with the down payment for her house, because he'd helped Ruth as well, even though she and Morgan technically didn't need it. But it did bother her to see a big water stain on the wall just above some warped floorboards, and she'd also noticed a piece of cardboard taped over a broken window in the living room. Glancing out the kitchen window, she saw a large branch had been torn from the maple tree, leaving a ragged wound in need of a neat cut and a coat of protectant, and— *Really, Lizzie!* Ruth thought. *It would be a shame to lose this tree, the one thing that gives your asbestos-sided house a bit of gravitas.*

But was she going to say anything? Today, with Murray in the hospital and her sister already under scrutiny for the stunt she'd pulled yesterday morning?

Sigh.

Instead, she forced herself to take a kinder approach, to which end she complimented her sister on her cinder-block bookshelves. "I love seeing all your books," she said. "Morgan thought our books were cluttering up the place so we got rid of a lot of them. Now I miss them. Oh look, you have Mom's fairy-tale book." She squatted and tipped out a worn volume. "Good for you. I'm glad you have it." She paused. "Just don't lend it to Gavin."

Her joke just popped out.

"Not funny, Ruth," said George, not looking up.

Dammit.

"I also like the way you keep your dishes on those open shelves," she said. "I like that look. Very French country. It's nice that you keep things simple. One set of dishes. One set of glasses. Morgan got rid of our books, but he can't touch the dishes he inherited from his grandmother, which aren't our style at all, gold-rimmed and all that, and they clutter up the cabinets, but whenever I say let's sell them on eBay, he says maybe we'll have a really big Thanksgiving dinner some year and invite all our friends—"

"Ruth," said George. "Stop with the comparisons, all right? Nobody's criticizing you for how you live."

"I was just trying to tell Lizzie what I liked about her house."

"Well, it comes off as bragging, for some reason," said George. "We're all different. Lizzie's a professor. I'm a nurse. You're a lawyer. We're all cool."

Which irritated Ruth. "You don't have to get all psychobabble about it." She really wanted to have a good morning with her siblings, but George wasn't making it easy, which sent her off in an ugly direction.

"Speaking of which," she said, "I know nobody wants to talk about this anymore, but have either of you been down in Dad's basement? There's mouse shit all over everything and it smells like a dead animal. I think he needs an exterminator."

"I'll set some traps," said Lizzie. "That's all an exterminator will do anyway."

"Okay," said Ruth, "but . . ."

"But what?"

Ruth could see it all. Lizzie would go and set some traps. Then she would forget about them. Murray wouldn't know where they were. Then: more dead mouse smell.

So she said what she was thinking. "Okay, but the exterminator will actually come back and check them."

"What's that supposed to mean?" Lizzie said.

Ruth contemplated a ball of dust that had migrated into a corner. *Like tumbleweed*, she thought.

"What did you mean by that, Ruth?" Lizzie pressed.

She could have used a cigarette right then. She smoked maybe one or two a week; she was that lucky kind of smoker, but nobody in the family knew. "I think sometimes you get tied up in your own life and don't make it down to Dad's as often as you say you do."

Lizzie applied some ChapStick. "I'm there more than you are."

"That's true," said Ruth, "but when you're there, what do you do?"

"I cook for Dad," Lizzie retorted. "I clean out his refrigerator and play cribbage with him and help him down in the sunflower field. But you're right, I guess I haven't been keeping up with my 'mouse extermination skills.'" She curled her fingers into air quotes.

"So he's letting food rot in the refrigerator? You see?" Ruth turned from one to the other. "Especially in the context of what happened this morning. He just shouldn't be living on his own."

"If he went to the Pines he'd still have a refrigerator to let things rot in," George noted.

"That's not my point. My point is, and I've already said this this weekend and I don't see why the two of you are so resistant to it, my point is that he should get himself resettled now. *Especially* now. What if he has that full-blown stroke that he's at risk of and no-body's there with him? You have to get help right away, you know. You can't just sit there and wait. At the Pines he'd be able to pull a string and presto, there's 911 banging on the door."

"So we'll get him one of those emergency things you wear around your neck," said Lizzie.

"They're not going to be as quick. And let's say he needs round-the-clock help. I'd rather have a plan in place than have to scramble at the last minute."

"Ruth," said George, "you seem to forget that I work in a hospital. I know what services are out there. We could get in-home help. And I can move on a dime."

Ruth shook her head. "You've both got your heads in the sand."

"Wait a second," said George. "Are you forgetting what Dad said last night? That he made it plain as day that he doesn't want to move? How would you like to be booted out of your own house? 'Hey Dad, choose your favorite chair, forget the sofa, there's not a whole lotta room.' And what's he going to do all day down there? He'd be bored shitless."

"Some of these places have gardens for the residents to tend," said Ruth.

"Like that'll excite him, growing carrots in a tub of dirt," George scoffed. "He wants to grow sunflowers by the acre, not a few rows of radishes. You think he can bring his tractor to a retirement home? You weren't here when he bought it. He was like a kid on Christmas. I thought he was going to ride all the way to Vermont, he was so excited. You can't count that for nothing, in terms of quality of life."

Ruth could not rebut this. But how much longer was their father really going to be able to tend his sunflower field? It had to be weighed against the advantages a retirement community could offer—now, before anything bad happened and they wouldn't let him in. She felt she was being reasonable. It was cost-benefit stuff, plain and simple. Why could her siblings not see this?

She had an idea. "Let's just visit one of these places," she said. "I can stay up here a few more days. We can drive down to Concord and have a tour. It might not be so scary for him, if he visited a place."

"I can't," said Lizzie. "I'll be in jail."

Oh please, cut the drama, thought Ruth. She had the distinct sense that Lizzie was still unwilling to own up to the foolhardiness of her stunt, and she was tired of it. "Do you see now how your little blowup complicates things?"

"You don't want to let this go, do you?" said Lizzie.

"Well," said Ruth, "I just wonder."

"Wonder what?"

"Whether the stress of this caused the TIA."

"Jesus, Ruth," George groaned.

"I'm just saying. Lizzie needs to take a little responsibility here."

"So it's Judge Ruth now?" said Lizzie.

"Maybe it's coincidental," said Ruth. "Then again, maybe not."

"Fuck you, Ruth," said Lizzie.

"Oh jeez," said George. "Come on, you two."

Ruth stood up abruptly. "Maybe it's time to go back to the hospital."

"With you guys at each other's throats?" said George. "I don't think that's a good idea at all."

"Well, actually, I for one would like some alone time with Dad," said Ruth. "If you guys wouldn't mind."

"Go ahead," said Lizzie. "Nothing says we have to hang out together this afternoon."

Ruth, who at work could make digs one moment and be shaking hands and laughing the next, was taken aback by the daylong scope of her sister's assumption. She wasn't suggesting they split up for the rest of the day! In fact she was still envisioning a more family-oriented time, and assumed she and Lizzie would get beyond their squabbling, for the sake of their father at least. That was the only reason she said all those mean things.

She felt it would be unkind to remind Lizzie that she'd spent $400 and foregone twenty billable hours and missed out on two soccer games to come up here this weekend.

"All right, then," she said tightly. "Let's go."

Lizzie got her keys and headed out the door. And Ruth wished, at that moment, that she'd rented her own car for the weekend.

BEFORE GOING into her father's room, Ruth stopped at the nurse's station, just to see if there were any changes in Murray's condition. What was his blood pressure now? When was the last time the doctor checked on him? She didn't find the nurses very friendly, but she didn't much care. Somebody had to be a patient's watchdog.

Heading down the hall, she found her father's door half-closed. A discussion was taking place within.

". . . the Inca Trail. On my bucket list for my entire life and I had to put down a hefty deposit and if I can't go, she should at the very least reimburse me for that as well."

"Fine, but criminal charges? You really need to go that route?"

"With a second-degree burn? You bet your ass."

Ruth pushed the door open. Murray's roommate looked at her without expression.

"You fucking look just like her," he said.

"And you must be Gavin," she said smoothly, and then: "How did this happen, Dad?"

"This is my daughter Ruth," Murray said. "She's the oldest of the bunch. The attorney."

"Lordy, lordy," said Gavin.

"They admitted you for just a second-degree burn?" Ruth asked.

"No, they admitted me because they claim I haven't been monitoring my blood sugar. Which is ridiculous. Can I help it if my blood sugar likes to shoot up every so often? Though we're talking about burns all over my goddamn hand, you know. Not good for a diabetic. Know what I just love about your sister? The way she acts like a nineteen-year-old."

His being diabetic reminded Ruth of the torts cases she'd read back in law school. You take your victims as you find them, even if they happen to be diabetic.

"If she acts like a nineteen-year-old, why did you ever get involved with her?" she said. "A guy your age, you're married, you're old enough for Medicare—is this your modus operandi? Screwing women half your age?"

"Ruth," said Murray.

"No, let her get it off her chest," said Gavin.

Ruth found that assessment insulting. How would her mother have responded? Her mother wouldn't have taken it, she was sure. "I'm not just getting things 'off my chest,'" she retorted. "I'm telling you something you need to hear. This whole thing with my sister should never have happened. You used her. You played with her feelings. What if she'd fallen in love with you? It was courting danger, what you did. And maybe that's how you like to live, but it's not right. You're just lucky that she's fine with the breakup."

"She didn't seem fine when she came over to get the cookbook," said Gavin. "She seemed pretty upset to me."

"Yeah—because you ruined something that was very important to us!" She wondered if they had a cause of action for negligent destruction of property.

"Oh, get over it," said Gavin. "It was a fucking cookbook. Besides, it wasn't really just about the cookbook."

"And what's that supposed to mean?"

"Ask Lizzie."

Her instinct was to snap back ("Oh please!"), but she caught herself. What else was Lizzie leaving out? Ruth turned her engagement ring so the diamond faced inward, as a reminder to follow up on this with Lizzie. In the meantime, she would deal with what she knew.

"This assault thing," she said. "Lizzie tells a different story. She says you tried to grab the teakettle and that's how you got hot water all over your hand. She wasn't trying to pour it on you."

"Of course she says that. What would you expect? But my daughter was there and saw the whole thing, and the fact of the matter is that your sister practically hurled the hot, excuse me, *boiling* water at me. I had to physically restrain her, and this"—he pointed to his mummified paw—"this is the result."

A growing sense of unease made Ruth break eye contact with the man. Did her sister really carry around that much rage? If so, over what?

"This whole unfortunate event could be settled with a new laptop," she said. "You don't have to get the law involved. Right, Dad?"

Murray had begun flossing his teeth. He grunted.

"Well, both of you are wrong," said Gavin. "Because frankly I want to see her sweat. I want her to worry about jail time."

"*That's* mature."

"Oh, get off your high horse."

"No, I think I'll stay up here for a little while," Ruth said. "What are you doing, staying married all this time? I'll bet your wife isn't too happy with all your dalliances."

"Stupid assumption," Gavin said. "I might as well assume your own marriage is a sham. You are married, right? Marriage is a complex institution. And people stay together for a host of reasons."

"Yours being?"

"Financial, if you want to know the truth. But since you're so righteous, you tell me: What keeps you married? Let me guess. Two point two kids. Double income. A hefty mortgage and Little League and music lessons and homework and dinner to cook every night and is it really fifty-fifty? Do you tell each other everything? Do you find time for love? What keeps you together?"

Ruth didn't know what to say. In truth she was stung by his words, because he had a point, especially in the context of her conversation with Abe. There were in fact a lot of things she didn't tell Morgan. Little things, like the way it bothered her that he clipped his nails over the kitchen sink. And bigger things, like how she was afraid of waking up at the age of seventy and feeling like she'd wasted her whole life in a law firm, arguing with people and trying to keep big corporations off the Justice Department's radar.

Yet she didn't tell Morgan any of this because what if things came out on his end, things he himself wasn't happy about in the marriage, and then she would bring up Charlene, and he would say,

You won't let it go, will you?, and both of them would find themselves staring at one another over their toothbrushes some night, realizing that maybe what they had was a hollow enterprise.

Because what *did* keep them together, besides the children? Not sex; they were always too tired. Not common activities; Morgan had his biking group, his running group, and his ski buddies, none of which included her, since she was far too out of shape to keep up with them. Shared values, she told herself—then remembered that time at the shore when Morgan (uncharacteristically frisky) had wanted sex one evening and was willing to let the boys download a movie even though they'd made a pact beforehand to say no to digital entertainment at the beach house. It was a little thing, but to Ruth it meant that Morgan was willing to compromise his values if it made things more convenient for him.

She suddenly wanted to call Morgan right now and get on a plane and fly home and fall into bed with the man she'd married, not the man he was now but the man she'd fallen in love with twenty years ago in law school who clowned around when everyone else was somberly forming study groups and worrying about who owned the fox; who rode his bike in circles around a courtyard in a top hat and offered her an identical hat if she would climb on the back and ride along with him; who invited her upstairs to his third-floor apartment and cooked her Chinese noodles and later, when they were in bed together, drew his finger down her ski jump nose and told her he'd been waiting for this moment since the first day in Contracts, when she'd croaked in front of the entire class upon being asked to state the facts of the very first case.

"Don't answer my question," said Gavin. "But I'm going to guess it's not like it used to be. You've got a job, a couple of kids, you're earning megabucks and can't imagine giving up the life you have just because the earth doesn't move anymore."

How did he know all this? Lizzie may have told him some basic facts, but she wouldn't have had access to Ruth's emotions. Even *Ruth* didn't have access to Ruth's emotions much of the time.

"You don't know jack about my life," she said coldly.

"My point exactly," said Gavin. "So don't give me any lectures on how to conduct mine."

Not wanting to appear shaken, she looked over at her father and saw that he'd closed his eyes. His hands were folded over his stomach, the skin loose and mottled, mapped out with ropey blue veins.

"Dad?" she said softly. "Are you sleeping?"

Without opening his eyes, Murray adjusted his hearing aid.

"I'm going to see about getting Gavin moved," she said. "Why they doubled you up is beyond me."

"Like the nurses know our personal history," scoffed Gavin. "But be my guest. By all means. I'd much prefer being in a room with someone who doesn't remind me of your sister. What a case," he said, shaking his head. "What . . . a fucking . . . *nutcase*."

BEFORE TALKING TO THE NURSES, Ruth placed a call to Morgan. He still didn't answer his cell, so she called their landline. Kyle, the younger, answered.

"Where's Dad?" she asked.

"I don't know," he mumbled.

"He's out, though?"

"I guess."

"And he didn't tell you where he was going?"

"Maybe he told Caleb."

"Put Caleb on."

In a moment Caleb came on the line. "I have this weird pain in my knee," he began. "Whenever I bend it, I get this shooting fiery feeling down to my toes."

Caleb had a lot of aches and pains, and Ruth had finally concluded that the best way to deal with them was one dose sympathy, one dose Tylenol, with instructions to stay off the internet.

"Where's your father?" Ruth asked.

"He said he had a meeting."

"On a Sunday?"

"Don't yell at me, Mom, I'm just the messenger. And my knee really hurts."

"Did he say what time he'd be back?"

"No. When are you coming home?"

"I don't know. Your grandfather had a little stroke." She expected Caleb to freak out. He didn't. "I was going to come home tomorrow night, but I might have to stay a little longer to get some help for Grampa. I would really like to talk to your father, though."

"Call his cell."

"I did, and he isn't answering."

"Ma, chill. What about my knee?"

"Go take a Tylenol and ice it," said Ruth. "Don't Google it."

"I already did," said Caleb, and she thought she detected a sniffle. "Bone cancer starts with leg pain."

"You don't have bone cancer, Caleb," she sighed. "You have growing pains. Please have Dad call me when he gets home."

She hung up and pictured Morgan in the shower at the fleabag hotel, sudsing up with hotel soap to erase the smell of another woman before heading home, and Charlene out in the room, slipping the magnetic key into his jeans pocket, a calling card for Ruth to find a week later, doing laundry.

13.

Tick Tock Talk

IF THERE WAS ONE THING GEORGE HATED, IT WAS COMparisons. Who's got a bigger house, a faster car. Who's earning more money. Who ran the fastest marathon, who's the favorite child—who's got a bigger dick, essentially; that was the question, and George didn't like it at all.

And he had a nose for subtext. He could spot the scales in someone's thoughts before they even realized they were weighing things. So that when Ruth started complimenting Lizzie on her bookshelves and her kitchen decor, he cut her off, because he knew that in her mind she was thinking: *I'm glad I make enough money to afford a two-story wood-frame house with built-in painted bookshelves and a waterproof roof. I'm glad I'm not sentenced to live up here in northern New Hampshire with all these Trump rubes. I'm glad I'm the oldest,*

most serious child because I would never want to fall prey to an emo-
tional outburst ... like pouring hot water on my ex's laptop.

Something like that.

As George saw it, Ruth had turned pretty snobby since moving away. First she'd gone to a small college over in Maine, where she learned to like the green stuff in a lobster. After that it was down to New Haven for law school, where she began using words like "notwithstanding" and "albeit" when talking on the phone. And after that, she'd headed to DC to work for a big law firm, and clearly she had no interest in returning to her roots up here in New England. Which would be fine, if she didn't keep trying to sneak her Great World experience into conversations. She used the foreign pronunciation of everyday words, like "croissant" and "Buenos Aires" (Buenos *Eye*-rays). If they went out to eat, she asked for a poached egg on her salad (which George thought was rather gross), and could the waiter please bring some sriracha sauce, hoping (in George's view) that the uninitiated would ask what sriracha sauce was, so that Ruth could let it drop that she'd grown addicted to it in Bali.

"And hold the croutons, please," she would add, which annoyed George, because he thought this whole low-carb thing was nonsense and would have gladly added them to his chili.

He'd visited her a few times, and he had to say: Ruth and Morgan certainly did things in style. They had an aerator for their red wine. They had a private bathroom off the guest room, with heated towel racks and two lush white robes. Ruth kept fresh flowers on the table in the front hall, replacing them weekly with whatever suited her fancy, and the sectional sofa in the family room was deep enough for a giant. It was like visiting a bed-and-breakfast, Ruth's house, and it didn't hurt that Morgan's NordicTrack faced a giant flat-screen TV.

George himself rented a small apartment in Concord Heights. Since he spent much of his disposable income on travel, he'd never saved enough to buy a house, which didn't bother him, although it did bother Murray, who kept offering to "lend" him money for a down payment. "I'll just deduct it from your share of the inheritance," Murray said, but George didn't want to own a home. He didn't want to caulk windows and worry about frozen pipes. He liked his life the way it was, free and noncommittal in every sense of the word, going into the hospital four days a week for his shift, and then taking off for a modest twelve-mile run, or going home and communing online with other runners.

Including Samantha, until lately. Samantha was forty-two and divorced, and lived in Boston with her eight-year-old daughter. He'd met her this past June during a race in Colorado, when they'd happened to set a pace together. George, like Lizzie, had been in a long-term relationship in his thirties, but it had fallen apart a few years ago over the issue of children. His girlfriend had wanted them; George did not. They made you too vulnerable, he felt; they gave you too much to lose.

But maybe if it was a stepchild he wouldn't feel so vulnerable, was his thinking last June with Samantha, and so during the course of the summer, he'd allowed himself to have dinner with her several times. In early August they ran a half marathon together. They spent the night in a bed-and-breakfast. Things looked promising.

Then George got spooked. Samantha invited him to the beach with her daughter, and George watched the girl frolic in the waves and all he could think about was the undertow. Clouds built in the sky and he worried about lightning. They ate burgers and he worried about *E. coli*. He was a ninny, even with an eight-year-old girl he'd just met. Imagine if he got more attached, or had one of his own!

So suddenly George had plans for the following weekend, and over Labor Day, when Samantha suggested a camping trip, he told her he was headed up north to be with his father. He didn't invite her along, and he spent the weekend splitting and stacking a cord of firewood, and lay in bed alone all night, shoulders burning with pain.

SHORTLY AFTER NOON, George and Lizzie headed back to the hospital, having agreed that Ruth had had enough alone time with Murray. As they got off the elevator, they saw Ruth arguing with one of the nurses. Frantically she motioned for them. "Guess who's in with Dad!"

For a moment it didn't register with either of them. Then George exclaimed, "Gavin?!"

"That's right!" Ruth said triumphantly.

Lizzie blanched. "Why is he still here?"

"I don't know, some issue with his blood sugar. Though why they suddenly had to put him in Dad's room is beyond me, and I'm trying to get that changed. So that's where things stand. Not good for Dad's blood pressure, I'm sure."

Lizzie started down the hall.

"Wait, Lizzie," George called. "I'm not sure that's a good idea."

"It's not a good idea at all," Ruth declared. "He's still talking about pressing charges."

Lizzie turned around. "Are you fucking kidding me?"

"Like I said, it's his word against yours, and he has a witness," said Ruth.

"Bitch," said Lizzie.

George could see where all this was going: Gavin would dig his heels in, Lizzie would take any bait he held out, and Murray's carotid artery would clot off. "Don't go down there," he said. "Think of Dad's health, Lizzie."

A look of incredulity spread across Lizzie's face. "He's going to send me to jail," she marveled. "Because of him, I'm going to have a criminal record. This is totally unbelievable."

George was very, very glad that Ruth didn't step in and remind her that if she hadn't poured hot water all over Gavin's laptop, none of this would have happened.

"You're not going to go to jail," said Ruth. "You'd get a suspended sentence with some kind of probation, and that's *if* he went ahead and pressed charges and you pleaded guilty to something. And frankly I get the sense he's just making noise to scare you. It's bluster. Hold on, I'm going to go check with the nurses again for another room."

"Um, actually, why don't I check?" said George.

A sheepish look crossed Ruth's face. "Right," she admitted.

At the nurse's station, George learned that the reason Mr. Langley was in the room with Mr. Blaire was to prevent infection; this was a small hospital, and the other rooms on the wing were occupied by patients who were contagious. "They're stuck with each other," the nurse said. "They'll just have to duke it out, whatever's going on between them."

Which George reported back to Ruth and Lizzie.

"Look," he said, "why don't you two go get a cup of coffee or something, and I'll go sit with Dad." This might give the two sisters a chance to mend their ways from the morning's tiff, he thought. "I'll just pull the curtain. I've already had my two cents with Gavin. I don't have anything else to say."

"Don't tell him that Lizzie's here," said Ruth. "Don't tell him that the police came to our house. But you can tell him that Lizzie has a lawyer."

George closed his eyes. "Could you stop trying to control every little thing right now?"

"I happen to know the significance of every little thing that could come out of our mouths," Ruth said.

George sighed. "I know. But could you just shut up for a while?"

Without giving Ruth a chance to respond, he left his two sisters by the elevator and went into his father's room.

Gavin raised his eyes from his Kindle. "Great. You again."

While George checked the heart monitor, he kept his hand on Murray's shoulder. George and Murray didn't have what you would call a very physically demonstrative relationship; it was not Murray's style to issue hugs except maybe during significant arrivals or departures. But as a nurse, George knew the healing power of touch, and he wasn't going to change his approach just because the man in the bed happened to be his father. Murray craned his neck.

"Am I still alive?"

"As far as I can tell," George replied.

"How about me?" said Gavin. "Maybe this is all a bad dream."

George ignored him. He pulled up a chair and sat by his father's side and handed him a lidded plastic jug with an accordion straw.

"Drink."

Murray obligingly puckered his lips around the straw. There was an intent with which he performed this simple task that suggested unsureness, a need to focus. A bit of water dribbled down his whiskered chin and Murray wiped it aside and then dabbed his finger on the sheet.

"You know that blood pressure unit you have at home?" George said.

Murray made a face.

"That's right, I want you to use it every morning. Keep track of your numbers. And I want you to get a MedicAlert."

"What's that?"

"One of those devices that can call for help if you fall."

"Stop treating me like an old man," said Murray.

"Yeah," Gavin said. "I agree."

George went and pulled the curtain around Murray's bed. Even though it did nothing to keep Gavin from hearing them, it lent some semblance of privacy.

"Look, I don't want you to move into assisted living," George said. "But you have to be sensible. With a stroke, you have to get help very quickly."

"My uncle died of a stroke," Gavin offered, from behind the curtain.

"I'm not asking much," George went on. "Just take your blood pressure and wear a MedicAlert. It'll put our minds at rest. You want that, right? You don't want your kids to worry."

"Fine," said Murray. "But don't start telling me to stay off ladders or stop working my sunflower field."

"You going to put sunflowers in again next spring?" Gavin asked.

George peeked through an opening in the curtain. Gavin's gown had slipped down his chest, revealing wiry gray hair. "Do you mind?"

"I'm just interested in sunflowers, is all," said Gavin.

"So go online then," said George, over his shoulder.

"They take a lot of water," Murray said. "Birds love them."

Gavin nudged the curtain further open. "When do you plant?"

"When the black flies come out—so, mid-May. And plant them north to south; you get a better yield, I've found."

George was growing irritated. To combat this, he asked himself, *What did it matter, if these two old geezers wanted to talk sunflowers?*

"There's an outfit over in Vermont that makes deck stain out of the oil," said Murray. "Market's pretty good these days, if you're interested in selling."

"Nope," Gavin replied, "I want to make my own biodiesel."

George turned around. "Oh? Giving up writing, are you?"

"A man can't sit at his desk all day," said Gavin.

"So go raise sunflowers," said George. "But do your own research." He snapped the curtain shut again.

"I can still hear every word you say," said Gavin.

George fumed. He wanted to talk a little bit more with his father about health issues. Now was the time, while Murray was a captive audience. When was his last colonoscopy, for instance? His last skin check? But was he really going to raise these issues with Gavin listening in?

He suddenly had the terrible feeling that time was running out. There was much, much more he wanted to say to his father. How much he loved him, of course. That he wanted to be like Murray when he was eighty-one, active and interested in things like growing sunflowers. What was it like to enter the last stage of life? Did he have a bucket list? Did he worry about death? Did he believe in an afterlife? And the ultimate question, the most important one of all: How did he ever get through the grief of losing his wife and child?

And what if it happened to him?

How could he ask his father any of this, with Gavin lying less than ten feet away?

He took his father's hand. Murray, startled, drew back, but then relaxed and let George hold it. With his fingertips George gently massaged the pad at the base of his father's thumb, then moved outward, working each finger into a state of relaxation. He noticed that the baby finger stayed kinked. Arthritis, probably, but George hadn't known that Murray had arthritis. What else didn't he know about his father?

Murray had closed his eyes and after a while he shifted and gave George his other hand. George settled in closer and massaged it as well, the fingers curling reflexively. George recalled Murray standing behind him when he was a boy and showing him how to hold a bat and swing, those same hands broad and knuckly from all the time spent writing longhand on a yellow legal pad. He remembered his father's smell in the summers of his youth, an evening smell of sweat and gin. Now his father smelled sour, tinny, unwashed.

As if reading his mind, Murray asked George if he could see about getting a toothbrush. "I wouldn't mind another cup of coffee, too," he said.

"I'll see what I can do," said George. He gave his father's shoulder a squeeze and left the room. The time for saying all those important things had passed, and as much as he wanted to blame it on Gavin's presence, he knew much lay with his own reticence around his father, when it came to emotional matters.

Be better, he told himself. *Stop waiting. Tell Ruth you actually respect her. Tell Lizzie you can't always be there for her. Tell Samantha you were just a little scared.*

And tell your father that you kids will survive, as a threesome, once he's gone.

14.

Point One One

NOBODY LIKES BEING IN A HOSPITAL. IT'S NOISY; THERE are dings and dongs and bells and whistles and people on the loudspeakers all the time. You have no privacy. There are germs. The food is terrible. Needles abound.

Nevertheless Murray had a sense of gratitude for being here—even with Gavin Langley less than ten feet away. It had to do with feeling protected from his children, his main thought being that they wouldn't dare nag him now. Nor would they fight, he assured himself. After all, how tacky would that be?

Plus there was the service factor. He recalled Lillian's doctor having her stay in the hospital an extra few days after Lizzie was born. Murray had been surprised when Lillian didn't object; didn't she want to come home to her own bed? Be around the people who loved her? What she didn't say out loud—and what Murray didn't really grasp until now——was that being in the hospital meant someone brought her breakfast, lunch, and dinner in bed; someone changed the baby's diapers; there were no hungry mouths to feed, no permission slips to sign. She could take a shower without being disturbed. She could sleep.

He got it. It was pleasant, not having to plan his meals or pick up after himself. Because the fact was, things *were* getting more difficult these days. At times a weariness set in, making it hard, for instance, to feign an interest in that piece of salmon he'd bought with such good intentions; he'd overcook it, take a few bites, then scrape the rest into the garbage. Some days his checkbook mystified him. He couldn't keep track of automated phone options. Was it "press 2" or "press 3"?

So there was a certain comfort being in a place where you didn't have to negotiate with the real world——even if it meant sharing a room with Gavin.

Who was currently reading on his Kindle. Murray hadn't brought a book and he wished he'd thought to grab something on his way out of the house. Gavin had come prepared. Not only that but his daughter had stopped in with a latte for him earlier. Murray was philosophically opposed to spending five dollars on a cup of coffee, but he certainly wouldn't have refused one now.

Eventually, being without a book made him fidgety. George had left about an hour ago to join up with Lizzie and Ruth; their plan was to order a couple of pizzas and bring them to the hospital around six. Right now, looking out his window, he could see the soft shadows on the mountains deepening into late-afternoon blues and purples. Back at the house he would be helping Boyd with the milking.

He would be thinking of dinner. Planning his evening with the kids.

Finally he couldn't restrain himself. "So what are you reading?" he said through the curtain.

"Who, me?"

"Who else?"

"*Heart of Darkness*."

Murray considered this choice. "Great book, but kind of dense for the hospital, isn't it?"

"I read it every year," said Gavin. "And then I watch *Apocalypse Now* and feel happy."

Murray knew Gavin had been in Vietnam, but he'd made it clear he didn't like to talk about it. Murray, born in 1935, had been too young for Korea and too old for Vietnam. Whenever he met a vet, he always felt the need to apologize for his year of birth.

He left Gavin's comment unanswered and looked out the window. He contemplated a cloud in the sky that was shaped like a flying saucer. He gazed upon a blue spruce and decided that its color reminded him of the ocean on a dark winter morning. He thought, *You poet you.*

"What, you want me to read aloud to you or something?" Gavin finally demanded.

"I'm doing just fine," Murray protested. "You go back to your book."

Gavin managed to push the curtain aside so the two men could see each other. He snapped his Kindle shut. "How old are you, Murray?"

"Eighty-one. You?"

"Sixty-five." Gavin twisted around to reach his mini-jug of water. It was identical to Murray's, with the hospital logo, and it made Murray feel like they were on the same sports team.

He said, "Don't you think sixty-five is a little old for someone who's thirty-eight? I'm talking about my daughter."

"I know who you're talking about," said Gavin. "You think I'm some kind of moron?"

"No, I think you're someone who doesn't have very good judgment. Kind of robbing the cradle, in my view."

"Twenty-seven years is nothing. Plus she knew exactly what she was doing."

"Which was?"

"I hate to break this to you, but both of us understood it was never going to be what you would call a long-term serious relationship."

"Which is part of what bothers me," said Murray. "Call me old-fashioned, but—what do you call them, hookups?"

"Hookups are for college kids."

"But it was the same thing."

"We weren't in love, but we enjoyed each other's company. Let's just leave it at that. Too much information for you, anyway."

Probably right, thought Murray. He wanted to know, and he didn't want to know. The thought of the whole arrangement still needled him.

He felt a tightness in his neck and wondered if that was his blood pressure rising. Another TIA?

Meanwhile Gavin had kicked the sheet away and was examining

his leg, surprisingly thin for such a large man. Some of the hot water had burned his shin, leaving an angry red splotch.

"How's it doing?" Murray asked, welcoming the diversion from his daughter's sex life. "Painful?"

"Of course it's painful," said Gavin. "You know, if I need a skin graft on my hand, then in addition to criminal charges, I'll file a civil lawsuit for damages, and your daughter will be looking at millions."

"Definitely not millions," said Murray, who had tried a few cases involving damaged hands. "And Lizzie doesn't exactly have deep pockets. And really, why *are* you pressing charges? Why get the law involved?"

"It's the principle," said Gavin. "She came after me like a wild animal."

"If you don't mind, this is raising my blood pressure," said Murray.

"Well, take a deep breath, dude. You're going to have to deal with this issue at some point."

"Not when I've just had a stroke."

"Mini-stroke, and you sound like my mother. 'Don't argue with me; you're going to give me a migraine.' Got her out of a lot of conflict zones, that approach."

Murray tried to imagine Gavin as a little boy, eating peanut butter sandwiches, chubby legs swinging. "Is she still alive?"

"Technically. Alzheimer's."

"Well," said Murray, "well, I guess I'm sorry to hear that." And to his surprise he found he genuinely *was* sorry. "Your father?"

"He died thirty years ago, in a boating accident. How about your parents?"

"My mother got lung cancer," Murray replied, "and my father had a heart attack the week after she died." It had been a long, gloomy winter, with his mother hooked up to oxygen and his father puttering around in his soft, old-man slippers, waiting on her. They had retired to the beach house, and Murray spent many a Sunday down there with them, looking out at the cold, gray Atlantic. Gone in time were the celebratory family get-togethers, the long summer days of sand castles and clambakes and just enough sunburn to make you feel tight and radiant and alive. He could think of no place bleaker, sitting there with his elderly parents, and he was always glad to get back to his house with its view of the Franconia Range.

Gavin slurped noisily. Setting his jug down, he stretched back and folded his left arm behind his head. "Since we're stuck with each other, we might as well make it worth our time."

"Like what, sing camp songs?"

"No," said Gavin. "Let's see. Tell me something secret about yourself, Murray. Something that would surprise me."

"And why should I do that?"

"Because I'm bored."

"You first, then."

"All right," said Gavin. "When I was in Vietnam, I shot a dog. It had rabies. It was foaming at the mouth. Afterward I just left it there. The end. Your turn."

Murray licked his lips. They were crusted and chapped, and felt like they were going to split.

"What kind of dog?" he asked.

"What do you mean, what kind of dog?! Does it matter? It was a mongrel! A rabid mongrel! And I shot it in the head, and its legs twitched for two minutes before it went still. And now I dream about that fucking dog," he said. "Come on. Your turn."

Murray was stalling, because he didn't know what to say. He felt as though everything about him fell into predictable patterns, so that nothing would surprise anyone. Except, of course, what happened that night thirty-two years ago.

"Tell me what you regret then, if you can't think of anything," Gavin said. "Everybody has regrets. I regret not moving to Canada. Then I wouldn't have gone to Vietnam and shot that damn dog. I regret not having my daughter when I was younger. I regret not telling my cousin he couldn't touch my ding-dong at age nine."

"I'm sorry to hear that."

"So what about you? Lemme guess. You regret resigning from Congress just after you got elected. Yes?"

"I didn't resign; I was never sworn in. I withdrew."

"Whatever. So?"

"So no. I don't regret not going to Washington. I served in the New Hampshire legislature instead. Twenty-six years. I did a lot of good work."

"And that was enough?"

"Meaning what?"

"Big fish versus little fish. Must have kind of felt like you were missing out on things sometimes, by not playing with the Big Boys down in Washington."

Murray felt himself growing irritated. "What else could I have done? I'd just lost my wife and son. I had three children to take care of. I couldn't run off to Washington and leave the kids with a nanny every week."

Gavin seemed to contemplate this for a while, and Murray closed his eyes. He was ready for another nap. Gavin, though, had other ideas in mind.

"Tell me about the campaign," he said. "Now there's an ordeal to put your family through. Must have been kind of rough at times, being in the public eye and all."

Murray thought back to Daniel's face-plant in front of the Zipper being captured on camera; he thought of all those Saturdays, traversing the state in the Blaire-Mobile. Had it been so awful for his family? He recalled Lillian's outbursts—the one with the anti-abortionist at the teachers' meet and greet; with the reporter who dug up the vandalism incident in Northampton. It must have been hard for her, knowing that at any minute she could put her foot in her mouth. Plus she had to give up so much of her writing time. Still, she never complained.

"It wasn't that bad," he said.

"What did your wife do again?"

"She was a housewife. But she worked her tail off," he added quickly, because the term "housewife" still wore the cloak of Betty Crocker—of cookies, and floor wax, and well-made beds. He shouldn't have used it. Ruth always got on his case. Why didn't he remember?

"I know about housewives," Gavin declared. "My mother was a housewife, and anyone who uses the word 'just' in the same sentence ought to be shot. But wasn't she some kind of writer, too?"

"How'd you know that?"

"Elizabeth said something."

"She did write," Murray allowed.

"What did she write?"

"Stories," said Murray. "Short stories."

"She publish them?"

The inevitable question. He used to think at times that it would have been easier to tell people Lillian was a writer if she had published something. He wasn't proud of this, but there it was: he wanted to be able to hold up a copy of *The Atlantic* and say, *See? My wife, in* The Atlantic! *How about that!*

It occurred to him—not for the first time—that maybe she'd have published something if he'd made things a little easier for her. But he hadn't, really. Oh, he'd encourage her, but then he'd go and dump a big household project on her, like refinishing the basement, which took up all her time. He never offered to grocery shop or cook dinner; if someone got sick, he never volunteered to stay home so Lillian could make time for herself.

This made him sad now, contemplating it.

He reminded himself that he'd been the breadwinner. The family depended on him. But in talking to Gavin now, he thought that maybe if he'd given Lillian more time, or at least made arrangements for a little help, all those hours spent in that third-floor guest room might have produced something worthy of publication. Something spectacular, even.

"No, she did not publish," he told Gavin. "And I could probably have made things easier for her. I guess I regret that."

"Too involved in your own life? Took yourself a little too seriously?"

"You could say that."

"So that's one regret. Tell me another."

"Why are we playing this game?" Murray said crossly. "I don't like to look back on regrets. I prefer to look forward."

"Because I find it interesting," Gavin said. "Everybody has regrets. It tells you something about the person."

"Then ask the nurse about her regrets," said Murray. "Leave me alone."

"As you wish," said Gavin, and he picked up his Kindle and began reading again.

Murray lay in his bed and fumed. Gavin had opened a door he preferred to keep closed, and now it was stuck. God damn it. God damn it all.

"You know what else I regret?" said Gavin.

"What?"

"I regret not being a little stricter with my daughter. You saw her. She's not very polite, is she? Too spoiled. I wish I'd taught her some better manners. You should have seen how rude she was to your son yesterday. I was embarrassed."

"Manners were a priority for my family," Murray said, proud to be able to boast a little. "When my kids answered the phone, they had to say 'Blaire residence; this is Ruth speaking.' Though Lillian was the strict one," he admitted. "I was the good cop. Except when it came to Daniel. Then we seemed to reverse roles. If Daniel wanted something, Lillian often made sure he got it."

He thought back to the day of the accident, Daniel wanting to take two cars to the rally so he wouldn't have to stay in town while Murray went to the VFW afterward (or, horrors, so he wouldn't have to walk home). Lillian had been against it—she thought it was a waste of gas—but then George had spilled chocolate syrup on his shirt, so she relented. He wished he'd stepped in that day and made the family go in one car.

That was a regret.

Not that he was going to share this with Gavin.

"Did Lizzie ever talk about her mother?" he asked, suddenly curious.

"Not a lot."

"Her other brother?"

"Only in the context of the accident."

"What did she say?"

"Now *there's* a lady with regrets. Mainly she regrets fighting with him in the car that night. Blames herself for the accident."

"Phooey," said Murray. "The accident wasn't Lizzie's fault. Lillian was used to the kids fighting. She could stay cool as a cucumber."

"It's not hard to imagine," Gavin went on, as though Murray hadn't spoken. "Kids horsing around while you're driving—it gets very distracting, and maybe she snapped. Once I was taking my daughter and a couple of her friends to camp and they started a pillow fight! Right there in the backseat! Feathers flying everywhere, I couldn't see anything out the rearview mirror and I had to pull over, I was so mad at them. Another time—"

"Will you please shut up?" said Murray. "Lizzie didn't cause the accident."

"How do you know? You weren't there."

"Never mind how."

"What, so now you're God?"

"Trust me," said Murray. "It wasn't her fault."

"Well, she certainly thinks it was. There was some kind of scuffle. Then boom, boom, out go the lights. Can't really argue with that, can you?"

"Well, Lizzie doesn't have all the facts," said Murray.

"What facts?"

"Important facts, okay?" He didn't like where this was going. There were certain things best left unsaid, partly for Lillian's sake but also for Murray's, because the less that was said, the less he had to remember. He wasn't keen on going down memory lane here. This approach had served him well for thirty-two years and he wasn't about to change it.

But Gavin was persistent. "You really want to keep me in the dark? You really want to keep your *daughter* in the dark? Let her go around shouldering the burden for something that's not her fault, supposedly? What's the big secret? You think I'm going to hold a press conference? God, you New Englanders, you're so tight-lipped—"

"Stop," said Murray.

"I'm not kidding! You—"

"*Stop*, I said." Something in his tone convinced Gavin to fall silent. Murray smoothed the corners of his mouth with his thumb and forefinger. He thought and thought, and realized that nobody was around to give a flying fuck anymore, except his children.

And so he said to Gavin what he'd never said to anyone. "Lillian was intoxicated."

Gavin waited.

"That's right," said Murray. "My wife was drunk." *What do you mean, she was drunk?* This to the coroner.

Gavin remained silent, and Murray gazed out the window. He watched a woodchuck waddle across the hospital lawn, heading for the nearby bushes. Odd time of day, for a woodchuck.

Finally Gavin said, "How drunk?"

Murray sniffed deeply, an inward sigh. "Point one one. It was snowing and she'd had a couple of cocktails, and she lost control of the car while going down a steep hill. Maybe the kids were fighting, maybe she got a little distracted, but the main reason was that she was DWI."

Gavin seemed to consider this without judgment. "How come this wasn't all over the front page? You were a candidate for Congress. It was right before the election."

"Because," Murray began, because really, fuck it, who cared anymore; he was eighty-one years old and could have another stroke any time and this had all happened thirty-two years ago, "because the coroner was a friend of mine. There was a toxicology report."

"And what, he changed it?"

"That's right."

"At your request."

"Correct."

Gavin gave a low whistle. "And so nobody found out she was drunk?"

"Oh, there was probably some speculation, especially among the folks who fed her the cocktails—who in my view were the real criminals, but that's another matter. In any case, no. Officially her blood alcohol level was listed as a mere point oh three."

"And nobody came forward, all these years?"

"Hey, we were all friends. Everybody felt sorry for me. Why would they want to tarnish Lillian's name?"

Slowly Gavin began to nod. "And the kids, they don't know either, do they? Which is why Elizabeth has assumed it was her fault."

"Nobody knows about the original report, except you, now," said Murray. "The coroner is dead. I'll probably regret telling you this," he added. "I'd appreciate your discretion."

"Why would I care to tell anyone? I may be an ass some of the time, but I'm not gratuitously mean."

"I'm not kidding," said Murray.

"Neither am I. But if you don't mind my saying so, you really should tell the kids."

"I'll tell them," said Murray, "but I'll tell them on my own schedule. You stay out of it."

"The sooner the better, I say. Tell them when they come back. You might be on your deathbed, you know."

Murray snorted. "Hardly." He looked at his watch. The kids were due in with the pizza in half an hour. It troubled him deeply that his daughter was going around shouldering the burden for the accident. That she had never said anything to him suddenly spoke volumes about his failures as a father, for being such a closed book about it all. For being unapproachable. In retrospect now, his nondisclosure seemed like a gross lack of judgment; he definitely should have told Ruth, who at seventeen could have comprehended the need for discretion. In due time he could have told George and Lizzie, too.

Instead, he didn't talk about it at all, partly because he didn't want the kids to think poorly of their mother, but mostly because he was afraid that talking about it would have unleashed all the anger and grief he himself was barely keeping in check. There were a lot of questions, for instance, that perpetually threatened to unhinge his sanity. *Why didn't you just tell Chuck no thank you? Why didn't you wait for me to get home? How could you have been so clueless about how drunk you were? Why, why, why? You took away my son, Lillian!*

And what do you do with questions like this? You put a muzzle on, that's what. Murray, after all, was a northern New Englander deep in his bones, prone to restraint and the cultivation of a calm demeanor; he was afraid if he opened up with the kids, the agony of it all would just quadruple in volume.

So he said nothing. Shared nothing.

Although at some point after the accident he did confront one person: Chuck White. He wanted a scapegoat. He fudged the facts a little. He didn't reveal Lillian's true blood alcohol level, but, knowing Chuck's tendencies as a host, he wanted Chuck to assume some of the responsibility. So he went to Chuck, got Chuck's version of the evening. When Chuck mentioned he was serving cocktails, Murray let his anger show. "What were you thinking?" he demanded. "Pushing a couple of drinks on her?" The family dentist drew back defensively. "I didn't push them," he said. "I merely offered, and she took. Besides, we all go out, have a couple of drinks, drive home. She was fine."

Well, no, she wasn't fine, he thought now, recalling the conversation. But he was right about the culture. Standards were different then. Forget any notions of designated drivers back in 1984. Unless you were falling down drunk, you drove.

Murray, incidentally, found a new dentist.

"Admit it," said Gavin. "You know I'm right. Tell the kids. Really, old man: What have you got to lose?"

He was right, and Murray knew it. Yet just thinking about telling the kids raised his heart rate—he could feel the pace pick up and hear the corresponding beeps on the heart monitor. To calm himself, he turned onto his side, away from Gavin, and closed his eyes and thought of that town in Mexico he'd looked at. Gavin said something, but he didn't answer. He pictured the sandy beach, the gentle waves, the salty, humid air. The smell of fish and coconut; the sun going down in a giant flaming ball over the Pacific. These images, culled from years of *Travel and Leisure* magazines, did in fact settle him down, and when Gavin said something else, he still didn't respond and Gavin must have gotten the message because he stopped talking and the room fell silent and Murray was left to float on his back in the warm waters of a southern sea full of colorful fish.

After a while one of the nurses came in to check his vitals. He opened his eyes. Her scrubs were printed with butterflies. He asked if any spare rooms had opened up.

"You're still wanting to get rid of me?" Gavin said to him. "After all we've been through together?"

"I would like a little privacy when my children are here," Murray said.

But he was told by the nurse that there had been a crash over in Vermont and the ER had three more admits. "So, no," she said.

"Maybe you could give this guy a sleeping pill," Murray joked.

The young nurse didn't have much of a sense of humor. She lifted Gavin's sheet and inspected his leg.

"Or maybe someone in another room would like to switch with me," Murray said.

"Dude," said Gavin. "Give it up. We're stuck with each other. When do I get to see a dinner menu?" he asked the nurse.

"Shortly," the nurse replied. She left the room with her entourage of butterflies.

"You know, it probably was a little bit of both," Gavin said.

"Both what?" said Murray.

"DWI *and* a scuffle," said Gavin. "*And* bad weather. The combination of all those things."

"Drunk driving trumps everything," said Murray. "Hey. Don't make me regret that I told you about all this."

"Don't be so paranoid," said Gavin. He adjusted the sheet around his legs, wincing as he did so, then squinted at his bandaged paw, as though reading an X-ray.

"I hope they're serving osso bucco," he said, to no one in particular.

15.

Fault Lines

LIZZIE NEVER WOULD HAVE SAID THIS OUT LOUD, BUT SHE thought Ruth should pay for the pizzas, since she was rich; and Ruth did pay, although she made a comment about how Dad would probably insist on reimbursing her, which Lizzie thought was incredibly tacky, since Ruth was rich. After the morning's argument, there was a fragile accord between them; Ruth's accusation that Lizzie had caused Murray's TIA still hung over her like a spectral presence. Had she? Was she just one happy trigger in the family? For the good of her siblings, Lizzie spent the rest of the day trying her best to ignore the accusation so she wouldn't get riled up again. In any case, they got the pizzas, and on the way to the hospital, she and Ruth teamed up to keep George from scarfing a piece.

And anyway, she had a more immediate worry on her mind, which was seeing Gavin. As they climbed the stairs to the second floor, she decided to wait out in the hall. "You guys are right, it's probably not a good idea for me to be in the same room with him."

She was met with no resistance: George promised to bring some food out to her—and wine, for Ruth had snuck in a bottle in her large purse.

"What do we say when Gavin asks where I am?" Lizzie said.

"We just say you're on your way. Let him wonder," said Ruth. It was a plan, and Ruth always liked a good plan.

So in the seating area just outside the door to the room, Lizzie settled into a tweedy chair while her siblings went in. "Shh," she heard her father say, and she got her hopes up because maybe Gavin was sound asleep and she could sneak in and just keep her mouth shut. But that would have been too risky, and anyway then she heard him cough and grunt and make a dry smacking noise with his lips; so she stayed where she was, and then there was the pop of a cork and she hoped George would bring her a good hefty glass of wine because the thought was boiling up again, what a dickwad Gavin was.

"I hope I'm invited to the party," she heard Gavin say.

Oh my God. Seriously?

"You're not," said Murray. "Where's Lizzie?"

"She'll be along," said Ruth.

"I hope she's not staying away because of me," said Gavin. "Why, thank you, Ruth. At least someone in the family has some manners. What is this, a Pinot Noir?"

Ruth!

"God, Ruth," said George. "Just a splash would have been fine."

"Ruth, maybe you could pull the curtain all the way shut, just to give us a bit of privacy," Murray said.

Lizzie heard the swish of curtain bearings. She figured it was safe as long as she didn't make any noise, so she went to the doorway, waved at her father, put her finger to her lips, and tiptoed in. Her father still hadn't had a chance to shave; his whiskers grew unevenly, giving him a splotchy, criminal look.

Carefully she took the wine from George and began to tiptoe away.

"Well, well, well," Gavin said through the curtain.

"Oh, for Pete's sake," sputtered Murray. "Have you no sense of social decency?"

Slowly Lizzie drew Gavin's curtain aside. There he was, his bed tilted up forty-five degrees. His bushy eyebrows were flattened and unkempt, like a poor Halloween disguise, and the craggy lines in his face had cloned themselves, a slow march to a contemporary version of the Marlboro Man he'd perhaps once aspired to. His hospital gown, printed with little blue posies, was loose at the neck, revealing the soft, crepey depression at the base of his throat. If she was not mistaken, she spotted a tremor in his hand as he lifted his wineglass to toast her.

And she'd been attracted to this man?

Gavin nodded at Lizzie's glass. "Don't pour that wine on my Kindle, ha ha."

Which made her want to throw it in his face.

"How is your hand?" she asked.

"Aren't you nice," he said. "Or are you faking it, just so I won't sue you? You do know I might need a skin graft, right?"

"So I heard," said Lizzie. She felt as though she had an enormous sense of power over Gavin, simply by being dressed in street clothes while he was lying there in a girly hospital gown. "You shouldn't have grabbed your stupid teakettle from me."

"You shouldn't have doused my laptop in the first place. Got a good lawyer yet?"

"Two."

"Family members don't count."

"Are you really pressing charges?" Lizzie demanded.

"Gavin. Lizzie," said Ruth. "This is really not good for Dad."

"I'm just not going to let you get away with claiming that I came after you," said Lizzie. "I don't care if your daughter was there. She's, what do you say—biased? And let's not forget. None of this would have happened if you hadn't ruined the book."

Gavin slammed his head back against the pillow. "Good God, it was just a fucking cookbook! I know it had your mother's notes in it but—really? All this? If you ask me, it's actually about the other issue."

"Yeah, well, fuck you," said Lizzie.

"What other issue?" Murray asked Lizzie.

"Nothing, Dad," she said.

"And convincing yourself that I made you do it," Gavin went on. "What a bunch of horseshit."

"You *did* make me do it," said Lizzie hotly.

"Okay," said Ruth. "I can't stand this. I'm getting a stomachache. Dad's blood pressure is I'm sure going off the charts. Whatever little secret you're talking about, stop it, you two. Just stop it. I call Quaker Meeting."

Lizzie glared at Gavin, who shrugged dismissively.

"I have a proposal," said George. "Why don't you two just apologize to each other, and let it go? Gavin, say you're sorry for drop-ping the cookbook into the sink. Lizzie, say you're sorry for pouring hot water on his laptop. Agree to disagree on whether Lizzie in-tended to pour hot water on your hand, or whether it was an acci-dent. Then let it go."

"Nice, George," said Ruth, surprised.

"Gavin?" said George.

"I'll think about it," he said. "But that's all I can promise."

"Lizzie?"

"Forget it," said Lizzie. "He's got so much to apologize for, I don't know where to begin. And no, I'm not going to go into it. I think I'll go back out in the hall," she told her family. "I never should have come in." She lifted her hair off the back of her neck, which had gone hot and prickly. "This is not conducive to good digestion, as Mom would have said."

"Wait," said Gavin, glancing at Murray. "Before you go, I think your father has something he wants to say to you."

Murray turned to stare. "Excuse me?"

"Dude," Gavin said.

"I absolutely do not," Murray said. "Lizzie's right, this is a terri-ble forum for anything of substance. And please don't 'dude' me any-more, either," he added. "I hate that word."

"What a family," said Gavin. "I think you'd all do well to say what's on your mind a little more often so it wouldn't come out in these twisted ways."

"Drop it, Gavin," Murray warned.

"Seriously—you've been carrying this big secret around for the last century. Your kids are grown adults. They should know."

"Know what?" Ruth asked.

Murray glared at Gavin. "Don't you dare try to orchestrate things like this. I don't need you pushing me. I don't need encouragement. I'll tell them in my own due time and you better believe it won't be in your presence."

"What big secret?" Ruth said.

"Ruth," said George in a low voice. "Leave it alone."

"But this is such a good opportunity," Gavin told Murray. "You've got everybody here, and if you get too emotional and your blood pressure goes wacky, you're in a hospital. I wouldn't wait a minute longer. If only for Lizzie's sake. You don't want her to shoulder the blame any longer than necessary."

Lizzie thought: *Blame?*

"For the car accident," said Gavin, reading her mind. "I happened to mention that you thought it was your fault."

"I'm gonna kill you," Murray told Gavin.

"It *was* my fault," Lizzie said, "and thank you, Gavin, but I'd appreciate you not blabbing about things we once talked about in private."

"Excuse me, people?" Murray said loudly. "Excuse me, all of you? I would like to put an end to this conversation. Right now."

"No you wouldn't," said Gavin cheerfully. "It's just that you wish I weren't here. If it weren't for my presence, you'd be relieved this conversation was about to take place. You'd feel like you were going to be getting a load off your shoulders. So! I have a proposal. Actually, it's not a proposal, it's a statement of intent, which is that I am just going to remove myself from the presence of this family."

"You can't leave," said Murray. "You've got that doohickey with the IV on your arm."

"So? Get me a wheelchair," he ordered George, and Lizzie watched in dismay as her brother obeyed this man as though he were his boss and vanished out the door. In less than a minute he returned with a wheelchair and deftly disconnected Gavin's IV from the buff cap and helped him get seated.

"And now," Gavin said, waving away George's offer of further help, "I bid you all adieu." And as though he'd spent years in a wheelchair, he used his arms to spin around in a three-point turn and wheeled himself out of the room.

Baffled by this sudden turn of events, and having no idea what to expect next, Lizzie turned to her father. "What the hell, Dad."

"Yeah, Dad," said Ruth. "What's going on?"

"Be nice, everyone," said George.

Murray shook his head, and regarded his hands while his children waited.

"Maybe we should leave," George suggested. "Maybe you're tired, Dad."

"No, don't leave." Murray rubbed his chin. "Look. I never thought I would be talking to you kids about this issue," he said. "I thought I would take it to the grave. But certain events in the past twenty-four hours have led me to believe that there is no sense in keeping mum for the rest of my life. Especially given the fact that you, Lizzie, seem to think the accident was caused by something you did."

He spoke calmly but firmly, and very rationally, like the lawyer he was. Lizzie began to object, but her father held up his hand. "The accident wasn't your fault, Lizzie."

Lizzie didn't want to argue with him. The accident was indeed her fault, but she didn't want to go into the details, which were best left with the therapist she saw once a month.

"You see, there's something I should have told you kids a long time ago," Murray said ruefully.

"Daniel was driving?" guessed Ruth. "I've always wondered about that."

"No, Daniel wasn't driving," said Murray. "I want you all to listen. And listen closely. Your mother was driving, and she was drunk."

The three Blaire children reacted in silence. They were, in fact, stunned. For Lizzie, the blunt force of the word felt like a punch in the chest. *Drunk*. Not *she had a little too much to drink*, but *drunk*. She tried to remember her mother stumbling, slurring her words. She couldn't come up with anything. She was only six, though! That was far too young to appreciate the nuances of cocktail hour.

George was leaning against the windowsill, arms folded. "Like, just how drunk?"

"Well, her blood alcohol level was point one one."

"Okay," said George, nodding, "okay, I guess that's pretty drunk."

Murray continued: "Remember how she stopped at the Whites' so Daniel could get his lab notes from their daughter? Well, they were having a little get-together with another couple, and they invited your mother in."

Lillian, my dear, you look like you could use a Manhattan.

"And according to Chuck, your mother said no but then changed her mind." *Oh, live a little, Mrs. Blaire.* "She made some comment about how she would call me for a ride home if she needed to. Or she would let Daniel drive if it wasn't snowing too hard. Daniel had just gotten his learner's permit, if you recall."

Ruth blew a puff of outrage. "'If it wasn't snowing too hard?' It was already snowing, the roads were a mess—and she was going to let him drive at night? With Lizzie in the car? I can't imagine letting Caleb drive under those circumstances. And I find it hard to believe that Mom would, either."

Murray shrugged. "It wasn't the best of plans. But I imagine she truly thought she'd covered herself. So she had one drink. Then another, according to Chuck."

"Two drinks?" said George. "And that gets her smashed?"

Lizzie recalled Dr. White handing her a glass of ginger ale with a maraschino cherry in it. *Say thank you, Lizzie.* She remembered the nubby, coarse texture of the fabric on the chair in which she was told to stay put while the adults conversed; her mother putting a cigarette between her lips, the oily smell as she flicked the stainless-steel lighter. The silver charm bracelet she'd been wearing, with its four flat silhouettes: two girls, two boys. What happened to that bracelet?

"It wasn't just two drinks, but I'll get to that," Murray said. "So they're having a good time, Daniel and Jennifer were upstairs in her bedroom, and outside the snow was building up and finally your mother decided it was time to go. She apparently looked out and made a decision and phoned the house, as planned, but I didn't answer—I was still at the VFW. No cell phones back then, remember. So on to Plan B. Chuck called the kids to come downstairs."

No, actually: that wasn't the way it happened. Lizzie herself went upstairs first, at Chuck's request. She remembered the glossy banister, the tightly carpeted steps with their brass rods against the instep. The locked door. The laughter.

"And this is where things got interesting," Murray went on. "The kids, it turned out, were upstairs getting high. And when they came down, everyone could see that a stoned-out fifteen-year-old with a learner's permit was in no shape to take a little driving lesson in the snow. At night, as you said, Ruth—with another child in the car. So your mother said she was fine to drive. And according to Chuck, she *was* fine."

"Still, Chuck was liable," Ruth said angrily.

"New Hampshire didn't have a social host liability law back then," Murray said. "Although believe me, I wished it did. But in any case, ultimately it was your mother's responsibility," he continued. "It wasn't just the two drinks, either. She'd been drinking before. You see, I found a flask in her purse later on at the hospital, half full of vodka. Which surprised me. Sneaky of her, drinking vodka. Of course I immediately wondered if she made a regular habit of this or if it was just that day. I'll never know, but regardless: she'd obviously been drinking before she got to the Whites'."

"Drinking enough to get her to point one one," said George.

"Exactly," said Murray. "And Chuck certainly had no idea your mother had been nipping at the vodka earlier. As far as he was concerned, she simply had a couple of cocktails, like everyone else. Which back then wasn't viewed as so bad."

The room fell silent again. Lizzie watched as Ruth went over to the sink and washed her hands. Really washed them. She flung the droplets of water off, then yanked two paper towels out of the dispenser. Lizzie thought there was a bit too much drama in her actions.

As did Murray, apparently. "All right, Ruth," he said. "What's the matter? Surely this doesn't come as a surprise to you. Surely you knew your mother had a bit of a drinking problem."

"I never kept count!" Ruth exclaimed. "Besides, what's the *matter*"—carefully wiping her hands—"is I'm just wondering why you haven't said anything all these years." She dropped the paper towels into the trash from on high, as though avoiding contamination.

"It was a mistake," said Murray flatly. "No good reason."

"And why now?" said Ruth.

"Because of what Gavin told me," Murray replied. "About Lizzie thinking it was her fault. It wasn't."

Yes, it was.

"Why wasn't this all over the news?" said Ruth. "'Candidate's Wife Driving While Intoxicated.' The media would have had a field day."

Slowly, and with great deliberation, Murray tapped his thigh. "Because I confiscated the flask before the police could find it."

"And the autopsy report?" said Ruth.

"I got Mo Green to change it."

"For the sake of the campaign?" said Ruth. "Great, Dad."

Murray looked up sharply. "Oh, I didn't give two hoots about the campaign at that point. I just wanted to save your mother's name. What's the matter now?"

"I'm fine," said Ruth, reclipping her hair; but Lizzie could tell from the haughtily raised eyebrows that she was decidedly not fine.

She herself didn't care if her mother was drunk or not. It still didn't change things.

"I'm totally fine," Ruth continued. "I just found out my mother drove drunk and caused an accident that killed my brother, and my father withheld evidence and falsified an official report."

"Don't go down that road," George advised.

"Why not?" Ruth shot back. "It's true. How could Mom have done that?" she demanded. "How could she have gotten behind the wheel? Why didn't she just ask for a cup of coffee? That's just common sense. And you, Dad! That's called tampering with the evidence. Just to keep her name clean?"

"And I would do it again, Ruth," Murray said evenly. "I wouldn't think twice about it. That's one regret I don't have. And it won't do any good to be angry at your mother," he added. "Believe me, I spent a lot of years being angry and it got me nowhere."

"Yeah, well, whatever. Because when I think of it, she screwed up our whole family with that accident," Ruth said.

George looked puzzled. "We're screwed up?"

"Yes, we're screwed up," said Ruth. "Lizzie still acts like a six-year-old. You refuse to have kids. And I have to look out for everybody because at the age of seventeen I suddenly had to cook dinner and make lunches and deal with nightmares and homework. When all I wanted was to go to Georgetown and wear my sweaters draped over my shoulders and volunteer as a page up on Capitol Hill."

"I'm sorry," said Murray.

"It's not your fault," Ruth grumbled.

"I know that," said Murray. "I'm just stating a fact. I'm sorry about all this. And anyway, we're not done."

"We're not?" said George.

"No, we're not. I don't want Lizzie leaving this room still thinking the accident was her fault."

"Oh, Dad," Lizzie sighed. "Please."

"Might as well dump your garbage on the table," Ruth told her. "Seeing as Dad did."

"I'm not Dad," Lizzie said.

"But you're carrying something around," said Murray. "It would help me to know what it is."

One reason she didn't want to tell them was because she hated remembering the details. They made her feel unclean.

"You're with family," George reminded her gently.

Lizzie saw that if even George was pressing her now, she would never get out of it. Maybe she could keep it vague, though. She cocked her head. "Look, I was a brat, okay? I was teasing Daniel and let's just say I took it a little too far."

"How so?" Ruth asked.

Leave it to Ruth. "Trust me, I just did."

"Like how, though?"

"Oh, come on, Ruth, really? I did something gross. Leave it at that."

"Gross like what?"

"I'd like to know, too," Murray said.

"How bad can it be?" asked George.

Lizzie felt herself grow hot with anger. Really? They wanted details? Fine, she'd give them details. And then *they* would be stuck with the image. *They'd* get to carry it around for the next thirty years.

"Fine," she said. "I was in the backseat, and Daniel was sitting up front, and I kept getting up and squatting behind him. 'Daniel and Jennifer, sitting in the tree,' I went, 'K-I-S-S-I-N-G.' Remember that one? And Mom was telling me to sit down but Daniel was ignoring me and I wanted to get his attention—" She paused abruptly, remembering the sensation. Warm. Oily.

"And so?" said Ruth.

"And so I poked my little finger into his ear, Ruth. Deep," she added. "Like Q-tip deep."

"Oh, ick," said Ruth.

"You want to make this as hard as possible for me?" said Lizzie evenly. "Keep judging me."

"I take it Daniel reacted," Murray said.

"Of course! He whipped around and shoved me, and I shoved him back, and Mom swung her arm out to try and separate us. Like a rogue turnstile," she said, recalling her mother's movement. "Twisting around, and then swerving, then braking, and—well, we know the rest. Satisfied now?"

"Lizzie, Lizzie," said Murray, shaking his head. "You were just a kid."

"A kid who didn't mind! If I hadn't stuck my finger in Daniel's ear, he wouldn't have freaked out, and Mom wouldn't have lost control. You have to admit I played a role that night. Right, Ruth? You're so quick to judge. Tell me it wasn't my fault."

Ruth didn't reply, and Lizzie looked at the ceiling. George handed her a tissue.

"Under better circumstances your mother wouldn't have lost control like that," Murray admitted. "But you really can't trace it all back to you. That's too heavy a load for a child to bear. And you've thought this your whole life? Oh, I'm such a fool for not telling you all."

Lizzie glanced at her father. Everything in his face—eyes, cheeks, jowls—sagged like Silly Putty. A queer, bruised light filled the room, a harbinger of winter skies even though it was only mid-September. Ruth had tucked her hands under her armpits, as though cold. George sat in the guest chair and cracked his knuckles. Everyone seemed like a stranger. Who was this family of hers?

Suddenly the door lever rattled. "Knock knock!" Gavin leaned around the edge of the door. "How're you guys doing? Can I come back in?"

"Has that son of a bitch been right out there the whole time?" Murray demanded.

"No," said Gavin, wheeling himself into the room. "I was down flirting with the nurses. Got a couple of phone numbers. Ha! Just kidding! But maybe we could switch places and you three could give Elizabeth and me a few moments."

"That," said Lizzie, "is the last thing I want."

Gavin raised his eyebrows. "I think we ourselves have some important issues to talk about."

"I'm talked out," said Lizzie.

"Oh, grow up," Gavin snapped. "Just because you were a brat then doesn't mean you have to be a brat now."

Had he indeed been out in the hall when she called herself a brat? To her dismay, Lizzie watched as George helped Gavin back into his bed and then wheeled the chair around to Murray's bedside. He unhooked his father's wires and Murray swung his legs down and with George's help he wobbled into the chair. Then George wheeled him out of the room, with Ruth close behind. Lizzie started to follow, but Murray told her to stay.

"Maybe you two can get to the bottom of your differences," he said over his shoulder. "And then we won't have any more family members pouring hot water on the enemy's laptop."

Mad at everyone now for abandoning her—for not understanding that one major disclosure was exhausting enough for the day—Lizzie planted herself in one of the chairs, slouching in a manly way with her knees spread wide. She crossed her arms and glared at Gavin.

"Well," said Gavin.

"Well yourself," she said.

"I will admit that there are hard truths here," said Gavin, "but ultimately I think that until you deal with them, as your father said, you're going to be pouring hot water on the enemy's laptop any chance you get."

"Oh, do *not* patronize me."

"I seriously don't mean to," he said. "But let's talk about what I think is really bugging you."

"Did you not hear what I just said?"

"The problem is, you think I pressured you into it, and you're mad about that."

"You did pressure me! I never would have done it if it hadn't been for you!"

Gavin shrugged. "I made my feelings known. I never said you had to do it."

"Well, guess what. That's the message I *heard*," she said. "You explicitly said you were too old to become a father again. And you made it clear it would be unfair of me to have the baby on my own, because you're such a saint that you'd feel compelled to be involved and then resent me forever."

"I never said any such thing."

"You implied it."

"Well, you should have asked if that was indeed what I meant," Gavin shot back. "Why are you regretting it so much, anyway? You had one when you were younger and it didn't bother you in the least, you said."

"I was nineteen! I'm thirty-eight now! Haven't you heard of the biological clock?"

"Oh, pshaw, you've got lots of good years ahead of you, honey-bunch. You know what I think? I think you're really mad at yourself for getting pregnant in the first place, for that day up at Gravity. And you're also angry for not having the balls to ignore me. Look, you gotta take some responsibility here. Quit making me out to be a monster. I simply told you my true feelings. You should have told me yours. And then you should have made the right decision for yourself."

"You're ignoring how overbearing you can be at times."

Gavin sighed with exasperation. "What can I say? You ought to know how to stick up for yourself at your age."

"I wish I'd never met you," Lizzie said.

"Do you really mean that? We had a good run for the last year and a half," said Gavin. "It wasn't love, but we were good for each other in a lot of ways. You made me feel young. I made you feel wanted."

She thought back to the days after Bruce left her, when she felt like such a hollow shell. She couldn't write. She couldn't teach. One day in class, she criticized a student so harshly for misinterpreting a passage in *The Sun Also Rises* that she later summoned him to her office and apologized. She would lie in bed at night full of self-pity, thinking: *I will never have what my parents had.* It wasn't rational to feel that way—she knew the chances were that someone else would eventually come along—but there it was. It was a low point in her life.

Enter Gavin, who could make her knees shake.

She asked, "Are you really going to press charges?"

"Oh, Elizabeth," he sighed, "why don't you just admit you tried to douse me with boiling water? Then maybe I won't feel so inclined."

"Fine," said Lizzie. "I tried to douse you with boiling water."

"No, you have to say it and mean it. You don't mean it. You're just saying it."

"Oh, who knows," Lizzie groaned. "The whole thing happened in a split second. Suddenly you were trying to grab the teakettle and maybe I—I don't know! And how was I supposed to know it was hot enough to cause a second-degree burn?"

"It had just boiled! There was steam coming out of the spout!"

And she was supposed to notice something like that, in the heat of an argument? "So are you going to sue me or not?"

Gavin regarded her with narrowed eyes. "The aggravation of a lawsuit alone would outweigh any benefit I might reap," he said. "So no, I'm not going to personally sue you. But that doesn't mean the law isn't going to come after you as a criminal."

"Ruth says they won't, if you don't want to press charges."

"It's up to them."

"No, Gavin. It's up to you. Ball's in your court. If you won't testify, they don't have a case. Do you really feel comfortable saying it was *all* my fault?"

Gavin regarded his knuckles. "I will grant you that I reacted with extreme emotion when I saw you pouring hot water on my laptop."

"Which I'll pay for, I told you."

"Darn tootin'."

"But there's still the ruined cookbook. You're not going to be able to replace that."

"Well, I guess I'll regret my clumsiness."

"'Sorry' not being in your vocabulary?"

"No," said Gavin. "Or yes. Because I'm truly sorry you're regretting what you did. I wish I could turn back the clock for you."

He looked at her from beneath his heavy-lidded eyes then, and she saw the face of a humbler man, a face that had probably always been there but that she had refused to see because a large part of her attraction to him had been based on his always being two steps ahead of her. In life. In wisdom. But he wasn't, really. He was just a guy with a complicated, mixed-up heart, like any other fellow. She should have seen him for what he was, all along.

"Thank you," she said. "I appreciate you saying that. I didn't think you had it in you."

Gavin shrugged. "I'm nicer than you think."

THE DOCTOR WANTED TO KEEP Murray overnight for observation, so Ruth, Lizzie, and George went back to the house without him. Lizzie found it unsettling, being in the farmhouse without her father. Strange places ticked. A pipe knocked. Windows rattled. His absence was tangible, from the unmade bed to the empty coat hook in the front hall.

Nobody asked her just what went on with Gavin in the privacy of the hospital room, but she did volunteer that Gavin wasn't going to sue her personally, and that he probably wasn't going to press charges with the police. Once home Ruth set about going through a box of their father's papers—his trust documents and will and various codicils—and George went to take a long shower, so Lizzie sequestered herself up in the twin bedroom and read through her students' papers. Halfway through, she found herself nodding off, so she went downstairs, where she saw Ruth presiding over multiple stacks on the dining room table, fuming that Murray as a lawyer hadn't organized things better.

"I hope Dad doesn't disinherit me for my little number with Gavin's laptop," Lizzie said, looking at all the papers. "Joke," she added.

"I know it's a joke," said Ruth. "I'm laughing on the inside."

Lizzie wondered if Ruth was any less angry at Lillian, now that she'd had time to digest the news about her mother's state that night. It had to be hard, she thought, for she knew Ruth had idealized their mother all these years. Ruth had some reckoning to do, but Ruth could bear a grudge like a Puritan, and Lizzie imagined her dismantling the shrines throughout her house. It could be another thirty years before she got over this.

But Lizzie didn't want to delve into the issue right now. There'd been enough wrenching discussion for one day.

"What time's your plane tomorrow?" she asked.

"Three o'clock," said Ruth. "I'm thinking of staying another night, though. Maybe even two. Though Morgan won't like that," she added. "He won't be able to get his daily bike miles in, and he'll be required to plan some meals. Horrors."

Morgan could be a real dick sometimes.

"But you know? Morgan can suck it up," Ruth added.

Lizzie wondered if this attitude had been born of its own, or if Gavin's comments about their family needing to get things out in the open a little more had had something to do with it. It was only later that evening, when listening to Ruth talk to Morgan and explain she wasn't leaving tomorrow, and tell him that she thought there were a few fundamental things wrong with their marriage, and would he finally agree to marriage counseling, because her needs weren't being met in more ways than one, and "No, Morgan, the fact that you cook breakfast on Sunday morning when nobody really even likes your banana pancakes isn't enough, nor is the fact that you keep telling me to go to the gym but don't make it easy for me to do so, and no, I don't *think* a divorce is in the cards, and this isn't about Charlene, and don't be ridiculous we shouldn't even be discussing custody—unless you have your own point to make—and this is why we need some counseling, and if you don't go, I'll go myself and the counselor will get a very one-sided story"—it was only after this that Lizzie saw Ruth as having undergone some kind of tectonic shift during the weekend.

At which point Lizzie felt like her eavesdropping bordered on snooping, so she went back upstairs. She started to walk past her father's bedroom, with its unmade bed and piles of clothes, then changed her mind and went in. The room smelled of menthol and old leather. After gathering up yesterday's clothes, she started straightening the sheets, and while she was doing this George joined her, and the two of them worked together to make up their father's bed, one on each side, pulling the sheets taut the way he liked them.

"I never make my bed," Lizzie said, giving a little grunt as she tucked in a corner.

"Waste of time," George agreed.

"I bet Ruth does."

"Every day. Sure as the sun comes up."

There was a brief pause.

"I had an abortion, George," she said, feeling a lump in her throat. "A month ago."

George straightened up. "Jeez. How come you didn't tell me until now?"

"I don't know. I really wish I hadn't, this time," she said, as tears welled up. "I want a child."

"I'm so sorry."

She took a tissue from the box on her father's bedside table. "I'll get over it," she said. "I just wish I'd put my foot down."

"Gavin didn't want it?"

She shook her head.

"We've all been involved with assholes, you know," said George. "Remember LuAnn?"

"Oh! She was a bitch."

They drew up the bedspread, making sure its hem was even all around.

"What's happening with that woman you were seeing this summer?" Lizzie asked, in need of an abrupt subject change.

"It's on hold."

"Don't be a fool, George. She was nice. She was decent."

"It's the kid thing. Unlike you, I'm too afraid to have one. Crazy, isn't it?"

"No shit. Get over it."

"How?"

"Do the math. Dad had four kids, and then there were three. You think he regrets any one of us? Worry is a fact of life, George." She threw away the used tissues that Murray had left crumpled on his nightstand. "Did you know Mom was drunk that night?"

"No. Maybe it occurred to me later, when I was taking driver's ed and they were making such a big deal of us not driving drunk. It probably crossed my mind. But I figured we'd have heard about it, if she were. It would have been a huge scandal."

"Do you think she was an alcoholic?"

"If she was, she was pretty high functioning. She got breakfast. She made our lunches. She wrote all day and then fixed dinner and cleaned up and put us to bed with a kiss."

Lizzie recalled her mother tucking her in, glass in hand. *Mom's soda.* Once Lizzie took a sip, and Lillian whacked her bottom.

Now she tried to plump a pillow, but it simply folded back on itself. "Why does Dad have such ratty pillows?!"

"He's cheap."

"They'll discharge him tomorrow, won't they?"

"That's the plan."

"He looks so old sometimes."

"He is old."

"Just not old enough for the Pines," said Lizzie.

"I don't think he'll ever be old enough for the Pines," said George.

16.

Whose Business Is It, Anyway?

WHEN THE ORDERLY CAME IN THE NIGHT TO MOVE GAVIN to another room, Murray was free-floating, recalling the time that Lillian broke her ankle while skiing. She'd fallen on a steep slope and skidded most of the way down, then got up and skied to the bottom with pain in her foot, insisting it was nothing serious. Only when her ankle swelled up like a baseball that night did she agree to get an X-ray.

They ate a lot of pot pies during those eight weeks when she was on crutches, and the kids got used to walking everywhere, since she couldn't drive. Murray recalled how she had him move her typewriter from her third-story room down into their bedroom. White pages began littering the floor. She gave him one story to read, but when he made a few suggestions, she took it back without a word and that was the end of her showing him her work. At the time he got huffy. He was just trying to help! Now he looked back and realized she didn't want help, she simply wanted an audience. Someone to say, *Hey, I enjoyed it!* That was all. Why couldn't he see it then?

Why hadn't he ever been more attuned to her needs? Why had everything always been about him?

And what good had it done to be angry at her, all those years after the accident? He recalled the nights after the first year or so, when he would lie in bed with his hand on the depression next to him, his anger seeping into the mattress like his own tears. It ate away at him without his realizing it. He took it out on his kids. Yelled at George for a little dent in the car. Grounded Lizzie for talking back to her teachers. Eventually, several years after the accident, his state of mind reached a point where, at the suggestion of one of his partners, he sought the help of a therapist. He'd never felt so weak and diminished in his life. It humiliated him to sit there in her office and try to articulate his anger. She told him to punch a pillow. Snap a rubber band against his wrist. Finally she suggested he picture his anger as a wave on the ocean, and let it pass by. This seemed too simple to work, but over time he did find that it helped. One morning he woke up and ran his hand over Lillian's side of the mattress and found that he couldn't locate the depression any more. He stopped yelling at the kids. He said yes when Ruth, a sophomore in college at the time, asked if she could go to Florida over spring break. He unpacked from storage the framed photo of Lillian sitting in the wicker chair in her yellow dress and placed it back on his bureau.

Now, thinking of that photograph as he lay in bed, Murray wished he had it with him. He made a note to himself: If he ever had to go into the hospital for an extended stay, he would make sure to bring it. As well as some photos of the kids: all four of them. *Aren't they a good-looking bunch*, the nurses would say. *Aren't you lucky.*

Was he?

Daniel would be forty-seven by now.

A book with a missing chapter. A court case with a hole. A *life* with a hole. You never get over it.

The orderly tried to be quiet as he helped Gavin into a wheel-chair, but Murray was wide awake. He could see Gavin's slumped figure in the chair. Why did people look so vulnerable, from the back? And why did they have to move him?

"Why do you have to move him?"

"I don't know, I just do what I'm told," said the orderly.

"Off to greener pastures, dude," said Gavin over his shoulder.

"Heal," said Murray. "Watch your blood sugar. And drop the case."

"Toodly-oo," Gavin said.

Alone in the room, Murray's ears rang in the relative silence. He felt the blood pressure machine squeeze and release. He tasted sludge and wished he could brush his teeth again. In a short while, somebody new was brought in—a groaner, as it turned out. Murray pretended to be asleep.

But he was never asleep. At one point he pictured the fishing village in Mexico again. He saw a marina, a rocky cliff, a long sandy beach lined with hotels that twinkled at night. There was a travel agency he'd been checking out online, because he wasn't quite sure how this Airbnb thing worked, but he wanted something other than a hotel room on a beach. He wanted street life, markets, a hot plate in his room at the very least to cook foods he'd never seen before. You could eat cactus, he'd heard!

He'd never been very good with languages, but he'd been studying a little and was sure that if you gave him a month in a Latin country, he'd be fluent in Spanish. The locals would compliment him. He imagined getting to know the real estate market: *Se vende*, *se rente*. If he stayed there long enough, maybe he would buy a *casita* and become a full-time resident. Drawn to him as always by the laws of gravity, the children would come to visit, and they would marvel at his independence, how easily he negotiated with the tile vendors, with *el plomero*. They would take back everything they had warned him against and listen in awe as he bargained at the market. He would arrange to take them all deep-sea fishing, and at the end of the day they would grill their catch, drinking *cervezas* and *vino blanco*.

"Dad," they would begin.

"Papa," he would correct them.

In his head he dialed the travel agency.

"Buenas Aventuras," he heard them say. "How may I help you?"

THE CALL CAME AT 2:58 A.M. Ruth knew the time because she'd turned the illuminated clock on the bedside table to face in her direction so she could get up and do some yoga before Lizzie and George made their morning appearances.

No middle-of-the-night phone call ever brought good news.

"Is this the Blaire household?" said the woman on the other end.

Ruth began to quake.

"It's about your father," the woman went on, "he suffered a massive, fatal stroke."

Ruth heard herself say, quite stupidly, "But is he all right?" and the woman on the other end said, "No, you must not have heard me, dear, I said it was *fatal*."

Across from her in the other twin bed, Lizzie had propped herself up on her elbow and turned on the light.

"Please, no," she begged.

Ruth hung up the phone. She looked at her sister and nodded, but the nod turned into her shaking her head, and Lizzie knew because she sat up and put her hands over her face and made no sound.

Okay, Ruth thought, feeling her heart thump. *Okay. It's happened. What do we do? What comes next? Why am I not sobbing? Why isn't Lizzie? What is wrong with us?*

"What happened?" Lizzie asked in a muffled voice.

"Another stroke. This time massive."

"We have to tell George."

Together they padded barefoot down the hall to George's room. Unlike the two sisters, George cried out a choked "No!" that made both sisters finally cry and the three of them crowded onto the double bed with their arms interlocked and heads bent close.

"We should have moved him to Concord," George lamented, and neither sister could contradict him.

Despite their grief, they all agreed there was no point in going to the hospital until morning. There would be numerous decisions to make. Whether he wanted to be cremated, and if so, where did he want his ashes scattered? Or did he want a traditional burial? They all felt extremely foolish for not following through on their discussion Saturday night.

"Should we have a celebration of life, or a church funeral?" Ruth wondered aloud.

"He doesn't belong to a church," said George.

"What did we do with Mom and Daniel?" Lizzie asked.

Ruth looked surprised. "You don't remember?"

"All I remember is pans of lasagna and mountains of brownies," Lizzie replied. "Bosomy ladies squeezing my shoulder. And Dad outside, smoking."

"We had a church funeral," said Ruth. "You really don't remember that part? The two coffins, side by side? All those white lilies? It was horrible."

"Dad wore dark glasses," said George.

"Dad was a wreck," Ruth declared.

"We were *all* a wreck," said George.

Ruth covered her face with her hands. "I can't believe this," she sobbed. "We just had pizza. Do you think that did it? Or the wine? Maybe we shouldn't have given him wine."

It was a terrible thought, and they all shared it, and again, nobody could contradict her for second-guessing that which had already happened. It seemed that fault had to be assigned for them to begin to grasp the fact of Murray's death, which was a dreadful state for them to be in.

Finally Lizzie admonished them all. "Guys," she said, "this kind of thinking isn't going to do us any good. We have to keep reminding ourselves he was eighty-one. He went out on a good note. He got to see all of us, right up until the end."

Ruth blew her nose. "Yeah, at least none of us went and died on him first."

Lizzie thought that was a pretty morbid understatement.

"Because it would have killed him to lose another child," Ruth went on, nodding at her own wisdom.

"I think we should try and get some sleep," said George. "Who's going to get up and tell Boyd when he comes?"

"I will," said Lizzie. "I don't think I'm going to be able to fall asleep again."

Back in the twin bedroom, Ruth and Lizzie settled under their covers. There was no moon, and the room was very dark, although an indigo glow filled the one window. Lizzie lay on her back with her hands folded on her belly. Phase Three of their lives had now begun, that of orphanhood. She wished she'd had her own alone time with her father in the hospital—Ruth had had it; George had had it; despite the fact that she saw him most every week, she felt like she never got to say the important things on her mind, things you might say to someone who has just survived a close call. Like, for instance, how sorry she was for all the acting out she did as a teenager. Sorry for taking a semester off in college to drive around Mexico in an old school bus with faulty brakes. No cell phones then, just a weekly call home to check in with Murray, who happened to also be dealing with a dying mother. Had Lizzie really needed to "find herself" just then, and add to his stress like that?

She turned onto her side, away from Ruth, and bunched up her pillow. Her father had often said that all he wanted was for his three children to be happy in their lives. Was Ruth happy? Things with Morgan didn't seem too romantic these days, and she was always working so hard. George? He had a decent job, a passion for running, but his love life was stalled. As for herself, eighteen months of shenanigans with Gavin had gotten her nowhere. She might've at least had a child to show for her time.

Trying to sleep, her mind flitted from one irrelevant matter to another. Student papers, her gutters, Clinton, her mother's old sweaters. "Hey," she said over her shoulder. "You remember that charm bracelet Mom had?"

"The one with the silver silhouettes?"

"Right. Don't suppose you know what happened to it."

"I don't have it. I'm sure George doesn't. Maybe Dad lost it. Or gave it away. Maybe he *threw* it away."

"Oh, I hope not," Lizzie said darkly.

"There's a box somewhere," said Ruth. "Like Daniel's box, with some things of Mom's. I bet it's down in the basement or up in the attic. We can check tomorrow."

"I didn't know there was a box," said Lizzie. "I'm always poking around and I've never seen a box of Mom's."

"He just told me about it," said Ruth. "When I was in with him yesterday. He wanted me to go and find it and bring it into the living room when he came home, so he could go through it."

"Are you tired?" Lizzie asked.

"No. Are you?"

"No."

They lay in silence for a while.

"If you want the army parka, you can have it," Lizzie said.

"No, you and George figure it out," said Ruth. "I'd never wear it in DC."

"Really?"

"Really."

"Okay. That's pretty nice of you, Ruth."

"I can be very nice sometimes," said Ruth.

OVER THE YEARS Ruth had spoiled herself with good sheets, choosing high thread counts and one hundred percent cotton, and she took a simple pleasure in climbing into bed each night and moving her feet about between the cool, silken layers. Up here in New Hampshire, the sheets were old and thin and half polyester; she could tell from the pilling and the fact that she overheated at night. The pillows were old, too, all matted down, and she thought that since she was probably going to be spending a lot of time up here settling the estate, she might just go ahead and order some replacement bedding, so everyone could sleep more comfortably.

She would have to negotiate some time off from work. She used up her vacation time every year, with the trips to the shore in summer and Vail in winter. There was going to be a lot to do. Sorting the contents of the house, dividing things up and finding the best estate dealer, putting the property up for sale . . . She had no idea what the real estate market was like up here, but with all the little repairs that were needed (and she prayed it was not in fact black mold they were dealing with), she didn't foresee the house being ready for showing until at least next spring.

And the house was really packed, every nook and corner. When he'd moved out of the Concord house, Murray didn't get rid of anything; he simply transferred the contents to his new abode. No yard-sale cleanout for him. He had stuff dating back to before he and Lillian were even married—she'd seen a box labeled "Class Notes—College" up in the attic. They were going to be very busy.

Morgan was going to have to step up.

Maybe now wasn't the best time for marriage counseling.

Or maybe it was the best time ever.

As she lay there, she heard a truck rumbling up the long driveway; that would be Boyd, here to start the milking. She heard the springs creak as Lizzie climbed out of bed.

"I can go, if you want," Ruth said in the darkness.

"No, I'm wide awake. Stay in bed."

"Wake me at seven?"

"Will do."

Her sister closed the door, and Ruth lay in the dark, and wept.

SEARCHING THROUGH his father's cupboards for some decent coffee the next morning, George found the shelves punctuated by little black droppings. Some of the cracker boxes had been nibbled through. He got out the vacuum cleaner and shut the kitchen door to keep the noise from escaping, and by the time Ruth got up, he'd cleaned all the cupboards, top to bottom.

Ruth looked terrible; her hair was straggly, her eyes red-rimmed and puffy.

"Coffee," she groaned.

He appreciated her not saying anything about Murray's lack of housekeeping. The whole issue of the Pines was moot now, anyway.

"In a minute," he said. In cleaning he'd found a package of Starbucks that someone must have brought as a gift, and now he got out his father's percolator and poured grounds into the upper cup and filled the base with water. Often they tried to talk Murray into an automatic drip machine, but Murray had always resisted. "If it ain't broke, don't fix it," he'd say.

Soon the coffee was burbling up in the little glass dome, as though nothing were different today.

"Want some waffles?" he asked.

Ruth gawked at him. "Do you *ever* not have an appetite?"

George thought.

"Can't remember a time," he confessed.

Just then Lizzie came in the back door, followed by Boyd, a short man, thick around the middle, bearded, heavy-browed, with caramel-colored teeth. He wore a John Deere hat, which left a dent in his hair when he removed it.

"Just like that?" he said, shaking his head. "No warning?"

"I told him about Sunday morning," Lizzie explained. Boyd didn't work on Sundays; another man took care of the milking that day. So he hadn't known about the TIA.

"A darn shame," said Boyd. "I'm sure going to miss him. He was a good man to work for."

"Well, nothing's going to change, as far as work is concerned," said George. "We still need you."

"I appreciate that," said Boyd. "Is there going to be a service?"

"We're still tossing around ideas," said Ruth. "We'll let you know."

"If you need a tent or something for a get-together, I know some guys."

"Thanks, Boyd," said Ruth.

"You want some coffee?" asked George.

"I could use a cup," the man said.

Afterward he stood and put his hat back on, carefully locating the dent. George wished he'd spent more time in the barn with his father and Boyd, so he knew a little more about the dairy business. His father belonged to some co-op, but George had no idea how things worked. He decided not to worry about it now, to just let Boyd do his thing, and when a decision had to be made, Boyd would explain things.

Still.

Was there ever a death that involved no regret? As an ICU nurse, George had seen his share, with loved ones wailing or quietly weeping, some numbly quiet; but more often than not, what he first heard in their moment of grief was the word "should." *I should have brought him in sooner. I should have fed him more fish. I should have warned him about the rickety rung . . . the steering wheel problem . . .*

Poor Lizzie, thought George. She'd carried the weight of regret around for thirty-two years. *I shouldn't have been teasing Daniel.* George wished that he could take that regret away from her, but he sensed it was in her bones. He tried to picture the scenario. He himself hated people touching his ears, and he imagined Daniel whipping around, and Lillian reacting. Blowing her stack. She didn't do it often, but when she did, things could get physical. Once he and Daniel had been horsing around in front of the stove while she was stirring a pot of pasta. After telling them to stop for the third time, she whacked them both over the head with the pasta claw. "There's a hot burner right here, you awful boys!" she cried. George didn't bleed, but Daniel did, and he threatened to call the police on her for child abuse. It took a less frazzled Murray to calm the boy down.

Meanwhile, as the coffee brewed, Ruth was going through the sundries that George had pulled from the cupboard. Most were jams and compotes and exotic salsas that she'd brought back from her travels, gifts for a father who didn't need more stuff but could always use something to eat, or so she figured.

She held up a bottle of steak sauce, its paper seal intact. "I bought this in Argentina. It slowed me down in customs. He should have passed it on to you, if he didn't want it."

"He would have been afraid your feelings might have been hurt," said George. "You'd come home and look in the cupboards and not find it."

Ruth surveyed the collection of gourmet sauces and seasonings, then gathered them up and threw them in the trash.

"What are you doing?" George exclaimed.

"They're all expired by now," she said. "You don't want them."

"I might," said George. He began going through the containers. "A small fortune in hot sauce," he said, removing some of the bottles. "This stuff never goes bad. Jeez."

"Have at it," said Ruth, yawning.

THE SKY LIGHTENED, the rest of the world got up, and the three Blaire children drove over to the hospital. Murray's body had been moved to a small room in the basement, and together they went in for one last look. He lay on a gurney, covered with a white sheet, and the nurse lifted it off his face and folded it gently across his shoulders and left them alone.

The first thing George noticed was that his father's hair had been combed back off his forehead in little rows with some kind of gel, a Brylcreem man at rest. This looked entirely wrong because Murray's hair was always falling over his forehead in a messy dart, so now George used his fingers and mussed up the styling so Murray looked more like himself.

Meanwhile, they regarded him in silence. For all his experience with people dying in the ICU, George nevertheless found himself thinking like a child: that any moment now his father would wake up. That he could put his mouth to his father's, and breathe life into the old man's lungs. "It was just a joke!" Murray would crow. "Now get me that damn coffee!" He looked for a twitch, any twitch, in his father's eyelids.

Ridiculous.

After a while Ruth bent over and kissed his forehead and left the room. Lizzie did the same. George stayed by his father's side. He fumbled around under the sheet for his hand, found it, and smoothed the cool, papery skin with his thumb, recalling the massage he'd given him the previous day. He cupped his other hand around his father's face and stared at his features. He'd always felt a distance with his father, owing to Daniel's death and Murray's hopes all being rolled into the one remaining son. So much pressure: Go to law school. Join the firm. Run for office. Do good things. Well, he'd found another way to do good things, but he always sensed a disappointment on his father's part that he'd gone into medicine rather than law.

For which he wasn't sorry.

Still, he wished his father had said, just once, "I'm proud of you, son."

BACK AT THE HOUSE Lizzie went up to the attic in search of the box that Ruth had been talking about. It was stifling under the eaves, and the air had the charged smell of overly dry wood. At the far end was a little window, cobwebbed and buggy, which she cranked open, and then, working her way down the length of the attic, she moved aside broken chairs and stacks of boxes but couldn't find anything labeled "Lillian." There were canoe paddles and life-jackets, old lamps and a porcelain sink; there was a big old trunk in which she found the army parka in dispute, but when she tried it on, it set off a sneezing attack, so she quickly bagged it up and left it by the stairs, to be taken to the cleaners for George.

She gave up on the attic and went down to the basement, where on carefully constructed shelves Murray kept cancelled checks and old mortgage statements and several defeated-looking tangles of cords and adapters. Against one wall a clutch of old skis threatened to topple over. Who wanted old skis? No one but the hippie crafts-men who used them to make Adirondack chairs. Between the attic and the basement she felt overwhelmed at the job ahead of them. She wanted to put a sign out by the road: "Free Shit, Come and Get It."

But she couldn't find a box with Lillian's name on it.

She was starting upstairs when she happened to glance into the dark, spidery area under the stairwell, filled with a jumble of softball mitts and knee pads and bicycle helmets. Behind all this, a light surface caught her eye. Squatting down, she shoved everything aside to reveal Daniel's box. So that's where it was all this time! She pulled it out and was about to lift the lid and go through the mementos, when she happened to glance back into the darkness and noticed another banker's box. Waving away cobwebs, she leaned far in and hauled it out. It was much dustier than Daniel's. There was no label. She tipped up the lid.

The box was filled with paper.

Eaton's Corrasable Bond, to be precise, stapled together in bundles of ten to twenty pages. She pulled the box out into the light and lifted out a stack and fanned through the pages. "Guidance: A Story by Lillian Holmes." "Home Repair: A Story by Lillian Holmes." And so on. She made her way down the stack and counted fourteen separate stories, each with four or five red-penciled drafts. At the bottom was a dog-eared manila folder. She didn't open it just then. Instead she hoisted the box and triumphantly lugged it upstairs and called for Ruth and George.

"Oh, did you find the bracelet?" Ruth asked, coming in from the kitchen. She was wearing an old pair of jeans that made her look bowlegged.

"No," said Lizzie. "Something better." She set the box on the floor and lifted the lid. "Mom's stories!"

Ruth peered down. "Holy shit. Where did you find them?"

"Under the stairs, in the basement! Behind Daniel's box!"

"Wow. I thought Dad got rid of them." Ruth squatted, knees popping. She reached down and ruffled through the stack. "That's a lot of work. I'm still mad at her, you know," she admitted.

Hearing this, it was all Lizzie could do to keep from hurling her water bottle across the room. "Ruth!" she cried, and she leaned over and gripped her sister's face between her hands. "I just found a box of Mom's stories that nobody knew about! This is a gift! And you're going to pout? At this point in your life? With Dad gone now? She was our mother! She fucked up! We all fuck up! But Dad said it himself—what good does it do to be angry about something that happened a zillion years ago?!"

Ruth's face had grown somber.

"I can't help it," she said in a small voice. "Even now. How do I stop?"

Lizzie sank back. "I don't know, Ruth," she sighed. "Maybe you just go outside and . . . and scream it to the stars."

"And then what?" Ruth was desperate for a good plan, Lizzie could tell.

"Then you forget about it," she said gently. "Simple as that."

Ruth looked doubtful, but before Lizzie could think of more words that might be of use to her sister, the kitchen door slammed, and George appeared in the doorway. "What's this?" he said, kneeling down.

"Mom's stories!" Lizzie exclaimed. "Fourteen of them! Rough drafts and all!"

"Wow," said George. "I thought Dad got rid of them. Sure beats a cookbook, doesn't it?"

"I don't know about that, but—where are you going, Ruth?"

"To scream at the stars," Ruth said over her shoulder.

"Huh?" said George.

Lizzie silenced him with her hand. They heard the kitchen door open and close, and then they heard a primal throaty roar that echoed off the mountainsides, frightening animals and triggering avalanches and calving glaciers five thousand miles to the north.

"Ruth getting something off her chest?" George inquired.

"Indeed," said Lizzie.

And then Ruth came back inside, now with the bottle of their father's gin, and the three Blaire children sat in a circle on the floor with the box of their mother's stories in the middle. For the next hour they passed the stories and the bottle around, Ruth trying mightily to keep the drafts in proper order. They skimmed and read and sometimes they interrupted one another with a passage they wanted to share. There was a story called "The Neighbors" about a couple trying to reignite their marriage by having sex by the neighbors' pool. A teenage boy getting drunk.

"Wonder where the idea for that one came from," George drawled.

And there was a story about a young woman having an abortion. Lizzie's eyes narrowed as she read. The imagery itself was vivid, haunting (and not even close to her own experience): a young girl waiting on a soiled sheet on an unpadded table in a ramshackle apartment. She tried to keep reading but her mind was careening. Had her mother once . . . before Ruth . . . ? Quickly she scolded herself for jumping to conclusions, for failing to credit her mother with simply having a very good imagination. It didn't matter, *had she or hadn't she*. It was just good writing, and full of empathy, a word Lizzie wouldn't have known at the age of six, and sitting there in the living room she felt her mother's presence, like a radio wave, or light beyond the visible spectrum, there to reassure her that the laws of the universe were on her side, and things would be okay.

At some point when all the stories were out of the box and circulating, Lizzie opened up the manila folder from the bottom of the box. Inside was a sheaf of rejection letters. Some were form letters, preprinted notes that broke the bad news on a mere strip of paper; others were more personally composed pieces of correspondence: ". . . not right for our needs . . ." "Readers found much to admire, but . . ."

"What are those?" George asked.

"Rejection letters," said Lizzie.

"Ouch," said George.

For someone who had weathered her share of rejection letters over the years for her scholarly work, it pained Lizzie to think of how much negative feedback her mother had endured. Some of the letters came awfully close, and she pictured her mother at the stove frying onions after getting such a letter, swallowing her disappointment in order to put another casserole on the table for dinner. There wasn't time for wallowing in self-pity when you had six mouths to feed.

Lizzie was about to put the folder back into the box when a thin, cream-colored envelope fell out. She picked it up. The return address showed it was from *The Northern Review*, a long-standing literary magazine Lizzie knew well, from people in the Creative Writing department.

Curious, she opened the envelope. She read the letter once, then read it again, and then she passed it to George, who upon reading it made a little O of his mouth.

"What is it?" Ruth asked.

"Ain't no rejection letter," said George, passing it to Ruth.

Ruth skimmed the letter, frowning, then looked at the date. "October 29, 1984," she breathed. "Right before she died. She must have just gotten it."

"Do you think Dad knew about it?" George asked.

"He would have told us, wouldn't he?" Ruth said.

"He must have just shoved everything into this one envelope," said Lizzie.

"But why wouldn't the editors have tried to get in touch with her again?" George asked.

Lizzie shook her head blankly. "Who knows. Disorganization, is my guess."

"What's the title again?" Ruth asked.

"'Whose Business Is It, Anyway?'" Lizzie shuffled through the pile of stories and found the story in question and read the first line aloud.

"Lucy wanted egg salad but Eleanor was saving the hard-boiled eggs to make deviled eggs for the party that night." Suddenly a thought occurred to her. She went to the kitchen and got the cookbook, which she'd left at the house on Saturday morning. She slid her fingernail between the pages to gently pry them apart, and turned to the recipe for deviled eggs. *Lucy/egg salad/Mother/D.E.,* read Lillian's notes.

She came back and passed the cookbook to Ruth, whose eyes went wide. "She must have had the idea for this story while she was making deviled eggs!" she exclaimed. Ruth loved solving a mystery.

"Read more," said George.

Lizzie picked up the story and continued:

"Eleanor hoped this wouldn't trigger a meltdown with Lucy, but it

did, and she spent the next half hour trying to calm the screaming child, who at six was way too old, in Eleanor's view, for a tantrum."

"Oh! That's you, Lizzie," said Ruth, nodding eagerly. "You had a lot of tantrums!"

Lizzie blushed and continued:

"But Eleanor didn't give in, and eventually Lucy fell asleep, which gave Eleanor time to make the deviled eggs and then clean up the kitchen for the caterers, who were due to arrive at four. (Her own deviled eggs were the one concession to food preparation that Eleanor had made for the party.) Her husband would get home from coaching football at five, and the guests were due to arrive at six, including the Governor and his wife."

"Mom hated giving parties," Ruth noted. "It was like a phobia."

"Shush," said Lizzie.

"This was an important party for Eleanor because people were paying $500 to attend, to raise money for Eleanor's reelection campaign. Eleanor had the support of a lot of people and groups. She had the support of the labor unions. The teachers. Three of the state's newspapers. The Governor. But there was one small problem: she didn't have the support of her husband.

"John had liked being the congresswoman's spouse for the last year and a half; he'd liked staying home with Lucy while Eleanor commuted to Washington. But he felt it was taking its toll on the family. 'Look at Lucy's tantrums,' he said. 'Where do you think they come from?' And he didn't like her being away for three nights each week. 'It's lonely,' he said. 'We need you.'"

"Wait," said George. "Who is Mom in this story? The wife? Or the husband?"

"Just listen," said Lizzie. *"When in fact Eleanor herself was having a ball down in Washington. She shared an apartment with a congresswoman from Oregon. The two of them drank wine late into the night, grousing over stalemates. Sometimes they went to restaurants together, sometimes they ordered pizza at ten o'clock. There were always position papers to read, the newspapers as well. Eleanor had never felt as well-informed as she was these days . . ."*

She glanced up. "Should I keep going?"

"Definitely," said George.

"Yes, do," said Ruth.

So Lizzie kept on reading. The story took an ugly turn when, during the party, Eleanor got a phone call from the national press. A photograph had surfaced showing John and Eleanor smoking pot. Did she care to comment? She hung up, but the issue wasn't going away. After the guests left, John glumly said there were probably more photos where that one came from. Eleanor told him that was awfully pessimistic. John said their lives were going to be lived under a microscope from now on. Eleanor accused him of leaking it to the press, to sabotage her campaign.

Lizzie, reading aloud, lost herself in the story. She could see Eleanor's viewpoint, but she could see John's as well. It was hard work, she knew, pulling off these contrasting points of view, and her mother had gotten no credit for it except one editor's set of admiring eyes.

A stalemate: a couple in crisis. A child waking from a nightmare. Parents competing for the right to console the child. And then at the end, Eleanor running a bath, locking the door, lowering herself into the tub, and settling back into the hot water and lighting a cigarette.

"*She exhaled dragon puffs through her nose and listened closely,*" Lizzie read. "*She could hear John out in the bedroom opening drawers and closing them; the clink of change into a dish on his bureau. In a moment he would be in bed with his library book. Sex? Not on your life, tonight. But as she took a long drag, she imagined him in the morning, off for a run while she and Lucy ate the rest of the deviled eggs for breakfast, and when he came back, they would craft an appropriate statement for the press together, saying yes it was me, and no I don't regret it. The laws are wrong, no one got hurt, and whose business is it, anyway? It was a bold approach to take, but she wasn't going to hide who she was, she wasn't going to lie, and if she lost votes, well then, that was the price of honesty.*

"*By this time the water in the tub had grown tepid. Eleanor was shivering. Using her big toe, she nudged the plug away, then stood up and reached for a towel as the water drained around her ankles.*"

Lizzie set the manuscript down.

"What?" said George. "That's it?"

"That's it," said Lizzie. "The end."

"That's awfully abrupt," said Ruth.

"And what does it all mean?" George asked. "Was Mom mad about Dad's campaign? Or was she wishing she could run for Congress herself? Did she have skeletons in her closet that we weren't supposed to know about? What does it all mean?"

Lizzie didn't want to be the professor right now. "It doesn't have to 'mean' anything."

"But do you think they're going to be all right?" George asked anxiously. "John and Eleanor?"

"Oh, George," sighed Lizzie, "what do you think?"

"I think they are," said George.

"I think they are, too," Ruth agreed.

"Well good, then," said Lizzie. "Maybe that's the effect she was looking for." Carefully she straightened the stack of stories on the rug. Her foot had gone to sleep, and she labored up from the floor, then limped over to the patio door and slid it open. It was midday, and white streaks feathered the sky. Slowly she breathed in the dry September air. Orange rose hips dotted the rosebushes, and a lone scarlet branch slashed the deep green of the maple. She waved to Boyd, out by the barn. He waved back.

"What are we going to do with all these?" Ruth asked.

The three Blaire children were stumped by this.

"We could make a book out of them," suggested George, after a while. "We could scan them into the computer, and get them printed up. *Collected Stories*, by Lillian Holmes."

"That's an idea!" Ruth exclaimed. "We could make three copies, so each of us has one!"

"I'm not sure how Mom would feel about that," Lizzie warned. "Writers can be very particular about which pieces they want to share with the world."

But as Ruth pointed out, they weren't going to share them with the world. "They would be just for us."

She was right. And it would be nice to have them all in one volume. Lizzie glanced at the title to the story again. "Whose Business Is It, Anyway?"

"Okay," she said, "I'm in."

"I'm in," said Ruth.

"Then it's settled," said George. "We all agree. Amazing."

Then Lizzie pictured her mother giving a reading to a group of admirers: standing at a lectern in her yellow shift, a pair of tortoise-shell glasses perched on her nose. Her voice might crack for an instant, but then she would continue, strong and clear.

"It'll be a sensation," Lizzie said.

Acknowledgments

As with every book, many heartfelt thanks are in order. To my crew at Putnam, deepest gratitude for all your support, with a special thanks to my editor, Alexis Sattler, whose vision and enthusiasm guided me smoothly through the editorial process. Many thanks to the Art department as well for designing such an elegant, classy cover.

To the fabulous Molly Friedrich, agent extraordinaire: thank you so very much for hanging in there with me, and for your tireless energy and welcome common sense. Thanks as well to Ellen Gomory, Lucy Carson, and everyone else at the Friedrich Agency for your insight and advice.

To Laura Uhls: I'm certain you were a star editor in a previous life! Thank you so much for your detailed and dead-on comments on an early draft. Lisa Halperin, MD, thank you, as always, for both your medical advice and your editorial guidance, and for brainstorming at all hours of the day and night. Thanks to Alison Trules, for your specialty expertise in grief counseling; and to Jenny Timbas, for helping me remember Concord politics through a clear lens.

To Mark Haimes, MD: thank you for consulting on all the medical issues, for giving me the right language and, heck, since I'm at it, for being such a great family doctor all these years.

Thanks and love to my beloved sisters, Jane Malone, Sara Eidenbach, and Sue Winn. How lucky I am to have grown up one of four girls—I cherish you, and always will. (And no, you are not the siblings in the novel!) Thanks to my father, John Hyde, for your love and unfailingly dry sense of humor. To my mother, Betty, wherever you are, thank you for your love as well, and for all your handwritten recipes, some of which came from Fannie Farmer, whose cookbook you may have stained but never dropped into a sinkful of dirty dishwater.

And amid all these thanks, a random acknowledgment: when Murray hears in his mind the saying "If you want to make God laugh, tell him your plans," he doesn't remember who said it. I first heard it from Anne Lamott (with God as a woman), but apparently Woody Allen said it as well. It's also an old Yiddish proverb and may have originated in the Bible itself, which Murray never read.

Finally, deepest love and gratitude to my husband of almost thirty-four years, Pierre Schlag, who pushed me every step of the way, who argued, who advocated, who helped me from going astray, and who has always been there for me, holding the torch.